MISTLETOE, MERRIMENT, AND MURDER

"Sara Rosett's Ellie Avery series is a winner. Rosett always delivers a terrific mystery with believable characters and lots of heart. The insider's look at the life of a military spouse makes this series a fascinating read. I look forward to each new book."
—**Denise Swanson**, *New York Times* best-selling
author of the Scumble River and Devereaux's
Dime Store mystery series

"Intriguing characters, a strong setting, more than a dash of humor and a suspenseful plot that ably keeps us guessing until the end. . . . Yet, what places air force wife Ellie Avery at the top of my list are the poignant descriptions of what military families face every day."
—**Katherine Hall Page**, Agatha Award–winning
author of *The Body in the Boudoir*

MIMOSAS, MISCHIEF, AND MURDER

"What fun is a funeral without a corpse? Ellie Avery steps into snooping mode, and not a moment too soon. . . . Rosett's grasp of the minutiae of mommyhood is excellent."
—*Kirkus Reviews*

"A winning mystery . . . A rumor of hidden money, secret letters from a famous recluse, a fire, a threatening message, and a crazed gunman add to the cozy mischief."
—*Publishers Weekly*

"Charm, Southern sass, and suspense abound in the sixth delightful cozy mystery in Sara Rosett's series featuring Ellie Avery—mom, military wife, part-time professional organizer, and amateur sleuth."

—*Fresh Fiction*

MINT JULEPS, MAYHEM, AND MURDER

"A nifty mystery . . . . Fans of TV's *Air Force Wives* will especially appreciate Ellie, a smart crime solver who successfully navigates the challenges of military life."

—*Publishers Weekly*

"Some cozies just hit on all cylinders, and Rosett's Ellie Avery titles are among the best. Her books recall the early Carolyn Hart."

—*Library Journal*

"Tightly constructed with many well-fitted, suspenseful turns, and flows like a country creek after an all-day rain."

—*Shine*

MAGNOLIAS, MOONLIGHT, AND MURDER

"Rosett's engaging fourth Mom Zone mystery finds super-efficient crime-solver Ellie Avery living in a new subdivision in North Dawkins, GA . . . Some nifty party tips help keep the sleuthing on the cozy side."

—*Publishers Weekly*

GETTING AWAY IS DEADLY

"No mystery is a match for the likable, efficient Ellie, who unravels this multilayered plot with skill and class."
—*Romantic Times Book Reviews* (four stars)

"*Getting Away Is Deadly* keeps readers moving down some surprising paths—and on the edge of their chairs—until the very end." —*Cozy Library*

STAYING HOME IS A KILLER

"If you like cozy mysteries that have plenty of action and lots of suspects and clues, *Staying Home Is a Killer* will be a fun romp through murder and mayhem. This is a mystery with a 'mommy lit' flavor. . . . A fun read."
—*Armchair Interviews*

"Thoroughly entertaining. The author's smooth, succinct writing style enables the plot to flow effortlessly until its captivating conclusion."
—*Romantic Times Book Reviews* (four stars)

MOVING IS MURDER

"A fun debut for an appealing young heroine."
—*Carolyn Hart*, author of the Death on Demand mystery series

"A squadron of suspects, a unique setting, and a twisted plot will keep you turning pages!"
>   —*Nancy J. Cohen*, author of the Bad Hair Day
>   mystery series

"Everyone should snap to attention and salute this fresh new voice."
>   —*Denise Swanson*, nationally best-selling
>   author of the Scumble River mystery series

"An absorbing read that combines sharp writing and tight plotting with a fascinating peek into the world of military wives. Jump in!"
>   —*Cynthia Baxter*, author of the Reigning
>   Cats & Dogs mystery series

"Reading Sara Rosett's *Moving Is Murder* is like making a new friend—I can't wait to brew a pot of tea and read all about sleuth Ellie Avery's next adventure!"
>   —*Leslie Meier*, author of the Lucy Stone mystery series

"Mayhem, murder, and the military! Rosett is an author to watch."
>   —*Alesia Holliday*, author of the December Vaughn
>   mystery series

Milkshakes,
Mermaids,
And Murder

Milkshakes, Mermaids, And Murder

Sara Rosett

KENSINGTON BOOKS
http://www.kensingtonbooks.com

KENSINGTON BOOKS are published by

Kensington Publishing Corp.
119 West 40th Street
New York, NY 10018

All Kensington titles, imprints, and distributed lines are available at special quantity discounts for bulk purchases for sales promotion, premiums, fund-raising, educational, or institutional use. Special book excerpts or customized printings can also be created to fit specific needs. For details, write or phone the office of the Kensington Special Sales Manager: Attn. Special Sales Department. Kensington Publishing Corp., 119 West 40th Street, New York, NY 10018. Phone: 1-800-221-2647.

Kensington and the K logo Reg. U.S. Pat. & TM Off.

ISBN-13: 978-0-7582-6922-5
ISBN-10: 0-7582-6922-6
First Kensington Mass Market Printing: October 2013

eISBN-13: 978-0-7582-9151-6
eISBN-10: 0-7582-9151-5
First Kensington Electronic Edition: October 2013

10 9 8 7 6 5 4 3 2 1

Printed in the United States of America

To LR and JR

Chapter
One

I checked the display on my ringing phone and muttered, "This can't be good." Mitch, my air force pilot husband, should not be calling me right now. He should be in the air, flying back from a two-week military exercise in Europe so we could depart later today for our family Fourth of July vacation to Sandy Beach, Florida.

It was all timed perfectly, with military precision, in fact. Mitch was scheduled to land in three hours. By then, I'd have finished packing the minivan, and we could hit the road, escaping the muggy humidity of central Georgia for the sea breezes of the Gulf Coast.

Be optimistic. Maybe he's early, I thought as I answered. "Hey. I didn't think I'd hear from you until later. Are you down early?"

"Ah—no," Mitch said, and I knew from his tone our plans were about to change. "We broke. We're in Goose Bay."

"You're in Canada?" I said incredulously.

"Afraid so."

"Oh." I surveyed the beach chairs and suitcases wedged into the back of the minivan. "So, how long before you take off again?"

"Well, that's the deal. We're not sure. I delayed calling you because maintenance thought they had the part we need, but they don't. They're going to have to fly it in."

"Okay. Well, if it's just a day's delay, we can wait until tomorrow to leave," I said, watching our youngest, Nathan, who was walking around the driveway with his new sand pail on his head, pretending to be a robot. Our daughter, Livvy, in an unexpected burst of big-sister devotion, was playing along with him, poking him in the chest, pretending to "program" him. Livvy wore her swimsuit under her shirt and shorts. The ties of her hot pink tank peeked over the collar at the back of her neck. She had on her kid-size purple sunglasses and wore flip-flops with huge sunflowers near her toes. She was ready for the beach.

"I'm not sure I'll be back by tomorrow," Mitch said reluctantly.

"Really?" I asked in dismay, thinking of our prepaid hotel and all our plans: our days playing in the surf, the dolphin tour, the southern plantation surrounded with live oaks dripping with Spanish moss, not to mention visits with two relatives who lived in the area. Mentally juggling our agenda, I tried to calculate what could be rescheduled. I'd already dropped our dog, Rex, at the kennel where he was romping with the other dogs in the "playroom," and I'd made sure to clear my schedule of appointments with my professional organizing clients for this week. "Where is the part coming from?" I asked finally.

"Maybe England."

"Maybe?"

"Yeah, they're tracking it down now. So it could be a day or two. You and the kids should go on. I'll catch up as soon as I can. We're supposed to meet Summer tonight and Ben tomorrow—you don't want to miss that."

"You're right. I'd have two sad kids on my hands if they miss their sleepover." Mitch's sister, Summer, had a share in a condo in a town a few miles south of our hotel. Summer lived in Tallahassee where she worked as a congressional aide, but she spent several weekends a year at the two-bedroom beach condo, and she'd especially coordinated time off work to be there this week. She took her role as Aunt Summer very seriously. Because distance prevented the kids from seeing her frequently, she'd offered—practically insisted—they spend the first night of our vacation at her condo for a sleepover. She'd spent quite a bit of time on the phone with Nathan and Livvy, making extensive plans. I knew cookies, Disney movies, and kite flying were just a few of the things on the agenda.

The Gulf Coast had practically turned into "relative central" for us. My brother Ben, who had followed in Mitch's footsteps and become an air force pilot, was stationed at a military base about an hour away from our hotel. His assignment in the spring had been one of the reasons we'd planned the beach vacation. He wouldn't have much time off, but he had promised that he'd be able to get away for at least a day, maybe two, so we could spend some time together.

Nathan turned in a stiff-leg circle and set off on a path toward the mailbox. Livvy fluttered along in his wake, jauntily swinging her own pail. I sat down on the bumper of the minivan with a sigh. I knew the kids would have a great time with Summer. Their time with her was supposed to be a little interlude just for them, at the beginning of the vacation. We wanted the bulk of our time to be spent together as a family. Mitch and I spend so much of our time separated—sometimes for a week or two, but other times for months on end. The stop-and-go schedule made family time precious, and that's what we wanted this week off to be—time to-gether. "I really wanted this to be a family vacation."

"I know. I did, too. I'll get there as soon as I can," he repeated.

"I know you will. It just won't be as much fun until you get here."

A FedEx truck rolled to a stop at the end of our drive-way. Livvy and Nathan stopped playing and watched the deliveryman sprint toward me. Mitch said he'd call when he had more news, and we hung up. By the time I'd signed for the box, the kids were hovering.

"Who is it from?" Livvy asked.

"Who is it *for*? Me?" Nathan demanded. Because we lived far from our relatives, a package delivery usu-ally meant it was close to someone's birthday or a major holiday.

"No. This time, it's for me," I said. I recognized the name on the return address—Angela's Boutique, my favorite online source for designer handbags, my weak-ness. I'm not a fashionista, as my current attire showed: denim skort, sleeveless white shirt, casual sandals. With my hair pulled back in a ponytail, I was ready to pack the van and negotiate a six-hour road trip with two elementary-school-age kids in 90 percent humid-ity. Cool and functional, those were my watchwords when it came to my everyday clothes. I did dress up a bit for my organizing consultations, but when it came down to the nitty-gritty of actually sorting and organizing a client's belongings, I found that basic work clothes like jeans and tennis shoes were the best options.

My friend Abby, who did have a flare for looking spectacular, lamented my uninteresting clothing choices. "Basic, but boring," she called them. But she couldn't complain about my purses. They were my one indulgence. I loved designer handbags, especially ones that I found at thrift shops and online auctions, like the one inside this box. It was a Leah Marshall, a chic oversized tote. If the exterior cream leather with heavy gold hardware seemed a bit bland, the interior lining of stripes in hot pink, black, and kelly green gave the bag a fun accent.

"Oh, it's just one of Mom's purses," Nathan said with a sigh, and reversed course back to the foot of the driveway.

I pulled the tab on the box as I walked inside, already planning to switch to the new purse before we left. In the kitchen, I pushed the crumpled packing paper aside and pulled out the purse, expecting to inhale the aroma of leather. But all I could smell was . . . cardboard? The strap felt stiff as I twisted the purse around to examine it. The leather wasn't leather at all. It was a rough "pleather." The hardware was flimsy, the stitching on the seams wavered about, and the lining was a bumpy black silk that didn't lie flat against the structure of the purse. This wasn't a genuine Leah Marshall—even the name imprint on the small leather tag that dangled from the strap had the designer's name misspelled as "Lee" instead of "Leah." It certainly wasn't the purse I'd paid for. This was a knockoff.

I dropped the purse back into the nest of packing

paper and flipped the lid over to check the address. This wasn't like Angela. I'd bought several things from her and had never had a problem. In fact, she'd become a "cyber friend," one of those people I chatted with online and think of as an acquaintance, even though I hadn't met her in person.

I went to my computer and fired off a quick e-mail to Angela495, the e-mail associated with her online boutique. I also had Angela's private e-mail because in the last month or so, she and Ben had dated a few times. I scrolled through my old e-mail, looking for the first e-mail I'd received from her. I found it and clicked it open.

> From: FLPartyGirl@gmail.com
> To: Ellie@EverythingInItsPlace.com
> Subject: Question . . .
> Hi Ellie, I'm Angela Day. You know me as Angela495 from Angela's Boutique. This is going to sound kind of weird, but do you have a brother named Ben? I'm only asking because I met a really nice guy awhile back and I noticed you're listed as a friend on his Facebook account. He mentioned one time that his sister is a professional organizer, so I thought it must be you!?! Anyway, if it's not you, sorry to bother you, and I hope you're loving the Michael Kors purse—isn't it divine?

I added Angela's second e-mail address to the note about the purse, hit SEND and then returned to stowing the essentials in the car, the toys and books that would get us through the drive. As I placed a stack of *Nate the Great* books in the van, Nathan skidded to a stop beside me. "When are we leaving? How long until Dad gets here?"

I extracted myself from the minivan and leaned down, bracing my hands on my knees. "I've got some bad news. Dad's been delayed. He's not going to make it in today. He wants us to go on."

"Go without him?" Livvy, who was hopping from one crack on the driveway to another, stopped abruptly and spoke through the open door on the other side of the van. "He promised we'd make a sand castle together." Her shoulders dropped and her pail sagged to around her ankles.

"And he will. He's just delayed. He'll get there as fast as he can."

"What about Uncle Ben?" Nathan asked, obviously searching for some male companionship.

"Uncle Ben will still meet us tomorrow." At least, that was the plan. I ruffled his hair and told him and Livvy to get the small string backpacks of toys they had packed the night before. I went inside and packed juice boxes, grapes, and peanut butter crackers for road trip snacks. The computer chimed, indicating I had a new e-mail.

From: Angela495@BagTopiaOnLineAuctions.com

To: Ellie@EverythingInItsPlace.com

Oh no! I am so sorry! There was a mix-up with the purses. I asked my idiot brother—he's soooo not like your brother at all!—to mail the Leah Marshall bag for me and he sent the wrong one. A friend gave me an imitation Leah Marshall bag for my birthday, and I've been meaning to drop it off at

a charity shop for ages, but I never remember . . .
guess I could use some organizing tips when you
come to town! Anyway, Ben says you'll be in Sandy
Beach today (so excited!!!) That will be perfect. I'm
only a few minutes away in Costa Bella. Call me
when you get to town (279-319-4263) and I'll bring
you the REAL Leah Marshall to your hotel. Again,
so sorry!! Can't wait 2 c u and Ben!

I sent back a quick e-mail saying that she didn't
have to meet me at the hotel. I'd mail her the imitation
bag after my trip, and she could send me the real bag,
but before I had taken two steps from the computer, it
dinged with another message. It wasn't a problem. Angela would be in Sandy Beach tonight, right on the
beachfront road where all the hotels were, so she might
as well bring the purse.

I shrugged and murmured, "Well, if you insist," as I
put the box with the purse next to the snacks. I would
like to get the real purse, and I wanted to meet Angela
face-to-face. I wondered how much of her insistence
on bringing the purse in person had to do with her de-
sire to see Ben and how much it had to do with keeping
a customer satisfied. Seeing Ben probably won out in
that battle.

Nathan came into the kitchen, his string backpack
clinking along the floor as he dragged it behind him.
"Mom, are you sure Uncle Ben will be there?" he
asked, his chin tilted down and his dark eyes serious.

"Yes. He said he would. He'll be there. What have
you got in here?" I asked, picking up the backpack.
"It's awfully heavy." The string cut into my fingers and
metal clanked as I lifted it from the floor.

"Stuff I need," he said matter-of-factly.

I opened the flap and saw a jumble of about seventy-five Hot Wheels cars along with a scattering of various appendages of action figures sticking up through the metal. "Are you sure you want to take all of these? You have to keep up with them and you have to carry this backpack yourself."

He took the backpack from me and slung it on his little shoulders. "Yeah. Uncle Ben said he liked Hot Wheels." He walked out of the kitchen and out to the van.

I studied the ceiling for a moment, debating whether or not I should make him leave his cars at home. Odds were, he would lose some on the trip, which would cause much anguish and tears. And the backpack must have weighed at least ten pounds. I quirked my mouth to the side. Crying now or later? I blew out a sigh. I had to let him take the cars. He'd decided to take them, and he knew he had to keep track of them.

Sometimes letting my kids learn responsibility was as hard on me as it was on them. Well, maybe he'd surprise me and keep up with everything and not complain about the cords cutting into his shoulders. Probably long odds on that one, I thought as I picked up my cell phone and dialed my brother's number.

He surprised me and answered on the second ring.

"Oh. Hey, Ben. It's Ellie. I thought I'd get your voice mail."

"Almost. I'm flight planning now."

"Okay. I'll make it quick. Slight change of plans on our end. Mitch has been delayed, but the kids and I are driving down today anyway. Mitch will join us as soon as he can."

"That's too bad. Where is he?"

"Goose Bay."

"So . . . may be a few days."

"Looks like it."

"Well, I've heard they have good beer. There's a German unit up there."

"Great. That's just what I want to hear," I said.

"Aw, you know Mitch will get out of there as fast as he can."

"True. Okay, but you're still good with meeting us tomorrow?"

"Of course. This is my last flight and it's local. I'll be down in a few hours. I'll see you guys tomorrow. I even got a few days of leave and a room at your hotel, too."

"Great! And you're up for playing with Hot Wheels? Nathan packed every single one he owns," I warned.

"Sure. No problem. Tell him to bring his tracks, too."

"Oh no, I think the cars are enough."

"Spoil sport," Ben teased.

"Someone has to act like an adult this week, and I know how you get carried away with those tracks," I said, thinking of how Ben had covered the entire floor of our living room and kitchen with his tracks and cars when he was a kid. "Remember how you ran the tracks over the dining-room table and broke Mom's crystal candleholder?"

"Hey, you're not going to list everything I ever did wrong, are you? You know, as a life lesson kind of thing: don't do this or you'll grow up to be like your Uncle Ben."

"I think you turned out okay. Besides, you can do no wrong in Nathan's eyes—that's a big responsibility. Make sure you use your powers for good, not evil."

"Sure," he said, and I could hear the laughter in his voice.

"Oh—one more thing. Angela is coming by tonight, in case you have a chance to come early."

"What?" His voice changed and all teasing disappeared. "Did you say *Angela*?"

"Yes, there was a mix-up about a purse I bought from her. She's bringing—oh, it doesn't matter. I just wanted to let you know if you want to see your girlfriend, she'll be there tonight."

There was a beat of silence, then, subdued, he said, "She's not my girlfriend."

"Okay," I said slowly. "She sent me an e-mail, and it sounded like she was looking forward to coming to Sandy Beach. I got the feeling she was interested in seeing you."

"Yeah. Well . . . I won't be able to leave until tomorrow anyway." He finished up hurriedly and we said our good-byes.

This was going to be awkward.

"Here is your key to the beach boardwalk," the desk clerk said. "And the complementary breakfast begins at six tomorrow." She slid the packet containing our keys across the counter.

"I hope I'm not awake for that," I said as I hitched my large beach bag higher on my shoulder, pocketed the keys, and grabbed the handle of the rolling suitcase.

"We serve breakfast until nine."

"That's doable." I turned to call the kids to follow me, but they were ahead of me. Typical. In a few short years, they'd gone from the toddler stage with their unsteady gates and wobbly legs to zooming ahead of me at a pace I could barely keep up with. Except this time, they weren't running ahead. They both stood motionless at the threshold, their small rolling suitcases forgotten beside them as they gazed around the atrium of the hotel. Livvy scanned the fifteen floors rising above us, with greenery dripping from the ledges enclosing each floor.

"Wow," she whispered. Glass elevators skimmed toward the skylights. A waterfall burbled into a pool with orange koi flashing through the rocks. "It's like Muffy's house," Livvy said, her tone laced with awe.

I smiled at her reference to a character from *Arthur*, the children's book about an aardvark, which had been made into a television show. Muffy lived in a mansion and had a chauffeur.

"Yeah," Nathan echoed, his chin tilted up to take in the huge palms and elephant ear plants towering over us. "Awesome," he declared and gripped his suitcase handle. "I get to push the button in the elevator." And we were off again.

We dumped our suitcases in the room, slathered on sunscreen, and headed for the beach, toting beach chairs, shovels, and pails, not to mention our towels and sunscreen. I felt a bit like a pack mule. On our way back through the hotel, Livvy halted in front of a poster. "Look, Mom, it's Suzie Quinn." A young woman with a round, freckled face topped with dark curls smiled out from the poster. She wore a one-piece racing swimsuit in red, white, and blue with USA printed near the neckline. "She won a gold medal," Livvy informed me, as if we hadn't sat side by side on the couch and watched Suzie Quinn win several gold medals during the last Summer Olympics. An underdog, she'd pulled off two surprise victories and had spent her time since then endorsing everything from cereal to phones.

Lately, news about her had revolved more around her personal life than her athletic abilities. She'd been dating Nick Ryan, a movie star with a bad boy reputation and a sexy British accent. I'd seen her photo on the cover of several tabloids while I waited in the checkout line at Target.

"*Never swim alone,*" Nathan piped up, parroting the video she'd made to teach kids water safety. I'd been volunteering in Nathan's class the day they'd watched it.

Livvy read a line from the poster. "*Meet Sandy Beach's Gold Medal Olympian at Green Groves Festival of Fireworks.*" Livvy swiftly read through the dates and times of the appearances, then twirled toward me. "Mom, she's going to be *here,* in Sandy Beach. Can we go see her?"

"And there are fireworks every night, all week!" Nathan added.

"We'll see," I said, thinking that the kids' improving reading skills complicated our lives a bit. I guess we'd have to add the picnic at Green Groves to our list of things to do. The antebellum home was on our list of sites to see, but I hadn't planned on visiting it during a "community-wide celebration," which sounded a bit crowded. "Let's hit the beach," I said.

Our hotel was located on a narrow peninsula that ran between the Gulf of Mexico and Sandy Bay. A road lined with hotels, restaurants, and shops sliced through the peninsula, more often than not veering close to the gulf. Beachside hotels along the road were the priciest and guests of those hotels could step directly onto the white beach. The nonbeach side of the road backed up to a mishmash of middle class neighborhoods that filled the narrow mile or so of land between the beach road and Sandy Bay. Many of the neighborhoods had

been in place long before the hotels and tourists arrived to block the view.

We were on the more "cost effective" side of the
beach road and had to schlep across the busy two-lane
road to the hotel's special beach access gate, but the
price difference made it worth the short walk. We navigated through the slow-moving traffic to the gate, then
stopped at a shop selling beach paraphernalia so I
could buy a pair of sunglasses. In the rush and excitement of getting on the road, I'd walked off and left
mine on the kitchen counter at home.

The glare of the sun was intense, and I was glad
I'd made the stop. We'd only gone a few steps when
Nathan spotted a fast food stand, The Shake Shack. He
asked, and I succumbed. We were on vacation, after all.
The kids picked their current favorite, chocolate milkshakes, and slurped them down as we walked onto a
boardwalk over dunes covered with sprigs of sea grass.
At the end of the boardwalk, I paused to pull off my
flip-flops and glanced back at the kids. They were both
staring at the wide expanse of water lapping onto the
sand, the sea breeze fluttering their hair. Closer inland,
a sea of sun umbrellas in a rainbow of colors flickered
in the breeze. Kids kicked up sand as they raced
around prone adults, who were reading or rubbing on
sunscreen. And always in the background was the con-
stant roar of the surf. "What do you think?" I asked.

"Awesome." Nathan shoved his empty milkshake
cup into a trash bin and sprinted for the water, his plastic bucket banging against his leg as he ran. I smiled.
Two pronouncements of "awesome" in one day. Pretty
good. It was getting harder to impress the kids as they
grew up. I wished Mitch could see their faces.

The white sand was silky and hot between my toes

and sent up a blinding glare. Livvy walked tentatively beside me with her flip-flops clutched in one hand and her pail in the other. She looked a little scared. I could see why. Water sports weren't her favorite activity.

"Let's find a place," I said, and headed for an opening near the waves. We staked our claim on a square of sand with our chairs and beach towels, then joined Nathan, who was hopping over waves, grinning in delight. Livvy held back a few minutes, but Nathan grabbed her hand and said impatiently, "Come on, I can't swim alone."

I could see in her face she didn't want to be the "scaredy-cat," so she hopped into the clear water with him. I stood and watched them, the water swirling around my thighs. The water was amazingly clear. I'd heard that the Gulf Coast was beautiful, but I'd never seen water like this—so translucent that I could see the grains of sand being pulled back and forth over my toes as the waves came in. It was like looking through glass. I marveled as I watched a school of tiny fish dart around my legs, then reverse course in a flash.

I splashed with the kids some, then went back to rummage in my straw beach tote for a book. I squished the sand between my toes and settled in to watch the kids over the edge of my book, thinking the only way the day could have been better was if Mitch were here, too.

After a while, the kids came out of the water and set to work moving sand to create a sand castle. They didn't notice a man in the red and white lifeguard T-shirt sprint parallel to the water, shouting, "Out of the water! Shark! Out of the water now!" The heavy sea breeze whipped his words away and they didn't look up because they were arguing over where to put the moat.

I stood and moved around the kids. I figured this was not the time to share one of the wonders of nature with them—not if I ever wanted them to get back into the water during the next few days. The words "shark" and "out of the water" spread along the beach as if they were wind-borne. People high-stepped out of the water, lunging for the sand, while other spectators on the beach, like me, edged cautiously toward the waves.

I heard a shriek to my left. "There it is!"

I squinted in the direction several people were pointing and saw the classic shark silhouette undulating through the shallows, slightly beyond the point where the waves broke and spilled onto the beach. The shark was small, only one, maybe two, feet long. A few people clicked off photos on their phones as it swam by, seemingly following the path of the lifeguard.

People waited uncertainly on the beach, scanning the water for more dorsal fins. After a few minutes, a couple of brave—or reckless—souls splashed into the waves while others began packing their gear up. Nathan announced he was hungry, and I decided it was time to head back to the hotel. On our walk back, I vetoed requests for another shake and was glad of the distraction when Livvy asked, "Mom, do you think mermaids are real?"

No easy answer here. Livvy had already discovered Santa Claus was make-believe, but she'd watched *The Little Mermaid* three times since we'd announced our trip to the beach. If she was enjoying imaginary singing mermaids, I didn't want to be the one to pop that bubble. I took the coward's way out. "What do you think?"

She contemplated the sidewalk, glanced at Nathan,

then lowered her voice so he wouldn't hear. "Probably not, but I like to pretend they are."

Before I could confirm or deny, Nathan announced, "I heard you."

I hid a smile, and we debated the possibility all the way back to the hotel, which was fine with me. Hopefully, the more they thought about mermaids, the less they thought about sharks.

Two hours later, the sand had been washed away, the kids had been fed, and we were in the hotel lobby. The kids were toting their small rolling suitcases and string backpacks. Summer arrived and swept into the lobby with her arms stretched wide and a huge smile splitting her face. "You're here!" she said as she scooped the kids into a joint hug, then exclaimed over how much they'd grown.

She turned to me and I said, "You cut your hair," as I embraced her. Instead of her cascades of red curls, her hair hung straight and brushed her shoulders.

She released me and rolled her eyes. "Why does everyone sound so tragic when they say that? You'd think I'd cut off my arm, instead of five inches of hair," she said, but she was smiling and that took the sting out of the words.

"Sorry. I like it. It's a bit of a shock. You look very professional," I said, taking in her sleeveless pale turquoise shell, black pencil skirt, and black heels. She'd obviously come directly from work. Quite a change from the last few times I'd seen her when she was sporting a bohemian chic style. I supposed she had little need for the berets in Florida, anyway.

"Thanks," she said and turned back to Livvy, who was gripping her hand. "Looks like you're ready to go."

"We are. We're making sprinkle cookies, right?" Livvy asked.

"Of course!" She must have noticed that Nathan was hanging back and wasn't as giddy with excitement as Livvy. Summer leaned down until she was level with him. "I've got lots of board games. I thought we'd have pizza for dinner, and if you don't want sprinkle cookies, we might make s'mores in the fireplace, if it gets cold enough."

Nathan nodded slowly. He liked the plan.

"Since Mitch isn't here, I was thinking I'd come with you . . ." I stopped at the kids' disappointed chorus of *aww*. I'd called Summer during the drive down and told her Mitch was delayed so she knew the situation, but I hadn't realized the kids might be opposed to my change in plans.

"No? You don't want me to come?" I asked them.

"No," Livvy explained patiently. "If you're there, you and Aunt Summer will talk the whole time, and we won't get her to ourselves."

I raised my eyebrows. "I see. Well, that's probably true."

I glanced at Summer, and she said, "Didn't you say you had a spa treatment scheduled?"

"I do, but I'm sure I can reschedule it." I'd planned on a trip to the spa and then a late grown-up dinner with Mitch.

"You don't have to," she assured me. "Take some time on your own. We'll be fine and you can have a break."

"Yeah, Mom," Nathan piped up. "You need a break."

"You really don't want me around, do you?" I teased.

"Nope," Livvy said, and pulled Summer toward the door.

An hour later, I slid into a lilac-colored Adirondack chair and propped my sandaled feet on the matching ottoman. I flexed my toes, admiring my Seashell Pink toenails, and then surveyed the view from the hotel's veranda. A tiny sliver of the moon hung in the navy blue sky, but even at seven, it wasn't fully dark. The sun wouldn't set for about another hour. The two-lane road was busy, packed with cars inching along and families trooping back from the beach or off to dinner. I placed a call to Angela and left her a message, saying I was in town, but didn't expect to see Ben until tomorrow. I put the phone beside the not-a-Leah-Marshall-purse I'd brought down from my room and settled back to enjoy the view.

It felt odd to sit with absolutely nothing to do. No kids to keep an eye on, no e-mails to reply to, no bills to pay, no dinner to cook. I perused the bar menu and ordered a caesar salad with the dressing on the side and a tall peach ice tea. I wanted to fit into my swimsuit at the end of the week, but I did splurge with a piece of chocolate cake for dessert. I figured with the salad and the cake it was a zero sum game, calorie-wise. Mitch called and we chatted. I relayed the kids' reaction to the beach and their eagerness to spend time alone with Summer. Mitch said the part situation was unchanged, then he had to go—the guys were leaving for dinner and he wanted to go with the crew.

We hung up and I settled back in my chair. I alternated watching the parade of people on the street and the slices of the water I could see between the high-rise hotels across the street, but as the sun sank, I found my gaze drawn to the hotels. A checkerboard of lights glowed from the rooms, some with the curtains wide open despite the growing dusk. I felt a bit like Jimmy Stewart in *Rear Window*, peeking into the lives of people who either had forgotten to close the curtains or didn't care. In one room, two kids jumped on the bed, their hair floating around their faces. In another, a woman paced back and forth from her suitcase to the closet, hanging up her clothes. Farther over, a couple stood on their balcony, sipping from wine glasses. Were they watching me, watching them?

A movement above the couple drew my attention up to a balcony on one of the higher floors, where two figures were locked in a tight embrace. The single glowing lamp in the room behind them made their figures into silhouettes. Okay . . . enough voyeurism, I thought as I shifted my gaze away, but then the couple moved jerkily and I found myself watching them, despite the feeling that I should look away.

There was something wrong. The couple broke apart and I could see their outlines clearly against the low light, a tall man with broad shoulders and a smaller woman with short hair. Their stiff arms locked together as they shuffled backward. He pinned the woman against the railing, shoved her shoulders back, then he upended her, and she went over the edge.

Chapter
Two

Isucked in a breath, my hand instinctively covering my mouth as the woman plunged through the air, then disappeared into the mass of trees ringing the hotel grounds. The palm fronds rattled as she hit the tallest trees, the coconut palms, then I saw only a flicker of her body as she tumbled into the lower-growing trees and bushes.

It happened so quickly I didn't even scream or yell. I realized I was standing. I glanced around. The veranda was empty. I dashed into the lobby, yelling for the desk clerk to call an ambulance, then ran across the street where a small group of people was already gathering.

A man, who seemed to have medical experience, knelt beside the sprawled body and wouldn't let anyone move her. She was on her back, half suspended in a hedge of greenery. Her arms were flung out to the side, palms up. A sunburst tattoo on the inside of one wrist looked startlingly dark against her pale skin. Her legs dangled, one twisted in the branches of the plant at an unnatural angle. In the growing darkness, her short dark hair merged with the murky greenery of the bush, causing her face to stand out. She was young, probably no more than twenty-five.

I stepped back, aware of a siren drawing closer. Several hotel employees stood in the group. I grabbed the arm of the man nearest me in a hotel uniform. "There was a man with her on the balcony," I said. "I saw him push her." He stared at me a moment, then said, "You'd better come with me." Paramedics pushed by us as we went to the hotel lobby.

I hadn't been the only one who'd seen her being pushed over the railing. Along with two other witnesses, I waited in the dining area where the hotel served its free breakfast, the counters bare at this time of the evening. On the hotel food chain, this place was just above mid-range. Not bargain basement cheap, but not super luxurious, either. The manager was an overweight woman, with her flyaway blond hair pulled back in a ponytail, who kept tugging at her polo shirt with the embroidered hotel logo as she scurried in and out of the room, looking worried. Across the room, one of the responding police officers spoke to a woman in her forties who had been on her balcony above the couple. She had talked almost nonstop to me while we waited for the police to arrive, telling me how terrible the whole thing was and how awful she felt that she didn't get a good look at the man's face. "But how could I?" she asked. "I was on the floor above them and it was almost dark. I couldn't really see anything, except that it was a man shoving her over. It was definitely a man, and she was fighting him."

A retiree, who I though had probably been in the military, was the other witness. He talked quietly with the hotel manager. His gray hair was clipped short and squared off at the back of his neck per regulation, and he had a military bearing in his stance and walk. He moved back to wait with me as a few police officers strode into the lobby, calling to each other about who was covering which door. The retiree shook his head. "I don't know why they're even bothering. The guy is gone."

"He could still be in the hotel," I said.

"If he's smart, he left during the confusion," the man said, tilting his chin toward the entrance where people were still gathered even though the ambulance was already gone. "There's at least three exits to the parking lot, besides the lobby, where he could slip out," the man continued as he wrapped his arms across his chest. "He may not have even been staying here, either. It's not that hard to get into a room. He'd only have to keep an eye out for someone leaving for dinner, then tell the front desk he forgot his keycard, and they'd make him another one. Happened to me last night, and the clerk on duty didn't even ask to see my identification."

No wonder the manager looked worried. When my turn with the police officer came, I told him what I saw, but I wasn't any more helpful than the chatty woman. "Which floor were they on?" he asked. The officer had ginger-colored hair and a ruddy face. He looked up from his notes, his eyebrows raised.

"Um, well, there was a couple on a balcony—a different couple—I saw them first. The woman who was pushed . . . ," I paused, closing my eyes, trying to re-create the scene in my mind. Were they one floor up or two? About two rooms away . . . or had it been three? I opened my eyes. "I'm sorry. I don't remember exactly. Could I borrow your paper?" He looked surprised, but turned his small notebook to a fresh page and handed it over. I sketched a rough outline of the hotel and marked an "X" where I thought the couple had been. "Somewhere around here," I said, handing it back. "It's very general, but I didn't really count floors or notice anything, except when she went over." I got a sick feeling in my stomach. "Any word on how she is?"

The officer shrugged. "She survived the fall, that's all I know. Describe the man you saw who pushed her. You're sure it was a man?"

"Yes, I'm sure, but that's about all I can say." I described the lighting. "He was taller than her by several inches and bigger, too. Not husky, more . . . athletic. Broad shouldered."

"Hair color? Tattoos? Clothing?" the officer pressed.

"Sorry. I don't know. It was almost dark." When the officer dismissed us, I went back across the street to my hotel and paused in the lobby, feeling shaken and dazed. There was something else I was supposed to do . . . what was it? My foggy thoughts cleared. Angela! Had she come while I was across the street? I reached for my phone and realized I didn't have it with me. I didn't have the imitation purse, either. I hurried to the veranda and found my phone on the side table exactly where I'd left it beside the fake Leah Marshall purse.

I dropped into the chair and reclined against the wooden slats as I checked my messages. One missed call from Angela. I really wanted to go upstairs and curl up in bed, maybe lose myself in one of the books

I'd packed or flip through channels mindlessly, but I called Angela back instead.

"Oh good, you called," she said. "Give me five minutes, and I'll call you back."

I waited, watching the activity across the street. Some police officers left. Media trucks arrived.

My phone rang again, and Angela said, "I have the real purse on my arm, and I'm walking down the beach road right now."

"I'll look for you. I'm on the hotel veranda. Which direction are you coming from?"

"From Costa Bella. I'll see you—"

After a few seconds, I said, "Angela? Are you there?" I pulled the phone away from my ear and saw that the call had dropped. I called the number, but after several rings it went to her voice mail. I didn't leave a message. I would see her in a few minutes anyway.

The sun set and the scene changed. The families departed and a younger crowd—teenagers and college kids—took their place. Costa Bella was only a few miles down the road, and it was a hot spot for college kids on spring break. I was sure it was still popular during the height of summer. I watched the steady parade of young people stroll by, the girls dressed in tank tops or short sundresses, the guys in T-shirts, shorts, and boat shoes or thick sandals. It seemed almost everyone held an ice cream cone or had a shopping bag hooked in their elbow. Some people paused to stare at the hotel across the street. Others gathered around the news reporters giving their stand-up reports. A few people separated themselves from the crowd and came up the steps to the hotel, but none of them was a young woman carrying a Leah Marshall purse on her arm.

I realized I probably wouldn't be able to recognize

Angela from her fuzzy online profile picture. The only thing it revealed about her was that she had long blond hair and a deep tan. I'd probably spot the purse before I spotted Angela. After forty-five minutes or so, I called her back and said I'd be upstairs in my room. She could ask for me at the front desk. Seeing the woman fall from the balcony had shaken me. I wanted to stop looking at the hotel, stop replaying the scene of her body dropping through the air.

"No, I don't have any messages for you." This morning's desk clerk was a fiftyish woman with a deep southern drawl rolling through her words. "Sorry, darlin'," she said after I thanked her. I made my way to the breakfast area, and sat down at the table with Ben.

"Nothing. No word from Angela." I put my cell phone on the table and nodded at the waiter, indicating that I'd like another glass of fresh orange juice. "The cell phone reception in my room is terrible. I'd hoped I'd missed Angela's call and would have a message from her."

I'd already told Ben about seeing the woman pushed off the balcony. The local newscast, which was blaring from a television in the nearby bar area, aired a story on it and reported that the woman was in critical condition at a local hospital. Her name hadn't been released, only the information that she wasn't a hotel guest. Just as the retiree speculated, it appeared the man who'd pushed her was not a registered hotel guest either. Black and white security video showed the top of a man's head at the front desk, which would have been helpful if he hadn't been wearing a baseball cap pulled low over his face.

The reporter stated that the man told the desk clerk he lost his keycard. She made him a new one, but wasn't able to give a good description of him. It had been a busy time at the desk, and she'd only glanced at him. I looked away from the television and gave myself a mental shake. That tragic story had nothing to do with me, except that I happened to see it. I had other things to focus on, like Ben, who I rarely saw. And, there was that loose end from last night, Angela. "I wonder what happened to Angela," I said.

Ben's mouth was full. He shrugged one shoulder, then concentrated on cutting his Belgian waffles. I'd had pancakes and a bowl of chopped fruit while he had an omelet as an appetizer. Apparently, the waffles were the main course. I watched him work through his food, slightly amazed. "It's so unfair you can still eat like a teenager." His lanky frame didn't show an ounce of flab.

He swirled more syrup on his waffles and grinned. "It's not every day that I get a free breakfast buffet. Got to take advantage. You should have one of these waffles. They've got something in them . . . cinnamon, maybe."

"No way. If I eat like you, I'll be wearing a muumuu at the end of my vacation."

"Since when did you start counting calories?"

"Since I had two kids. And the big three-o is coming up. So enjoy that food. You can't eat like that forever," I said, raising my glass in a mock toast.

Ben wiped his mouth with the cloth napkin and asked the waiter if he could have the recipe for the waffles. I blinked. "You're cooking? With actual pots and pans?"

"Of course," Ben said, his forehead wrinkled. "You don't think I live on take-out, do you?"

"Ah—well, yes, I did. Do you even *have* a waffle iron?" I'd never seen his small apartment near the base. I'd pictured it as spartan.

"Sure. The person who lived there before me liked to cook. Worked in one of the restaurants on the beach, but got a job in New York and couldn't take all his stuff. The landlord was going to send it to Goodwill, but I said I'd take it. I did the ramen noodle and pizza thing in college, but I like to eat, you know? There's nothing like a good steak or spaghetti Bolognese."

"*Bolognese?* You make spaghetti Bolognese?"

"Yeah," Ben said as the waiter returned with a print-out of the recipe. Ben thanked him and tapped the page. "Cinnamon. I knew it. And vanilla sugar . . . interesting."

I sat back in my chair. "My brother, a foodie. Who knew? Aren't you the same kid who refused to eat roast because Mom cooked it with a bay leaf?"

"That was a long time ago," Ben said, but he was smiling.

"I know." I leaned forward. "It's for a girl, isn't it? You want to impress someone."

"No, I like to eat good food." Ben folded the paper and tucked it in his pocket. "So how are the kids?"

I noted the obvious conversational dodge, but went with it. I figured I'd already ribbed him enough over the cooking issue. "We've already talked about the kids and about Mitch. I want to hear about you. What's going on with you?"

"Flying. I had a TDY to Japan last month. That was cool. I got Mom a tea set."

"She'll like that. What else?"

"Not much. Same old thing."

I rolled my eyes and muttered, "Guys," in exasperation. "Would it kill you to give a few details?"

"There's not much to tell. I go to work. I go out with the guys. I go to the gym. You know, normal stuff."

"And people think the life of a pilot is so exciting."

Ben snorted. "Yeah. It's just like the movies. *Top Gun* all the time."

My phone chimed. It was the kids, but they didn't have long to talk. They were simply calling to check in because Aunt Summer had insisted. Nathan informed me that Aunt Summer didn't have a night-light, but it was okay because she'd left the bathroom light on *all night*. Livvy's news involved a report on the status of the cookies (delicious) and their plans for the morning (beach, movies, and more cookies).

I hung up and clicked through the various screens on my phone. "Still nothing from Angela," I said.

"Really? No texts?" Ben asked.

"No. I think it's odd that I haven't heard from her at all." I had bought several bags from her, and she had always been prompt in her replies to any questions I had. Lately, she'd sent me occasional e-mails, sometimes updating me if she had a new bag for sale, but more often than not, to share one of the funny stories or photos that make their way around the Internet. There had also been an uptick in the cute puppy photos she shared. She was seriously thinking of getting a dog and wanted my take on owning a big dog since we have a rottweiler. I'd advised her to get a smaller dog since she lived in an apartment, but she'd replied almost instantly, "Purse dogs are too clichéd for words, Ellie. No itty-bitty outfits or jeweled collars . . . if anyone's wearing jewels, it will be me! What do you think about a Weimaraner?"

"Do you know if she got a dog?" I asked.

Ben checked his phone as he murmured, "Hmm?"

"She wanted a puppy and mentioned Weimaraners."

"Weimaraners?" Ben looked up from his phone, perplexed.

"The gray dogs with the blue eyes. Really pretty. That's all I know about them, and that's what I told Angela."

Ben nodded in a distracted way, then checked his watch. "Want to go for a walk down the beach road? You're not getting the kids until later, are you?"

"No, they'd run at the sight of me. Livvy informed me I'm not to arrive a minute before noon so I don't cut into their time with Summer."

"Okay then," Ben stood up. "Angela works in a store about half a mile down the beach road. Why don't we walk by and see if she's there? She probably ran into friends or something and got distracted last night."

"Sure," I said. "Let me run upstairs and grab the purse she's exchanging for me."

The sun was already hot when we emerged from the hotel, and I slipped on my sunglasses. The crowds were lighter than they had been last night, and we were able to walk side by side. Boogie boards, racks of T-shirts and postcards, along with all sorts of sea-related kitsch, like seashell wind chimes and plaques declaring MY OTHER HOUSE IS A BEACH HOUSE, spilled out of the stores onto the sidewalk. The smell of sunscreen permeated the air, except when we walked by the fudge shop. I breathed in deeply. "Got to come back here later," I said as the aroma enveloped us.

"You and your chocolate."

"At least it makes me easy to buy for," I said, moving to the side as several kids trotted down the street, their flip-flops slapping the ground. Their parents followed at a slower pace, pulling a wagon loaded with a cooler, toys, folding chairs, and a huge furled beach umbrella.

Ben said, "They look like they're prepared for a siege."

"You wait. Soon, that will be you."

"God, I hope not. At least, not for a long time." He gestured to a small store called The Sea Cottage. "We're here."

The store had wide wooden floor planks in a pale blond wood. White walls and images of the gulf made the small space feel bigger than it was. Stacks of clothes in taupe, pink, gray, and cream sat atop tables of weathered white wood. Gauzy scarves and long necklaces dangled from driftwood displays on a glass counter at the back of the store. A light airy soundtrack, mostly flutes, played softly in the background. It was the kind of store that catered to wealthy middle-aged women, and it surprised me that Angela worked here.

A girl in her early twenties came around the counter. Her name tag identified her as Cara. She had a thick swath of bangs combed across her forehead that dipped into the crease of one eyelid. She wore a short-sleeved cotton shirt, tied at the waist over a pale pink tank with gray pants. Three inches of thin gold bracelets jangled on both wrists as she moved across the wide plank floorboards. "Can I help you?"

I said, "We're looking for Angela. Is she here?"

Cara's lips pressed into a thin, disapproving line. "No. Are you friends of hers?" Now that she was close to us, I could see that she had a piercing near the corner of her mouth and several along her earlobes, all empty of jewelry.

Ben hesitated, so I said we were.

"You can tell her she better call in, or she won't have a job."

Ben asked, "So she was scheduled to work today?"

"Yes. And I'm not covering for her anymore." Her heavy bangs slipped over her eyelashes, and she tossed her head, flicking them back into place. "And after I closed for her last night, too. Like I'll be doing that again for her."

"So what time did she leave last night?" I asked.

"About eight-fifteen. We're not supposed to close up alone, but she got a phone call and said it was like super important, so I told her to go ahead." She sighed and crossed her arms over her waist. Her short nails were painted a glossy black and contrasted with her white shirt.

"That was probably me," I said, glancing at Ben.

"So have you tried her phone?" Ben asked.

"No, I texted her," she said.

I wondered how many more years I had before Livvy began using that tone, which implied we were stupid for even asking the question. "No personal calls at work," she explained.

"Does she usually text you back?" I asked.

"Yeah. Right away. Her phone is, like, glued to her hand."

I exchanged a glance with Ben. "Maybe she's at home. She could have overslept or maybe she's sick."

Cara's forehead wrinkled into a frown. "You think she's okay, don't you? I mean, it *is* kind of weird that

she didn't call or anything today. That's not like her."
Her irritation had ebbed away, replaced with concern.

"She's probably delayed," I said, going into soothing-mom-mode. "Or, her phone battery is dead."

"No, she would never let that happen," Cara said as she raked her dark fingernails through her bangs. "She might miss a call."

"So she had her phone with her when she left last night?" I asked, wanting to make sure Angela knew we were trying to reach her.

"She was, like, texting as she walked out the door. Maybe she got her big payoff," Cara said in a quiet voice, more to herself than to us.

"Payoff?" Ben asked.

"Yeah, she was talking about some big find. She said she'd have tons of money soon," Cara said.

"Was she listing something online, something exclusive?" I asked, wondering if Angela had found some rare designer outfit or bag, maybe a Birkin or something along those lines.

"I don't know, but I don't think so. She said it wouldn't be like her allowance from her dad, but *really* big money. Enough to buy a house on the water or travel anywhere she wanted. She said when it came in, she would book a flight to Paris for the fall shows."

Even a Birkin bag wouldn't pay for a house with a water view. "Was it an investment, something like that?" I asked.

"No idea," Cara said. "I didn't believe her. I thought it was all talk, but now that she's gone . . . well, maybe it wasn't made up."

We left the store and retraced our steps toward the hotel. "That didn't seem like a place Angela would work," I said. "She seems more like a pulsing music and bright colors kind of girl."

"That's what she likes when it comes to clubs," Ben said. "But she needed the money. Her dad works overseas. He does something in electronics or computers. He sends money to her and her brother every month. She's not that good at managing it and usually runs through it pretty fast. She'll get her money from him and buy some designer dress or purse, then a few weeks later, she's out of money."

"So does she go to college?"

"She took a couple of classes last semester, but said she wasn't into campus life. I think she mostly hangs out on the beach or works in the store when she needs extra money to make it until the next check from her dad. Then she hits the clubs at night. If she runs through her money, which happens quite a bit, she sells some of her designer duds online to tide her over until the next check arrives from her father."

"Designer duds?" I asked. "I would recommend not describing designer clothes as *duds*, especially around Angela."

"Yeah, I got the lecture. I guess you could say I view clothes as something to wear and she thinks of them as . . ."

"An art form?" I supplied.

Ben nodded. "That's one way to put it. We're not on the same wavelength." I looked at him out of the corner of my eye, but didn't ask anything else. I could see from his face that he wouldn't have any more to say on the subject, but I had to wonder if Angela's rather carefree approach to life was why Ben seemed to have distanced himself from her.

It had taken Ben a few years to find his niche. After

high school, he'd worked in sales for a plastics company, then he'd found a job as a tour guide for a company that coordinated trips abroad for high school students. That job ended when the economy shriveled and parents' disposable incomes dried up. He'd returned home with a host of useful phrases in five foreign languages and a list of the best restaurants in European capitals—so maybe his interest in food wasn't that unexpected, I thought tangentially. He'd enrolled in college when he returned from his tour guide stint. He'd graduated with honors and a degree in engineering, then secured a slot for pilot training through the Reserve Officer Training Corps. Ben was more focused than he appeared at first glance. It sounded like Angela was more of a party girl than I'd realized.

"Where's her mom?" I asked.

"South Beach. Divorced. Sounded like it was messy. Angela said she hadn't talked to her since her high school graduation."

"Wow," I said, trying to imagine a life without family connections. We might not live close to our families, but we talked on the phone and visited as much as we could.

"I know," Ben said.

We walked a few paces in silence, then I asked, "Do you think we should call her home phone—just to check? Or, is that kind of weird, for us to check up on her? For all we know, she could have gotten an unexpected inheritance and jetted off to the French Riviera."

"Somehow, I don't think that's where she is." Ben took out his phone. "She doesn't have a home phone, just her cell phone. That's why it's odd that she's not answering or texting. She might go a few minutes without calling back, but, like Cara said, she's *always* texting. I'll try her cell phone again."

Ben walked a few more paces, then stopped and scanned the sidewalks. A bald man nearly bumped into him, but Ben didn't even notice the man's glare as he stepped around him. "Do you hear that?" Ben asked. "That music?"

I could faintly hear the notes of "Girls Just Want to Have Fun."

"Yes, I do."

"That's her ringtone." Ben looked around. I scanned the people in our immediate area, but didn't see anyone reaching for their cell phone. The song cut off mid-note, and Ben pulled his phone away from his ear. "It went to voice mail."

Ellie's Digital Organizing Tips

Organizing Computer Files

The key to organizing computer files is to create a tiered system that works for you. If you save everything to your hard drive, you'll have an overwhelming number of files to sort through when you want to find a file. Take a little time to think through how you use your computer, then pick an option that works for you.

Organize by category—If you work from home, you could start with two separate folders, Work and Home, then use subfiles to categorize within those broad groups. If you use your computer for only home-based files, you can still use the same principle. For instance, create folders for Finances, Kids' School Work, Photos, Music, Hobby/Craft, and Recipes.

Organize by individual—Another way to organize your hard drive is with a folder for each family member. This system works well for families who share a computer. Under each name, use folders to group files together. Kids can have a folder for each school subject under their name.

Chapter
Three

"Call it again," I said.

Ben had already hit REDIAL. The notes sounded again and we both moved down the street a few steps, then paused over one of the large flowerpots that lined the edge of the sidewalk. "It's louder here." I pushed begonias aside.

"Here," Ben said as he ended the call, simultaneously putting his phone in his pocket and picking up a small phone with rich, dark soil almost obscuring its shiny gold case. He activated the screen, and I grabbed his arm to lower it so that I could see. "Thirty-six missed calls? Fifty-two text messages?" I asked in astonishment.

"I think that's normal for Angela."

"But Cara said she had her phone with her when she left the store. She got all those calls and texts in a few hours?" My mind reeled. I was old, I realized. I couldn't imagine having that many missed calls, much less texts, in a few hours. I doubted I'd have that many calls when we returned from our vacation.

Ben punched some buttons and scrolled through the incoming calls. "There's mine," I said. "At eight-twenty."

"Lots of incoming calls after that. Several from you and me through this morning." He switched over to the list of sent calls. "Nothing after eight-thirty last night."

I studied the street, looking toward my hotel. It wasn't in sight because the street curved gently back on itself and our hotel was hidden behind several other high-rise hotels. "How far do you think it is to the hotel?"

"Maybe a quarter mile."

"What are the chances that she dropped her phone by accident?"

"And she didn't realize it?" Ben asked. "Zero." He shook his head. "If she'd dropped her phone or lost it, she'd go back and look for it. And if she couldn't find it, the first thing she'd do is go buy a new one today, even if it was a cheap disposable one." He punched some more buttons. "I'm calling her brother."

"I think that's a good idea." I leaned against the flowerpot as Ben pulled up the number from Angela's contact list. After a moment, he said, "Chase, this is Ben. We met in June when I came to pick up your sister." He explained how Angela hadn't arrived at the hotel last night, her no-show at work, and how we'd found her phone with no outgoing calls or texts since last night.

I examined the strap on the fake Leah Marshall purse as he talked. This morning, I'd switched to a Fossil crossbody wallet bag in light tan so I'd been able to take the Leah Marshall purse out of the box and carry it on my shoulder.

I listened to Ben's one-sided conversation. "Right,

but would she go off without her phone?" he asked. "Without calling in to work or telling you?"

His jaw tightened. "Was she home last night? Oh, well, don't you think—"

He threw his head back, studied the sky, then paced away and back, murmuring, "Right. Okay, well, I don't agree with you . . . but you're her brother. Sure. You're on your way there now? I'll meet you."

Ben turned to me and said, "He doesn't get it. He says she's checked out before—picked up and left without a word to anyone, so we should 'chill.' He thinks she'll turn up in a day or two."

"She didn't go home last night?" I asked, fiddling with the zipper on the fake Leah Marshall purse, which was caught at the halfway point.

"Chase was out of town, so he doesn't know if she was there or not, but apparently that's nothing to worry about."

I picked up on the edge of disdain in his words. "You don't like him?"

Ben shook his head. "I only met him once, but he's . . . slick."

Interesting description. I processed that information silently, then said, "Well, like you said, he is her brother and if he thinks everything is fine, then . . ."

"I know," Ben said shortly.

"I wonder where her car is." I shaded my eyes to look up and down the street, which was filled on each side with cars parked in parallel slots.

"That's a good question. I'll check at the apartment. I know that sometimes she left her car there and walked to work. It's not that far, and parking is a hassle on the beach road. Chase is on his way to the apartment he and Angela share. I told him I'd meet him there and give him Angela's phone."

"If her car isn't at the apartment, it could be anywhere," I said, gesturing to the beach road. "There're several public lots all along the beach." I glanced at my watch. "While you do that, I'll pick up the kids from Summer. By the time I get there, it will be almost noon."

We walked back to the hotel. Before I climbed in the van, I called, "See you in a little while."

He waved, pulled out of the parking lot in his sporty blue Mazda, and turned into the traffic slowly creeping to the east, the direction we'd walked that morning. I turned the opposite way and inched along. It was late Saturday morning in a Florida beach town on the week of July Fourth. We weren't going anywhere fast. After a few blocks, I took a road that cut north, away from the beach, and the congestion eased. My phone rang and I glanced at the screen—blocked number—before I answered the call with the speaker.

"Ellie? Is that you?"

I didn't recognize the female voice, but I got calls at all times of the day and night for my organizing business. Being a professional organizer was a bit like being a realtor. I wasn't ever really on vacation, even when I was out of town, and with the economic downturn, I couldn't afford to miss any potential clients. "Speaking," I said.

"Ellie. Thank God you answered." A sound came over the line, a raspy gulp like the kids make when they are trying not to cry. My "mom sense" went on high alert, even though I knew it wasn't one of my kids on the phone.

"Angela?" I asked.

"I need you to take the purse, the fake Leah Marshall—this is really important—take it to my apartment," she said. Her breathing was rough and there was a tension in her words, an urgency that had me sitting up straighter.

"Are you okay?" I asked.

There was a slight hesitation, then she said quickly, "Yes, I'm fine. Don't worry about me. Just take the purse, okay?"

"Sure," I said. "I'm on my way to pick up my kids. I can drop it by later—"

"No!" she cut me off. "You've got to do it *now*." Her breathing was ragged and her words vibrated with . . . fear, I realized. My heartbeat sped up. I pulled off the road into a Publix and stopped at the far end of the parking lot with the van slewed diagonally over the lines.

"Do you understand?" she asked, her voice tense. "You can't wait a minute. Take it *now*."

"Okay. I can do that. What's your address?" I asked, opening the van's console where I keep a pen and notepad.

"Thank you," she said as she blew out a breath. "12989 Sea Water Lane, Apartment twenty-nine B."

I jotted down the address. "I was worried about you when you didn't show up last night and I didn't hear from you this morning. Ben, too."

"I'm sorry. I—," she broke off. "I'm sorry. Tell Ben, I'm sorry . . . about everything," she said, her last words caught up in a sob.

"Angela," I said, using the same soothing voice that I spoke in when the kids were hurt or distraught, "where are you? I'm sure everything will be okay. Are you at home?"

"No. That's not important. What's important is you take the purse to my apartment and then leave. Do you understand?" Her voice trembled with intensity. "Don't stay. Just leave it on the porch and get out of there."

"Okay." I tapped the address into the GPS, which was still mounted on the windshield from the drive down yesterday. I put the van in DRIVE. "I'm turning around right now."

A dial tone sounded. I glanced at the purse, which I'd tossed on the passenger seat when I first got in the van. Why the panic, the fear? It was only a purse—and a fake one at that. It was worth probably about ten or twenty dollars total. I hit REDIAL on my phone, but got a message saying the call couldn't be completed.

The GPS routed me inland along the highway and then south, back toward the gulf. I made a quick call to Summer to let her know I'd be a little late, then called Ben. He didn't pick up. I was glad the route kept me off the busy beach road, and I made good time, pulling into the Sea Side Garden apartment complex a little after noon.

Located a few blocks inland from the busy beach road, the complex was misnamed, because there wasn't a drop of seawater in sight, only a shopping complex and a few gated neighborhoods with patio homes. Several high-rise hotels towered over the patio homes, cutting off any view of the gulf. The complex was well kept, with spotless cream two-story stucco buildings topped with terra-cotta roofs. The "garden" part of the name was accurate. The grounds were lushly landscaped with fringy pindo palms shading the walks, which were lined with the low-growing, sturdier sago palms. Purple bougainvillea mixed with ivy trailed over the stucco walls, draping down to low-growing shrubs and flowering ground covers.

I couldn't find a slot near Angela's building and had to park on the far side of the complex near the pool. There were several parallel parking slots running along the tall stucco wall that enclosed the property. My parallel parking skills were a little rusty, but I managed to pull into a space on my first attempt. I picked up the purse and hopped out of the van, feeling accomplished as I walked by the vine-covered wall that enclosed the pool. Through the wrought iron gate, I could see a slice of blue water sparkling in the sun. It looked like the pool was only slightly larger than a hot tub, but I suppose if you were only a couple of steps from the beach, you wouldn't need a big pool. I saw Ben under the residents' carport near a silver convertible BWM. The convertible's top was up and he was peering in the driver's side window. I looked at the number painted on the ground: 29B. "Angela's car?"

Ben straightened. "Hey, Ellie. What are you doing here?"

I held up the purse. "Angela called me and asked me to bring this by her apartment."

Ben closed his eyes for a moment and breathed out. "She's okay? What happened? Where is she?"

"I don't know. She wouldn't tell me anything. All she wanted to talk about was this purse. She said I had to get it here right away and leave it."

"Is she here?" Ben asked, starting toward the apartment building.

"No. She said she wasn't home."

He took a step closer to me. It was already shady with all the palm trees and it was even dimmer under the carport. "She wouldn't tell me where she was and she sounded . . ." I paused, trying to think how to sum up Angela's state. "Distraught" and "afraid" came to mind, but I didn't want to voice those words. "She was . . . upset," I said, knowing it was a pretty mild description, but I couldn't quite overcome those sheltering, big sister habits. Ben was already worried and I didn't want to add to his concern.

"Upset, how? Crying? Angry?"

I sighed, realizing that he wasn't going to let me gloss over her reaction. "I don't know her that well. Today, she sounded . . . scared." I watched his face and said, "You're really worried about her . . . that she's in trouble?"

He put his hands on his hips and stared down at the car as he said, "Angela's kind of like this car—you can't drive it slow, you know what I mean? She's crazy and fun and wild . . . I'm worried she got herself into something . . . over her head."

He nodded to the empty slot next to the car. "The neighbor just left, and she told me the car has been here all night—at least, it was here when she walked her dog late last night and early this morning."

"It's a nice car," I said, taking in the leather trim and sleek lines. "Are you sure Angela had money problems?"

Ben shrugged. "I don't think she's making payments on this. It was a gift from her dad."

"I guess she could always sell her car if things got really rough," I said as we walked to the apartment. "Her brother isn't here yet?"

"I don't think so, but let's check." We walked up the curvy path and followed the little signs pointing us around the corner to Angela's building. "How did you get here so fast?" he asked.

"I didn't take the beach road."

Angela's apartment was a secluded ground-floor apartment on the end of the building, a prime spot. It shared a concrete patio with the opposite apartment, which had a pot of petunias beside its front door and a mat that read, WIPE YOUR PAWS. Angela's door, with only a dry, crinkled palm frond caught under the threshold, looked bare in comparison.

Ben raised his hand to knock on the door, but paused and leaned closer. "That's odd," he said, pointing to several deep gouges between the doorframe and the handle of the door. He rapped on the door, and it swung open.

Chapter Four

"**I**s Angela messy?" I asked.

"Not like this," Ben said, carefully edging the door open with the back of his hand, revealing tumbled couch cushions and a lamp on the floor.

"Angela?" Ben called, and stepped slowly through the door.

"We shouldn't go in," I said. "We should call the police."

"What if she's in there? She might be hurt," Ben said.

"She said she wasn't home—"

He shook my restraining hand off of his arm. "Chase?" he called.

I followed him inside the small entry area. Ben stepped over a large leather cushion from the couch and moved toward the kitchen. From the entry, I could see through an open door to a bedroom decorated with a feminine flare in shades ranging from pale yellow to deep gold. It was in even worse shape than the living room. Clothing hung from gaping drawers and was strewn across the floor. An overturned nightstand lay in the middle of the room, and fashion magazines rested on top of everything as if they'd been flung into the air like oversized, glossy confetti.

A breeze stirred the lemon curtains in the bedroom, catching my attention. No one leaves windows open in Florida in July. "The window is open in this bedroom," I said as I stepped carefully around several throw pillows. Ben moved that way, too. I stopped on the threshold of the bedroom while Ben swept aside the curtains.

A pale gold comforter had covered the bed. It was piled on the floor, along with eyelet-edged sheets. It looked as if a small explosion had taken place inside the double-door closet, scattering clothes, shoes, bags, scarves, and hats across the floor. A Mac laptop had been knocked off the desk, shattering the screen. "I guess money wasn't the motive," I said, pointing to the computer. "I bet that would have been easy to sell online or in the paper."

Ben examined the window. "The screen is outside on the ground."

"But if the front door was already open, why . . . ," I trailed off. "Do you think they were in here when we got here?" I whispered as I reached for my phone. "They could still be outside."

Ben spoke softly, too. "You call 911. I'll call Chase." We both moved back to the living room. I pulled the purse off my shoulder, then stopped. "I don't have my phone. It's still in the van." I'd been so wrapped up in what was going on, I'd forgotten I was carrying the imitation purse. I'd taken off the Fossil crossbody bag when I climbed in the van. It was still there. Ben waved a hand to stop me. "Let's stay together. Chase didn't pick up." Ben left a terse message, then dialed the police.

There was a sharp knock on the door and a voice called, "Hello?"

I twirled around and saw a teenage guy in a T-shirt embroidered with the words COSTA BELLA FLOWER SHOP, holding a huge bouquet of mixed flowers. "Delivery for Angela Day," he said, holding out the flowers to me. He glanced around. "Must have been a good party."

The gorgeous arrangement of roses, lilies, lilacs, and gardenias wobbled in midair as he held it one-handed. I took them, but said, "I'm not Angela."

He consulted a piece of paper. "But you are in twenty-nine B. Enjoy." He gave a little salute before he left.

A trim man in a pale gray suit shoved past the delivery guy. "What the hell is going on here?" he barked as he surveyed the room.

"Chase," Ben said, quickly crossing the room. "I tried to call you."

Chase pulled off his Ray Ban sunglasses. "Oh. Ben, is it?"

While his sister had golden blond hair, Chase's hair was paler, almost white, and was cut close to his head. A mustache and goatee framed his lower face and I wondered if he'd grown it to distract from his rather pointed nose. If he had, it didn't work because the added facial hair only emphasized his nose, and with his small dark eyes, he reminded me of a mouse. He gave the flowers a curious glance.

"That's right." Ben quickly introduced me as his sister and explained we'd found the door unlocked and the apartment ransacked. As Ben explained, Chase made a quick circuit of the apartment, twirling his sunglasses by the earpiece.

"Ben called the police," I said.

He twirled the glasses faster. "Good. Good. That's good." His dark gaze darted around the room, and I got the feeling that he was anything but pleased about the call.

"Here's Angela's phone," Ben said.

Chase took the phone, then tossed it onto the kitchen counter. "Thanks for bringing it over. Angela will turn up soon. She always does." He walked toward us, obviously intending to usher us out the door, and I got a close look at his face. My initial thought had been that he was older than Angela, but up close I could tell he was closer to twenty than thirty. It must have been the suit that gave me the impression of his maturity.

Still holding the flowers with one hand, I pulled the purse off my shoulder. "Angela called me. She asked me to drop this off—" I broke off and turned to the front door, which was still open. A high-pitched voice was wailing, "Ohmygod, ohmygod, ohmygod. Someone help! She's dead."

We all froze for a second, then moved to the door. I jerked to a stop, put the flowers on an end table, then hurried after Ben and Chase out the door. Ben sprinted across the patio to a woman who stood, her arms and legs visibly trembling, in the parking area near the pool, a beach bag discarded on the asphalt behind her. She was wearing a bikini under an open-weave cover-up. She was probably about eighteen and looked as if she were about to throw up.

"In the pool." She paused and swallowed hard. "There's somebody dead in the pool." Chase and Ben both took off to the pool, leaving the poor girl shivering and alone.

I put a hand on her shoulder and steered her to the curb beside the residents' parking spaces. "Sit down here," I said, and she collapsed like a puppet whose strings had been cut. "Would you like some water or something?" I asked. She shook her head and buried her face in her shaking hands. I picked up the beach towel that had spilled out of her bag, but left everything else exactly as it was. I shook the towel out and wrapped it around her shoulders. It was at least ninety-five degrees and humid, but she was shivering with shock.

"The police will be here soon," I said, thinking of the call Ben had made and wondering if we should make another call. Somehow I thought a call about a break-in might not get as quick a response as a call about a dead body, but I couldn't make the call unless I knew for sure what I was reporting, and then I'd have to get my phone out of the van.

I squared my shoulders and hurried across the parking lot to the pool. As soon as I stepped through the wrought iron gate that yawned open, I saw Ben standing fully clothed and completely soaked. At his feet, two bodies huddled at the rim of the pool. Ben was panting. Water trailed down from his hair into his face and dripped into his eyes, but he didn't wipe it away. I stepped around a lounge chair and saw that Chase had the limp form of a woman gathered to his chest, her blond hair sagging over his arm as he swayed back and forth. She was fully clothed but wet, as well. Little rivulets of water were snaking across the bumpy pool deck. My gaze locked with Ben's, and he shook his head. I closed my eyes and dropped down onto the end of a lounge chair. Ben gave Chase's hunched back a long look, then came over and sat down on the lounge chair next to me.

"I had to pull her out. In case . . . just in case," he said, his tone dazed and, although he was staring at the far side of the pool, I knew he wasn't seeing Chase. He shook his head. "She was so light . . . so easy to move through the water."

I pressed my hand to his shoulder. "I'm sorry, Ben."

He looked up at me like he was surprised to find me there.

I said, "I'm going to get some blankets and my phone." He nodded and wiped his hand down over his face. I met the apartment manager, a woman with in-flated gilt-colored hair, on my way to the van. She was horrified when I told her what had happened and looked like she wanted to sprint back to her office near the front of the complex. "Call 911 and tell them what's happened, then keep an eye on that woman over there," I said, pointing to the woman huddled on the curb. I hurried to the van and grabbed my phone along with a thick Mexican blanket we kept in the back for days at the playground or picnics.

I slipped back inside the pool gate and went directly to Ben, who was sitting with his head in his hands. I wrapped the blanket around him and rubbed his shoulder. What could you say in a situation like this? There weren't any words that seemed adequate, so I stayed silent. Chase was weeping on the other side of the pool, and I felt awkward, witnessing his grief. I heard sirens and breathed an internal sigh of relief. I perched on the end of the lounge chair and tried to look any-where but at Chase. That's when I saw the purse. It was on a little end table positioned between a pair of lounge chairs a few feet away. I knew, even at a distance, that it was a gray Chloe shoulder bag with a long, thin strap. It was just the sort of bag I'd expect Angela to carry. The mouth gapped open, revealing the hot pink lining. It looked rather like a beached trout. The contents were scattered over the table. I stood and walked over.

A pair of sunglasses, a long, thin cream-colored wallet, several bits of paper, hair clips, breath mints, a movie ticket stub, and a small prescription bottle had tumbled out. I didn't touch anything. I'd barely sat down at the foot of the chaise lounge when a police officer arrived, took one look around, and spoke into his radio.

The police officer escorted Chase out of the pool area, took my name and Ben's name, and then told us not to move. It was only about ten minutes later that a fortyish sandy-haired man wearing a cream-colored guayabera shirt with black pants strode into the pool area. "Hey, Austin, how's fatherhood? Getting any sleep at all?" he said to the young police officer with shoulders so broad that I wondered how they found a uniform to fit him. With his build, he looked like he should be stepping into a cage match.

"Not much," the officer said. "I've got a cigar with your name on it."

"Terrific." The guy in the casual clothes had a badge clipped to the hem of his shirt and from the way the police officer quickly got down to business, outlining the situation as they walked around the pool to the body, I figured he was a detective.

Voices carry over water, something both guys must

not have thought of as they stood over Angela's body. I could clearly hear their conversation despite their lowered voices. "Body was removed from the pool by a Ben Evanworth," the police officer said, consulting his notes. "Says he came running after being alerted by the woman in the parking lot, a Carrie Sanchez. She says she doesn't know the woman, only saw the body in the pool and screamed for help."

The detective squatted on his haunches to look at Angela's body. I glanced at Ben, but if he could hear the conversation, he didn't seem to be taking it in. He'd moved only slightly. He was still hunched over, staring at the ground, his hands clasped between his knees. Now that Chase wasn't bending over her, I could see more of Angela's body. A tangled mass of blond hair covered most of her face. A few strands of it trailed over the edge of the pool, the ends still moving slightly with each ripple of the water. She was wearing a sky blue dress shirt, with a long gold chain that would have fallen almost to the waist of her black trousers, and two-inch open-toed gray heels. Work clothes, I thought.

"Do we know who she is?"

"According to the man who pulled her from the pool, this is Angela Day. Her brother, Chase Day, was also on the scene when she was found. He's waiting in the apartment they shared, twenty-nine B. They had a break-in."

"Busy place." The detective stood up. "We have confirmation on the identity from the brother?"

"Yes. He's distraught. There's also a purse over there," the police officer said, and they both glanced across the pool. I lowered my gaze to my hands.

"Who's the woman?"

"Sister of the guy who pulled the woman out of the

water. Ellie Avery. She says she got a call from the victim this morning. Told her to come here."

"Good grief. Sounds like a family reunion. Okay, I'll start with the brother. Got a place we can go?"

"Yes, the apartment manager says you can use her office. And one more thing," the police officer added as the detective moved to turn away. "I've seen her," he said. "I work two clubs on weekends as a bouncer. She was a regular."

"Party girl?"

He nodded and even across the pool I could see a shadow cross the officer's face. "Shame when the lifestyle gets them this young."

The detective tilted his head. "You think it was drugs?"

The police officer shrugged. "Seems likely. Who goes swimming fully clothed? And drowns in a three-foot splash pool?"

Thirty minutes later, Ben and I were waiting in the reception area of apartment manager's office. I couldn't see the pool, but I could see the continual flow of people back and forth through the main entrance. I'd already called Summer and told her that I wouldn't be at her apartment anytime soon.

The small reception area had a battered desk, three uncomfortable molded-plastic chairs, and a small coffee table with a dusty plant centered up between stacks of *People, Us,* and *Celeb.* The bulky police officer who had secured the scene was seated at the desk, watching Ben and me. He had escorted us into the office and informed us that we weren't allowed to talk to one another while we waited.

I shifted on the seat and shot another glance at Ben. He was so still, his face pale, as he stared fixedly at the low-pile carpet. His clothes were damp and wrinkled,

but with the high temperature, they were already par-
tially dry. I gave him a long look, willing him to look
up at me, but he was lost in his own thoughts. I picked
up a magazine and flipped through it, more to give me
something to do with my hands than because I wanted
to catch up on celebrity news. I stared at a photo col-
lage that claimed celebs were just like normal, nonfa-
mous people: They shopped for yogurt! They pumped
gas! They parallel parked!

The door to the manager's office opened, and Carrie
Sanchez stepped out. She still looked shaken, but she
seemed more in control of herself than she had in the
parking lot. She held the beach towel, now folded
neatly, clasped to her chest. She raced out of the office,
and the plastic plant trembled in her wake.

The police officer consulted a list, then said, "Mrs.
Avery?"

I tossed the magazine on the table and followed him
into the small office where the man in casual clothes
sat behind a large faux-wood desk. A framed map of
the apartment complex hung on the wall behind him.
He reached over pictures of two kids, an open can of
Red Bull, and several bobblehead figurines to shake
my hand. "Detective Adam Jenson," he said with a
friendly smile. "You're Ellie Avery?"

I shook his hand and confirmed my identity, then
took a seat in the chair in front of the desk.

"So let's get the preliminary things out of the way."
He took down my name and contact information.

"Georgia?" he asked after I gave him my address.

"Yes, we're in town on vacation," I said, which led to
questions about where we were staying and how many
people were in our family. I explained about Mitch's

delay, then fell silent. I realized I was gripping my hands together in my lap and made a conscious effort to relax my fingers. It didn't matter that I hadn't done anything wrong—I was still as jittery as if I were a guilty party. It was an instinctual reaction. Even if a cop pulled me over and I knew I wasn't going over the speed limit, I broke out in a cold sweat.

Detective Jenson put down the gold pen he'd used to take notes. "Okay, so tell me why you're here."

"Because Angela called me this morning. She asked me to bring a purse to her apartment. She wanted me to leave it on her porch." I explained how I knew Angela through her boutique, how we'd exchanged e-mails, and about the mix-up with the purse. "She also dated my brother a few times," I said.

Jenson didn't say anything, just raised his eyebrows.

"I don't know much about that." I figured it was up to Ben to share that kind of information with the detective.

"What did he say about her?"

"Ben? Not much. Until this morning, we'd hardly talked about her at all. All I know is they went out a few times."

Jenson wrote notes without looking up. "But you talked about her this morning?"

"Yes. I thought it was odd that she didn't show up last night at the hotel. I've bought other things from her and she's always been prompt to answer any e-mails, and she shipped things as soon as she received payment. I'd never had a problem before, so it seemed strange that she'd offer to personally deliver the purse to me and then not show up, not even call."

"This is the purse?" Jenson asked, pointing to the

corner of the desk where I'd placed it when I first came in. I'd been carrying it around since Carrie Sanchez's cry had interrupted me when I was about to give it to Chase back at the apartment.

"Yes."

He picked it up, looked through the pockets, and examined the exterior, then set it down.

"She was very insistent that I bring it over right away. She sounded scared."

"What exactly did she say?"

"I can't remember it word for word, but she wanted me to bring the purse back." I closed my eyes in an effort to remember. "I asked her where she was, and she said it wasn't important. She said she was okay, but . . ."

"But what?"

"I didn't believe her. She sounded afraid. I told her we were worried about her, and she said she was sorry."

Jenson glanced up, his hazel eyes intent. "Sorry for what?"

"I don't know."

"Did she sound down or depressed?"

"No. She sounded scared," I repeated.

Jenson flicked a look at me, then went back to his notes. "How often had your brother and Miss Day seen each other?"

"I don't know. A few times, I think."

"Was it serious?" Jenson persisted.

"I don't know," I said with more emphasis. "You'll have to ask Ben."

"Okay. Now," Jenson leaned back in his chair as he said, "walk me through your movements from the time you left Georgia until this morning."

I described our drive down, sparing him the details of the argument the kids had gotten into over a Happy

Meal toy they'd discovered stuck in the seat cushion—even though it was the most eventful thing that happened. I recounted our time at the beach, and how I waited at the hotel for Angela, then described how I'd seen the woman pushed off the hotel balcony. He listened, his face expressionless. He asked if I'd spoken to a police officer about what I saw, and when I said that I had, he simply made a note. "Anything else?" When I mentioned that Ben and I had gone to The Sea Cottage, he perked up. "Why?"

"We were worried about her."

"I take it she wasn't there."

"No. Cara, a woman who works there, told us Angela left early last night and didn't show up this morning. She said it was unusual for Angela not to return texts or call in, if she couldn't make it to work. We found Angela's phone. That's when Ben called Chase. *He* wasn't worried."

"Really? Her brother wasn't concerned?"

"Yes, he said Angela had—how did he put it?—checked out before. He thought she'd turn up."

"Okay." Jenson closed the notebook over the pen, then leaned back in his chair and laced his fingers together behind his head. "So, Mrs. Avery," he said conversationally, "tell me about yourself."

"What?"

"What do you do? Got any hobbies?"

"Does this have something to do with Angela's death?" I asked, confused by the abrupt change in tone, not to mention topic.

He shrugged, his elbows still in the air. "It helps me get to know people. Gives me a feel for them. So . . . what are your interests? Your work?"

"My hobbies? At this point, laundry and grocery shopping."

He smiled. "Not much spare time in your life?"

"No. I'm a stay-at-home mom and I have a part-time professional organizing business." That sounded mundane. I didn't want him to think my whole life revolved around work and the kids. It pretty much did, but that didn't sound too healthy. I had other interests . . . didn't I? What else did I do? "I like to knit," I said as if I were a game show contestant and I'd suddenly remembered the answer to a question. I toned my enthusiasm down a notch and added, "I'm not very good at it. My scarves tend to have no ending point. I'm in a book club, too. That's about all I have time for."

He opened his notebook and jotted some notes. Was he seriously keeping track of my hobbies? He stood and escorted me out of the room. "Thank you for your time, Mrs. Avery." He handed me a business card and said, "Please get in touch with me before you leave town."

Digital Organizing Tips

File Names

Be consistent and concise when naming files. Pick a short, identifying title for each file. "Jane Doe Resume" is easier to identify than "Resume."

Dates in file names can save you time, too. It's easier to find your most recent resume if it's saved as "Jane Doe Resume 2013."

If you abbreviate words in file names, use abbreviations consistently. "Family Budget 2013" and "Fam Bdg 2013" can be confusing. Also, if you use the search function to look for files, it's easier to find a file named with a full word instead of an abbreviation because you might not remember exactly how you abbreviated the file name.

Chapter Five

I parked myself on the chair in the waiting room while Ben had his turn with the detective. By the time he was done, I'd flipped through all the gossip magazines and two women's magazines. I was up on my movie star hook-ups—speculation ran high that Suzie Quinn and Nick Ryan were planning a secret wedding—and I was now aware of three suspicious symptoms that could possibly indicate I had life-threatening illnesses. The door opened, and Ben stepped out looking dazed. I tossed the magazine down and made for the door with him.

We were already outside when Detective Jenson called out, "Mrs. Avery, you forgot this." He came down the sidewalk, holding out the imitation purse, which I'd left on the desk in the office.

I didn't move to take the purse. "But it was Angela's. She mentioned it when she called me."

He extended his arm farther. "At this point, it's not

relevant to our investigation. You can give it back to her brother. We can get it from him, if we need it in the future." I could tell by his tone that he thought the likelihood of that day ever coming was about as possible as a severe snowfall blanketing Sandy Beach.

"She mentioned it on the phone. Right before she died. It has to mean something. She was insistent about the purse . . . then she died less than a half hour later." While I'd waited for Ben, I'd worked out the time in my mind. I'd gotten the call from Angela and driven straight to her apartment. My phone logged the call at eleven forty-five, and I figured it took me about ten minutes to get to her apartment since I went the traffic-free back way. Ben was still in the parking lot when I arrived, so it couldn't have been much longer than that. We'd stood near Angela's car and talked for a few minutes, then gone into her apartment. We'd only been in there a short time, probably less than five minutes, when Chase showed up. A few more minutes and we'd heard the screams from the parking lot.

So, figuring ten minutes for driving, five minutes in the parking lot, and five in the apartment, that was only twenty minutes total. Twenty-five, at the outside. I'm sure the detective would check the time of Ben's call to 911 about the break-in, but I bet it wouldn't be much different from my estimate. Angela was alive at eleven forty-five, but dead at five after noon, possibly ten after. Somehow in that short span of time, she went from alive and worried to dead.

"Sometimes it doesn't mean anything. Everything we've got points to an accidental death," Detective Jenson said. Ben briefly closed his eyes.

He didn't look good, and I hated to prolong the conversation—part of me wanted to hustle him out of there—but I couldn't stop the question that popped out of my mouth. "You think she slipped and drowned?"

"No, Mrs. Avery, I don't."

He must have thought it was either an accidental overdose or suicide, I realized, thinking of what the cop at the pool had said about it being sad when "the lifestyle" got them so young. "Don't you want to keep it, in case you need it later?" I asked as Ben shot me a look that signaled he wanted me to stop talking. I'd seen the same look on his face when he was six and I was eight, and I'd told Mom that he'd made Jessica Dunlop cry at recess.

Detective Jenson sighed deeply. "If I take this, I've got to log it into evidence. It was not part of the crime scene. Right now, I only have your word that the victim spoke with you about it. Once it's in evidence, it's not coming out anytime soon. It will be logged and tracked until we decide we don't need it anymore. We already have a boatload of evidence to process, most of it useless goggles and fins that people forgot at the pool. No use tying up my techs with more items to process. I'll contact her brother if we need it," he said as he pressed it into my hands and turned away.

"Don't you get it?" Ben hissed as we walked through the parking lot. "They think she overdosed . . . either accidentally or on purpose."

There are some things that only a blood relative can say and get away with. I decided I'd go easy on Ben because he had just pulled the dead body of a woman he knew out of a swimming pool. "Of course I realized that, but not taking it is lax police work."

"And you're some sort of expert on police procedure?"

"Well, I know a few things," I said, hedging because my extended family didn't know quite how deeply I'd become involved in several investigations in the past. Mitch knew all about it—we didn't have any secrets from each other. Well, I had attempted to keep a few things from him, but that never worked out well, and I'd given up on trying to keep him in the dark. As for my family, there were some things they knew—it was hard to keep a secret when your name appeared in the paper—but for the most part, I'd glossed over the incidents, especially with Ben. He'd been out of the country so much and then busy with his flight training, I'd used the excuse that I didn't want to worry/distract him. Besides, if he knew what I'd been up to, I would never hear the end of the Jessica Fletcher jokes.

"From watching *CSI*? *The Mentalist*? Television is not a reliable source of information," Ben said as he followed me up the path to Chase and Angela's apartment.

"I know that." I knocked on the door. It immediately swung open to an empty apartment.

"He's gone, poor thing." The female voice came from behind us. Ben and I turned to a woman with a lined face dressed in a plunging V-neck jumpsuit that revealed a generous swath of tanned, leatherlike cleavage decorated with densely spaced gold chains. If I were guessing, I'd say she had probably already celebrated her seventieth birthday. No matter what her exact age was, her white jumpsuit wasn't age appropriate, as they say on those fashion makeover shows. Several geometric-shaped swatches of material were placed in strategic locations, creating cutouts at the midriff that showed more of her weathered flesh than I wanted to see. "Oh, it's you again!" she said to Ben as she shook her Veronica Lake sweep of hair off her face and grasped his hand, pulling him close to her side.

She looked up at him, her sunburned face breaking into a grin, sending deeper accordion-like wrinkles through her skin. "It's terrible. That beautiful girl, dead," she said, her expression shifting to sadness as she pressed her long burgundy nails into the back of Ben's hand. "And Chase so troubled, he can't bear to be here." She managed to break eye contact with Ben and glanced my way. "I'm Honey," she said, but didn't offer a hand for me to shake.

"Chase is gone?" I asked, since Ben was occupied with trying to pry his hand out of her grasp. I glanced inside the open door and saw that the flower arrangement had been knocked off the end table. The beautiful flowers now lay in a puddle of water on top of a magazine splayed open on the carpet.

"Yes. As soon as he answered the questions from the police, they let him leave to make arrangements at his job. He's off to get someone to cover for him at work for the day. I told him I'd keep an eye on things." Honey's gaze followed mine, and she dropped Ben's hand, then hurried inside, casually pushing the door open the rest of the way with the palm of her hand. "What a shame. Beauty should never go unadmired," she said with a significant glance at Ben as she bent to pick up the vase of flowers. I thought she was fishing for a compliment, hoping for a comparison of her beauty to the flowers, but Ben was flexing his fingers and didn't notice.

She righted the vase, shoving the flowers back inside, then pinched the wet magazine between her thumb and first finger. "So sad about the puppy," she said, and

I saw it was a magazine about dogs. "I guess Chase will have to call the breeder and tell them it's off," she said as she dropped the magazine in the kitchen trash, then filled the vase with water. "I'm sure he can't keep a dog himself. He's gone too much."

"So Angela had decided to get a dog?" I asked, a feeling of sadness sweeping over me. Everything had happened so fast. It hadn't really set in that Angela was dead. She'd been so enthusiastic about the puppy. It was hard to believe I wouldn't get an e-mail from her in the next few days with an attachment of a puppy photo.

Honey came out of the kitchen and nodded. "I'd never heard of the dog she was getting. Whiney or rhymey. Something like that. She was so excited, bless her heart. Could hardly stop talking about it when I saw her at the mailbox yesterday." She put the vase down and examined the flowers. "Oh, I hope the card didn't get wet." She fluffed the flowers into place, then plucked the card from the plastic pitchfork holder. She flicked a long nail under the flap and pulled it out, saying with a little wrinkle of her nose, "Cards that come with flowers are like postcards, they're meant to be read. Nope. It's fine." She waved it around for us to see its unmarred state.

Honey squinted, held the card at arm's length, and read aloud, *"Let's meet and discuss your find."* Her forehead crinkled like a crepe paper streamer. "It's signed Monica. Well, that's . . . interesting."

I wondered how close a friend Honey was to Angela. I hoped Honey was an acquaintance because she didn't seem sad at all. In fact, she was downright cheery. She replaced the card and turned to us. "I'm sure Chase wouldn't mind you waiting for him here, or you could come over to my place." She fixed her gaze on Ben like a puppy anxious for attention.

We were still standing in the doorway. Ben took a step backward. "No, we have to go. Appointments. Places to be."

"What a shame." Her gaze transferred from Ben to me as he moved out of her line of sight. Her gaze locked onto the handbag, and she closed the distance between us.

"Is that a Leah Marshall bag? From her fall line? Oh, I'm so jealous." She ran her hand over the fake leather.

Ben said, "Yeah, if you could give—"

"It's a knockoff." I cut Ben off.

"But not a bad one." She traced one nail along the stitching on the strap. "Nothing that would stand out."

"Thanks for letting us know Chase isn't here," I said, moving outside and then down the sidewalk. "We'll catch him later."

Honey pulled Chase's door back to the closed position, then leaned on her own doorframe and waved languidly.

"Why didn't you give the purse to her? She could pass it on to Chase," Ben said when where were out of earshot.

"Did you see the lust in her eyes? It would have gone straight into her closet, and Chase would never get it back. She didn't care that it was an imitation."

"Well, you could have left it in Chase's apartment."

"Yeah, and she'd be in there two seconds after we left, to take it. You saw how she walked right in."

Ben grabbed my arm and pulled me to a stop. "Ellie. What is up? It's just a purse."

I blew out a sigh. "It was what Angela asked me to

do. The detective may not think it's important, but Angela asked me to return it and now she's dead. It's the least I can do."

Ben nodded. "Okay, I can understand that. You sure you don't want to leave it on the porch? Isn't that what she said you should do?"

"With Honey as a neighbor? No, I'll come by tomorrow. Let's go back to the hotel. I need a few minutes to . . . I don't know . . . decompress, I guess, before I pick up the kids."

"Animal cracker?" I asked, offering the box to Ben.

He was slumped in the club chair in the living area of our hotel room with his elbows on his knees, his chin resting on his clasped hands. His room was on the same floor as ours, but we'd both walked by his door without a word, to my room.

I pulled out the rolling desk chair and sat down, propping my feet on the coffee table. I crunched through an elephant, tiger, and some unidentified headless animal, waiting to see if Ben would say anything. He didn't.

We sat like that for a few minutes. I couldn't get the image of Angela's limp and wet body sprawled on the side of the pool out of my mind. "I almost can't believe it was her. Probably because I never met her in person. It's hard to believe I won't get an e-mail from her in a day or two—I can't quite grasp that, even though we saw her . . . ," I trailed off, not wanting to complete the sentence. Instead, I finished off another handful of crackers and downed some Diet Coke while Ben stared at the soles of my feet. The imitation Leah Marshall bag sat on the coffee table between us.

I fished a Hershey's kiss from the bag I'd brought

with me and ate it. When all the chocolate goodness had melted in my mouth, and I couldn't stand it anymore, I said, "Ben, are you okay?"

No reply.

"Chocolate?" I offered.

"Contrary to what you might think, chocolate is not going to help me feel better," Ben said without moving.

"I didn't say it would help you feel better. I asked if you wanted some."

He lifted the fingers of his right hand, signaling he'd pass. I looked at him closely. I didn't think, technically, he was in shock. He wasn't shivering or disoriented or dizzy, but he was dealing with the death of a friend.

"Do you want to change your clothes?" I asked, noting that they were wrinkled, but completely dry now.

"Enough with the mom stuff. I'm fine," he said, then sighed and leaned back in the chair. "Sorry." He ran his hands over his face. "I'm not fine. I can't believe it, either. I talked to her two days ago. Of course, that's all the detective wanted to talk about. What she sounded like." Ben shifted in the chair, rearranging his long legs. They didn't seem to fit under the coffee table. He stood and walked restlessly around the room.

"He asked me that, too," I said.

"Yeah, but you didn't just break up with her."

I wasn't sure I'd heard him right. "You broke up with her?"

"Yes and now she's dead. Apparently, Detective Jenson thinks she may have committed suicide because she was depressed over the breakup. Wanted to know if she was moody, stuff like that."

"But that's—that doesn't sound like Angela."

"I know, but . . . I wonder . . ."

"Ben, I talked to her yesterday. Last night she sounded

fine. Happy, even. She didn't sound depressed at all. This morning, she was different—scared, but she wasn't depressed. Besides, she had an upbeat personality. At least, she seemed that way to me. I would have described her as sunny, not moody."

Ben watched me for a moment, then sat down in the chair abruptly. "She was upbeat—happy and fun and always excited about whatever was coming up, even if it was only a movie or going to a new club. She was almost like, well, I was going to say Livvy, but Livvy is a lot more restrained than Angela ever was," Ben said, cracking a bit of a smile. "*Moody* doesn't sound like her, but I have to wonder . . . you know what they say about manic-depressive-type personalities. High one minute, then bottomed out the next. Maybe she was like that, and I just didn't know it. Maybe I'd never seen her at a low point. Maybe today was a low point for her, and she couldn't stand it."

"Ben, she was getting a puppy. I don't think that's the hallmark of someone who's . . ." I let my voice trail off, not wanting to finish the sentence.

"Considering suicide?" Ben said, his eyebrows raised. "You're right," he murmured more to himself than to me. "She wouldn't do something like that," he said, his voice firmer. "She wouldn't. All that about why she was sorry had me wondering. The detective was really fixated on that, too."

I shrugged. "It was what she said. I told him her words as closely as I could remember them. She said she was sorry and, specifically, to tell you she was sorry."

He ran his fingers through his hair. "I have no idea why she'd say that. *I* broke up with *her*. She didn't have anything to be sorry about."

"Um, maybe I shouldn't ask this, but why did you break up with her?"

"Because we lived an hour apart. With my work schedule, I hardly ever saw her. And," Ben said, his voice quieter—I thought, *here it comes, the real reason*—"we didn't have that much in common. I like to have fun on the weekend as much as the next guy, but I'm more into hanging out with my friends, relaxing, watching the game. I'm not into clubs and staying out until three in the morning." He looked rueful and said, "I didn't tell the detective that last part, just that I broke it off because we lived too far apart."

"There's no other girl on the scene?" I asked as I put the bag of Hershey's kisses on the coffee table.

"What did you do, read that guy's notes? That's exactly what he asked."

"Well, thinking like him—like a detective—if you break it off with a girl, and then she found out there's another girl in the picture . . . if the first girl is emotionally fragile, then I could see how Detective Jenson would come up with that question."

"Wow," Ben said, backing off. "You do watch too many cop shows, don't you?" Before I could answer, he said, "No, there is no other girl. None. And, now that I've thought about it, I don't think Angela was fragile."

"I don't think so, either—I said that's what Detective Jenson was probably thinking." There was a thought circling in my mind, and I knew I needed to ask Ben about it, but I didn't want to. I leaned forward and said gently, "Don't take this the wrong way—I didn't know her as well as you—but could it have happened accidently?"

"No." He said it flatly, emphatically, not in that knee-jerk quick way that sometimes indicates you've hit a sore spot. "She wasn't into drugs. Steered clear of them. She was fun and she did like to have those girly drinks at clubs—what are they? Appletini or something like that—but that was it. She didn't do drugs. I don't know the whole story on it, but she wouldn't go near anything like that. Once when we were out, someone make a joke about oxycodone, and she came down really hard on the guy, said it wasn't funny. She went to the bathroom right after that, and her friend made some comment to the guy, saying he knew about Angela's mom, and he should know better than to bring up oxycodone, so I figured it had something to do with her mom."

I leaned back in the chair, my head tilted to the side. "Well, if it wasn't an accident, if she wasn't depressed, and she didn't accidently overdose . . ."

"Then it means it was on purpose. She was murdered."

I swiveled my chair around, knocking it against the desk. "Ben, that's quite a statement." A faint chime sounded, and I turned to my laptop, which was open on the desk. I must have jiggled the mouse when I bumped the desk because now the screen was bright. I had a new message in my mail folder. The sender was Angela495.

Chapter
Six

"That's impossible," I said.

"What is it?" Ben asked.

"I have an e-mail from Angela in my inbox. The time stamp on it is a few minutes ago. Could it be a crank e-mail?"

I opened the e-mail as he moved across the room to look over my shoulder. It was only one line long and read, Sorry I missed you yesterday. I'll be in the lobby in fifteen minutes. Can you meet me to switch purses?

"That's not a crank e-mail," Ben said, meeting my gaze. We both looked toward the purse on the coffee table.

"Why would someone want that?" I asked.

"Her account must have been hacked," Ben said at almost the same time.

"But why ask for the purse?" I picked it up and ran my hands over it much like Honey had. It still had the same wobbly stitching and dry, fake leather. "We need to call Detective Jenson," I said, moving back to the desk. "Why don't you do that, while I look up something."

I opened a new window on the computer and typed in the name of the purse, then scrolled through the list of hits. "There has to be something about this purse that's important. Something that would make someone hack into Angela's account and try to get us to give it to them. I have Detective Jenson's card, if you need his number. It's on the coffee table," I said, but saw that Ben already had one in his hand. He was dialing on his cell phone. I gestured to the phone on the desk. "You can use the room phone."

"I'm fine."

"You must have a different carrier, because I don't even get a line in here, much less a bar."

I scanned the results as I spoke, clicking on a few. They were all store sites or blogs about purses. I recognized some of them because I was a more than frequent visitor. My motto was that it never hurt to look, especially since I was keeping an eye out for bargains. I paged through a few more search results until the lists trailed off into sites that didn't relate to the purse. I typed in "fake Leah Marshall purse" and got another set of hits that didn't show me anything, except that there were plenty of fakes out there, some even worse than the knockoff sitting on the desk beside me.

Ben clicked his phone and moved to my side. "Not in," he said shortly, his gaze on the screen.

"You didn't leave him a message?"

"What was I going to say? Get down to my hotel right now because someone hacked into Angela's

e-mail and wants the purse that you didn't want?" He
shook his head. "I don't think I can leave a voice mail
message that adequately explains the situation. I'll try
him again in a minute."

I looked at the clock on the screen. Five minutes had
already gone by.

"Maybe it's not the purse itself. Maybe it's something *in* the purse," Ben said.

"It's empty." I picked it up anyway and looked
through the main compartment and the two small zip-
pered pockets. "Nothing." I gripped the purse by the
mouth and turned it upside down to illustrate. The lining shifted against my fingertips, and I frowned. I righted
the purse, and the slight bulge shifted to the bottom of
the bag.

"I think there's something in the lining." I put the
purse down on the desk so I could run my fingers over
the inside. "Here, in the corner," I said as my fingers
traced around a flat shape about an inch square. "How
did it get in there? I wonder if it was sewn in," I said,
more to myself than to Ben. He was on his phone
again.

I clicked on the desk lamp and moved it so that it
shined into the empty purse, then I checked all the
seams again until my finger slipped into a gap deep in
the corner of one of the inner pockets. Several of the
stitches were missing and I could just work the tip of
my index finger into the opening. I tilted the purse and
felt the object in the liner glance against my finger as it
slipped from one end to the other. I twisted the purse
the other way more slowly, letting the weight of whatever was in there move gradually along the lining to
the hole.

"No answer," Ben said shortly, and turned back to me. "We've got to take care of this ourselves."

I paused and looked at him, the purse suspended upside down in midair. "What do you mean, *take care of this ourselves?*"

"There's no way Detective Jenson will be able to get here in under five minutes. That's all the time we have left. We have to get down there to the lobby and see who shows up," Ben said, reaching for the purse.

I moved it away from him, putting it on the other side of my body from him, like I used to do with candy when we were kids, and he tried to swipe some of my M&Ms. "Whoever hacked Angela's e-mail and sent that message might have had something to do with her death."

"I know. That's why we have to get down there and see who it is before they're gone."

"That's not smart, Ben," I said, jiggling the purse.

"So we should just let this person . . . or people . . . whoever it is . . . go? We shouldn't make any effort to see who it is?"

"Just a second. I think I almost have it," I said, seeing an edge of plastic emerge from the opening in the seam as I hit the correct angle. "See if you can get it out." I turned back toward Ben. I had my hands full holding the purse and the lining, to make sure the object didn't slip away again.

Ben worked it lose. "A memory card," he said. We exchanged a glance before Ben plugged it into the drive on my laptop. I dropped the purse on the coffee table and leaned on the desk beside Ben as the files loaded. He clicked on the first one.

It was a photo of three smiling young women stand-

ing shoulder to shoulder with their arms linked loosely
around each other's waists. "That's Angela," Ben said,
pointing to the blond girl on the far right. "These are
recent. The date on the time stamp is three days ago."

"There's the girl from the store, the one she worked
with. Cara," I said, tapping the screen. "Who is the
third girl?"

"I don't know her," Ben said.

It was obviously a girls' night out. Angela wore a
sparkly spaghetti strap dress with three-inch heels and
the latest Belen Echandia bag. Cara had on a print sundress. The other girl was the odd man out. She had
short brown hair, a round face, and wore a jean jacket
over a black T-shirt and cargo pants. She flashed a
peace sign at the camera, showing off a sunburst tattoo
on the inside of her wrist.

"Wait." I leaned toward the picture, noticing the tattoo. "That's the woman who was pushed."

"The one who went over the balcony?" Ben asked,
his tone disbelieving.

"Yes, that's her. I saw her tattoo when she was on the
ground with her arm stretched out. I noticed it because
it stood out against her pale skin. Where are they?" The
background was dim and filled with people dancing.
The camera had been angled slightly upward, so there
was quite a bit of the ceiling in the photo. It was draped
with swags of white, purple, and blue cloth. There was
also a loft area that overlooked the dance floor where
the girls were posing.

"Club Fifty-two. It's—I mean, it was—one of Angela's favorite clubs," Ben said, pointing to the neon
logo on the wall, the number fifty-two sitting in the
curve of the letter C.

Ben clicked on the next file. More mugging for the camera. Ben opened several photos. They all were along the same lines, some with the same three girls, others with only Angela and another person. It looked as if she had made her way around the room, snapping photographs or asking people to take her picture.

"This isn't doing us any good," Ben said as he checked the time on his phone. "I'll go down there and see if I can find the person who sent the e-mail." He reached for the purse. "I can at least get a picture of them on my cell phone to show to the detective."

"Wait," I said, slipping into the seat. I selected the rest of the files as a group and opened them all. They popped up one after another, rapid fire. "There's got to be something here . . . hey, that looks like Suzie Quinn," I said, clicking like mad to get back to the familiar face. I recognized her tan body, her strong shoulders, and her freckle-dotted face under dark curls.

Ben paused, looked closer. "It *is* her. And she's at the club. That picture was taken up in the loft area, near the back corner."

Angela wasn't in the picture or any of the next few, which were all of Suzie. The way Suzie wasn't smiling at the camera—she was absorbed in talking with the people at her table—made me think that Suzie Quinn hadn't known she was being photographed. I clicked through to the last few photos, which had a bright yellow glow and seemed to be taken in a different area. A row of stall doors was visible on one side of the photo.

"That must be the restroom in Club Fifty-two," I said, moving the curser over another neon club logo on the wall, then switched to the next photo.

Suzie was in the next picture, too. She was seated on

a flowered couch, hunched over a thin line of powder on a glass-topped table, snorting the powder into her nose through a straw.

I sat back, stunned. "Suzie Quinn, doing drugs? That's . . . that's . . ." I let my voice trail off. I didn't want to think that America's swimming sweetheart was throwing her life away.

Ben reached around me and clicked on the next few photos. They were more of the same.

"Those photos could be worth a lot of money," Ben said quietly.

"I know." I chewed on the inside of my cheek. "You better call Detective Jenson again. These could be why Angela was killed."

Ben shot me a long look, and I shrugged my shoulders. "We both agree suicide wasn't something she would do. Detective Jenson didn't think she accidentally fell. That pretty much leaves murder, as you've already said."

I switched back to the e-mail to read it again. No wonder someone wanted the purse. "How could someone get into her e-mail so quickly?" I looked at my watch. "She's only been dead a short time. Could her account be hacked that quickly?"

Ben dialed again, listened, then shook his head. "Not in." He pointed his phone at the computer screen. "I suppose it doesn't take long, if you know what you're doing. But you're right, there probably aren't that many people with great hacking skills who already know what happened to her. So, it's probably someone who was there today at the apartment."

My mind skipped through the possibilities. I thought of Honey, but discarded her. Unless I was very mistaken about her, I didn't think her computer skills would go much beyond typing and Internet searches. But how would she even know I was supposed to switch the purses? We hadn't told her that detail, which only left one person. "Chase?"

"I think so," Ben said, nodding slowly. "Angela could have told him about the photos, that they were mistakenly sent to you, and that she was going to pick them up last night. Even though her laptop was damaged, Angela and Chase probably had the same Internet service provider with different e-mail addresses on the same account. He probably knew her e-mail password—or could find out what it was with a forgotten password request."

"I can't believe he'd be worried about photos at a time like this," I said.

"I have a feeling Chase is one of those people who sees the gray in everything. He's kind of shady himself."

"How do you know that? I thought you only met him once," I asked, but at the same time, I was thinking of the feeling I got that Chase wasn't happy that Ben had called the police about the break-in.

"Couple of things Angela said. She was worried about him. He had some friends that she thought might be into drugs and there was an incident at his work, a theft. I don't know the details, but it happened right before one of our dates. She was really stressed out. He could have been arrested. She said someone with his past would have a hard time convincing the police he didn't do it, which I took to mean that he'd been in trouble with the police before. But it turned out the thief was someone else. She was so relieved. I could tell she thought he was guilty. So if he did know about the photos, which wouldn't be impossible, then I could see how he'd put securing them above grieving for his sister. They're valuable. People do crazy things for a lot of money."

"How much money do you think they're worth?"

My e-mail dinged before Ben could answer. I had a new message, again from "Angela."

It read, I'm here! I've got your purse.

Digital Organizing Tips

Password Tips

As more of our daily activities go digital, we have more passwords to remember. Here are a few ways to keep track of all those user names and passwords:

High tech—Some Web browsers like Firefox will remember passwords for you, if you enable them to do so. There are password manager programs, which remember passwords you create or randomly generate passwords for you, then automatically fill in each sign-in page with the appropriate information. Password apps are available for your mobile phone or mobile devices.

Medium tech—You can create your own password manager, a spreadsheet with three columns: Account Name, User ID, and Password. Save it to your hard drive and e-mail a copy of it to yourself in case your computer crashes.

Low tech—Use the old-fashioned method and write your passwords down on a piece of paper, but don't keep the list under your keyboard. Find a more secure location for it. You might store it in a home safe or even in a file in your filing cabinet with an innocuous label, such as Keyword File.

Chapter Seven

"How is he doing that?" I asked, rotating the computer so Ben could see the new message. "Her computer is broken, but even if Chase had another computer, he still couldn't be e-mailing us from the lobby."

"He could if it was a laptop or if he used a phone app. If he knew Angela's password, it wouldn't be that hard. Once he logged into her account, he could change the settings and link her e-mail to his phone."

"But then that would be traceable. The police would be able to see he'd done that."

"It doesn't matter because right now the police think that Angela's death was an overdose or suicide, so there's no need for them to look on her computer, which, as you said, is broken anyway."

"It doesn't make sense," I argued. "Why would Chase e-mail us on her account? We know she's not sending the e-mail. We know she's dead."

"I don't know," Ben said impatiently. "Maybe he's trying to play on our curiosity—get us to bring the purse to the lobby to see who is sending the e-mails. Maybe it's a long shot, a last-ditch effort to get the purse, in case the police reevaluate Angela's death and decide it wasn't an overdose. It doesn't matter why he's doing it. He is doing it, and we have to get down there." Ben reached for the purse.

I was quicker and swiped it up. "It looks like someone killed Angela for those photos. It might be the same person, a dangerous person."

"All the more reason to get down there," Ben said. "I'm not going to give them the photos, just the purse. We'll keep the photos up here. It will take a few minutes for them to realize the photos aren't there. By then, I'll be long gone. Besides, it's a hotel lobby—a public place—nothing's going to happen to me there."

"That is crazy—" I broke off as my phone rang. I saw it was Mitch. Good. Maybe he could talk some sense into Ben. "Just a second," I said, answering the call as I quickly moved to the sliding glass door in the bedroom portion of the suite. It stuck, so I set the purse down, tucked the phone into my shoulder, and used two hands to wrench it open. I stepped out on the balcony, the only place I seemed to be able to get reception. The muggy air and brilliant sunshine hit me, and I immediately started to sweat.

"Mitch, I'm so glad you called. We're having a bit of a crisis. I need you to tell Ben to calm down." I glanced back over my shoulder and saw the door to the hallway slowly swinging closed. I looked down at the carpet just inside the sliding door where I'd dropped the purse. It was gone. I closed my eyes, tempted to mutter words that I wouldn't allow Livvy and Nathan to say.

"Ellie? Are you there?" Mitch asked.

"I'll call you right back."

I flew out of the hotel room and ran along the corridor, which had rooms on only one side. The other was open to the atrium area below. I stopped for a second and leaned over the edge then immediately regretted it. We were near the roof and looking down from the high floor made my stomach spin. There was no way I'd be able to pick out individuals or recognize someone. I hurried to the closest glass elevator, scanning the one on the opposite side of the hotel. I didn't see Ben anywhere. He'd probably taken the stairs.

I decided to take my chances with the elevator. There was no way I was pounding down ten flights of stairs. In the elevator I'd be able to see, and I doubted I could catch up with Ben on the stairs, anyway. The StairMaster was my least favorite piece of gym equipment.

I punched the DOWN button, practically jumping from foot to foot, doing a good imitation of Livvy and Nathan on their way to the beach yesterday. Livvy and Nathan! I'd completely forgotten to call Summer back. I'd meant to call her after the police interview. She was probably wondering where I was. I'd have to call her as soon as I dragged my brother back upstairs, but before we talked to Detective Jenson. I had a feeling the conversation with the detective might take awhile. The elevator pinged and I was in, repeat-punching the DOWN button before the doors finished gliding apart.

Thankfully, the elevator swooped down, only stopping once on the way. I burst out of the doors as soon as they opened, earning a severe look from an older couple in sunhats who smelled of coconut sunscreen. I slowed down long enough to make sure I didn't topple them over, then jogged to the lobby.

I paused by the waterfall, letting the feature, which was at least eight feet tall, hide me. In the far corner, near the sliding glass hotel entrance doors, I spotted Ben talking to a guy holding a large box. He was a kid of about twenty with gold-rimmed glasses and rumpled brown hair, wearing a blue Hawaiian shirt, cargo shorts, and a pair of flip-flops with thick soles. He looked like a young Magnum P.I. impersonator.

So, not Chase. Interesting.

Ben gripped the purse in two hands, like an old lady afraid she'd be mugged on the bus. I got a moment's satisfaction out of the thought that he did look silly carrying around an obviously female bag. The young Magnum guy gave the box to Ben, then snatched the purse when Ben held it out. Without another word, the Magnum wanna-be turned and ran out of the hotel, angling his shoulders to fit through the barely open sliding glass doors. Ben hurried after him, checking the box as he ran. It must have been empty because he dumped it on the floor, then pulled out his phone.

I rolled my eyes. "Of course, you chase him," I muttered and took off after Ben.

I cleared the glass doors and stepped into the sticky heat, squinting as I scanned the sidewalk, but I didn't see them. I spotted the blue Hawaiian shirt on the far side of the parking lot. Ben was a few steps behind him, his phone up, ready to snap a picture.

I took off after them. A ripping sound cut through the air, and I saw bits of thread and fabric flutter to the ground in the Magnum kid's wake as he literally tore out the purse's lining.

I hurried to close the gap. There were several rows of cars between the two men and me. Ben circled around a hatchback and clicked off a photo of the kid. Young Magnum's head whipped around. He dropped the purse and sprinted toward Ben. Ben took a step back, hands raised, palms facing the kid. He still held his phone in his hand as he said, "Hey, man, no need to get—"

The kid was about the same height as Ben, but he was stockier and had the advantage of momentum. He angled his shoulder into Ben's chest and hit him squarely, knocking Ben to the ground. Ben dropped his phone and it landed on the asphalt, shattering into pieces that spun away from the impact point. I could see Ben gulping, trying to suck air into his lungs.

The kid had collapsed on top of Ben. He pulled himself up, angled his arm back, and planted a punch squarely in Ben's face. I gasped. The ferocity of the hit shocked me. I started moving again, pressing my hands against hot metal as I sprinted between the cars.

The kid stood, pulling Ben up by the shirt to a standing position. Ben moved slowly, shaking his head as if to clear it. His lethargic movements made my stomach lurch. I rounded the hood of the last car, finally reaching the same row. I had no idea what I was going to do when I got there. I'd be useless in a fight. I'd taken a self-defense class years ago, but that only covered how to get away. I had no idea how to attack someone. Despite my mental misgivings, my feet pounded down the asphalt, fired on by a basic protective instinct. I'd do what I could. That was my brother.

Ben staggered back a step, shook his head again, then he put his hands back up in the "surrender" mode and walked a few steps with the kid behind him to a low-slung metallic blue sports car, one aisle over. I switched course and dodged through another row of parked cars. A horn blared as I stepped into the next aisle, and a bright yellow Volkswagon Beetle swerved around me. The driver, a teen with her curly red hair in a ponytail, wearing a swimsuit top and shorts, shouted at me. Ignoring the driver, I skipped around the back of the car as it accelerated away.

Where was Ben? I spotted him ducking into the sports car from the driver's side. I frowned and shaded my eyes. It looked like . . . yes, he was crawling over the console into the passenger side. I couldn't see him very well, but he looked dazed, as if he was trying to get his bearings.

I broke into a run, but then jerked to a stop as Mr. Hawaii slid into the driver's seat. The bright sunlight flashed on silver. He had a gun tucked up against his brightly patterned shirt, the barrel pointed squarely at Ben.

The car's engine growled, then it whipped out of the parking slot, turning away from me as it cut off another car to join the slow-moving traffic on the beach road.

I stood there for a second, my mouth literally hanging open. That was the craziest thing I'd ever seen. I forced myself into motion. I sprinted to the end of the parking lot, hit the sidewalk, and dived into the crowd. Shoulders swiveling, I pushed through the pedestrians to the next corner, but didn't see the sports car.

I stood there, hands on my hips, surveying the road. The traffic moved slowly, but it was moving. The car would have arrived at this corner in a few seconds, probably while I was standing still in shock, trying to process what I'd seen. They could be on the Interstate by the time I got back to the hotel.

I turned, pushed my way back to the hotel, questioning myself. The sun was so bright. Maybe I made a mistake—who pulled a gun on people in broad daylight, in the middle of a tourist area? This was a nice, upscale part of town, not some gritty neighborhood where people fear drive-by shootings. Maybe it hadn't been a gun? I shook my head. I couldn't think of anything else that would draw the hands-raised reaction from Ben.

I picked up the pieces of Ben's shattered phone from the parking lot and the battered purse, then returned to the coolness of the lobby. It seemed like another world with the ding of the elevator and the burble of the fountain the only noises. I marched to the front desk, pulling out my cell phone.

There was no one there. I called out, craned my neck, and looked into the room behind the desk. Empty. I'd have to call the police myself on my cell phone. I turned around, headed for the glass doors again, then slowed, my fingers running over the keypad, as I thought about how long it would take to explain the situation over the phone to an emergency dispatcher. I had no license number of the car, not even the make and model, only a general description. I'd been so amazed by what I'd seen that I hadn't taken in very much detail. And Ben was a grown man—it wasn't like he was a kid who'd been snatched. They might think that I was seeing things—heck, even *I* thought I was seeing things—and put off searching, reasoning that Ben might have gone off on his own, just like Chase thought Angela had left on the spur of the minute.

I reversed course and headed for my room, glad I'd slipped my keycard in my pocket earlier. Detective Jenson's card was on the coffee table. I'd call him.

I pushed into the hotel room and stopped short, surveying the second decimated room I'd seen that day. My gaze went straight to the desk, which was empty, except for the desk lamp and complimentary notepad and pen.

"No, no, no." I stepped into the room toward the desk, then jerked to a stop. If the laptop was gone, someone had been in here . . . could still be here.

I reached back and caught the door before it closed and stood motionless, listening. Nothing, except the whisper of fabric as the bedroom curtains stirred in the breeze from the open sliding glass door. The bathroom door was ajar and I could see there was no one in there. I stepped into the room and let the door sigh slowly closed.

The desk was the only tidy place in the room. The cushions were off the couch. The coffee table had been overturned, sprinkling silver-wrapped chocolate kisses across the carpet. My suitcase had been upended in the bedroom, and all the cabinet doors in the bathroom were open. I did a quick search of the room for the laptop and memory card. It was futile, I knew, but I picked up couch cushions, patted along the edges of the bed, even checked the cabinets in the kitchenette and bathroom.

Nothing.

The laptop was gone. I went back to the desk, looked under it again and beside the couch, but the only thing there was the power cord, still plugged uselessly into the wall. Someone either slipped into the room before the door completely closed when I pursued Ben—making sure the door closed had been the last thing on my mind—or someone had climbed over the balcony and come in the sliding glass door. Considering how high we were, I was betting on the first situation. Then, another thought struck me and I hurried over to the door to turn the deadbolt. Could someone have conned the front desk into making a duplicate keycard for this room? I hoped our hotel had higher security standards than the hotel across the street.

I turned on all the lights and walked slowly around the room, studying the patterned carpet, hoping that the memory card had fallen out when the laptop was taken. I knew the possibility of that happening was miniscule, but I looked anyway. Twice.

I was on the second pass of the room, crawling on my hands and knees, peering under the furniture, when I saw a pair of sunglasses under the couch. I pulled them out and sat back on my heels to examine them. Sleekly designed, the silver frames curved seamlessly into the earpieces, which were a blend of silver and bright green. I fingered the heavy nosepiece before slipping them on. They were men's frames and too big for me, but the sturdy nosepiece anchored them in place. I took them off and looked from them to the desk, then to the couch. The desk was only inches from the end of the couch where I'd found them.

It was possible the sunglasses belonged to the person who'd taken my laptop and the memory card. If someone set the sunglasses down on the desk while they gathered up the laptop, it was possible they might have knocked the sunglasses off the desk and left without realizing they didn't have them. I'd done it myself just the other day. My favorite pair of sunglasses was sitting on the kitchen counter at home. I folded the earpieces closed and stood up. It was also possible that they belonged to any prior occupant of this room.

I put them in my crossbody bag, then dropped onto the couch and wondered what to do. My laptop was gone and that normally would have upset me, but it paled in comparison to the loss of the memory card. Without that card I had nothing to take to the police. I had no way to convince Detective Jenson that Angela had very sensitive information, information that might have put her in a dangerous position.

And how would I explain what happened with Ben? What *had* happened with Ben? He'd been . . . what? Kidnapped? Snatched? Because he snapped a picture with his camera phone? Because the guy was angry about the empty purse?

I rubbed my forehead. Okay, prioritize, just like in organizing. What was most important? Ben, no question. I angled the coffee table upright. There was no need to worry about fingerprints now. I'd already touched every surface in the room during my frantic search for the laptop and memory card. I plucked Detective Jenson's card up from the floor and pulled out my phone. Two missed calls from Mitch. I needed to call him back. I was sure I hadn't sounded calm and in control when I'd abruptly cut off our conversation earlier, and he was probably worried. I guess I'd missed the calls in all the commotion of chasing after Ben, or they'd come in while I was still in the hotel where my phone didn't get reception.

Ben, first, I reminded myself, and moved to the balcony to make the call, but the room phone rang before

I stepped onto the balcony. I picked it up quickly. Maybe it was Ben calling. His phone was broken, after all . . . but how would he have this number? In fact, who had this number? Most people called everyone's cell phones now.

"Your brother is here with me. Don't go to the police." The male voice was rough, deep. I didn't recognize it.

"What? Who is this?" I demanded, all the questions in my mind colliding.

"Your brother is with me," the man repeated. "Don't call the police, and he'll be fine. Just bring me the memory card, and I'll let him go."

My palm felt sweaty on the handset. Was this the guy in the Hawaiian shirt? If it was, the voice didn't match his appearance. This man's deep voice suggested someone older, more mature. I glanced around the room, as if the memory card might suddenly appear.

"Okay. I can do that," I hedged, "but . . . it might take me a little while."

"You're not going to be difficult, are you?" The rough voice sounded weary, as if he didn't have time to convince me that this was important. "I do hope you're smarter than Angela. She didn't want to cooperate with me, either . . . at first. Your brother seems like a good kid, and I would hate to see him get messed up. He's a pilot, right? They need good vision. Be a shame if something happened to his eyesight . . ."

Was he saying he was responsible for Angela's death? And how did this guy know that Ben was a pilot? Ben had only been gone a short time. Was this someone who knew Ben personally, not a stranger? "No. No, I want to give it to you. There's just been a"—I drew in a breath because I felt light-headed—"a complication. Someone took it—"

"Well, I'm sorry to hear that," Mr. Sandpaper Voice said almost conversationally. "I know Ben will be disappointed when I pass that news on to him. Too bad he'll have to find a new line of work."

"No, wait. I can get it back," I said, improvising wildly. "I just need some time."

"Midnight. I'll give you until midnight."

Chapter Eight

I sat there with the phone pressed to my ear, dial tone droning. What was I going to do? Why had I said that? I didn't know where the memory card was or who had it. And the caller didn't want me to go to the police.

I checked my watch. One forty-five. I had less than twelve hours to find a tiny square of plastic. An urge to cry swept over me. This was beyond anything I could do—way beyond my abilities. Sure, I could sort out a closet, help organize paperwork so tax prep was a snap. I even had handy tips on how to schedule your day to save time and cut your gas bill in half. But I had no idea what to do when a scratchy-voiced man called and demanded I hand over a memory card that someone had stolen.

I broke out in a cold sweat. The air conditioner clicked on, and I shivered as the frigid air hit me. Why hadn't I asked where Ben was?

Why hadn't I asked to talk to Ben?

I'm not exactly sure what I did for the next few minutes. I think I raced around the room, searching again for the memory card, panic my primary emotion.

My phone rang, snapping me out of the fog of anxiety as abruptly as if someone had tossed a glass of water in my face. It was my cell phone, not the hotel phone, and I was filled with a mixture of relief that I didn't have to talk to the rough-voiced guy again and despair that I didn't have the chance to ask to talk to Ben.

I didn't recognize the number. "Hello," I said cautiously. Did Mr. Scratchy Voice have my cell phone number, too?

"Ellie, I don't have a lot of time. I need you to listen—"

"Ben," I shrieked, my voice probably carrying to the rooms across the atrium. "What is going on?" I had my hand to my chest where my heart had suddenly jumped into high gear as the words came tumbling out. "Are you okay? Where are you? Did that guy really have a gun? What were you thinking?"

"Ellie!" Ben said sharply, and I realized he was speaking very low, almost in a whisper. "Listen to me. I'm fine."

"Where are you?" I asked, trying to match his even tone. He sounded so calm. I saw my reflection in the mirror over the desk. My face was pale, my clothes rumpled from crawling around on the floor as I'd looked for the memory card, and my tangled hair was shoved back behind my ears. My eyes narrowed. Ben sounded awfully calm . . . maybe too calm? "This isn't a prank, is it? You better not be punking me because—"

"No, this is real. The gun was real."

"Where are you?" I asked again, edging over to the coffee table and lowering myself down. My legs felt wobbly.

"Some plush hotel near the beach. I can see the beach from the window, but I'm not sure exactly where I am along it. They took the phone out of the room and everything else with a logo that would identify the place. Look, I don't have long. He thinks I'm unconscious."

"Unconscious!"

"Yeah, he clocked me pretty good in the car once he pulled away from the hotel."

"He hit you again?" I asked, incredulous.

"Yeah, I let my guard down. I wasn't expecting it in the car. Knocked me out. I didn't really come around completely until we were in a hotel corridor. He was dragging me into a suite when he tripped, and I went down. I let him think I hit my head on the table by the door. That's why he thinks I'm unconscious again."

"Where is he now? Can you get out of there?" I asked, half rising. I realized I was whispering.

"Of course I could get out of here, but I don't want to. These people have something to do with Angela's death. I can tell from what they said when I was dragged into the suite. I'm going to stay here and figure out what it is."

"What?" I was stunned that he would even *think* of staying there.

"I don't have time to go into it right now," Ben said.

"I didn't mean what did they say. I meant what are you thinking? That's crazy. You should get out of there now. A man called me, said you were with him, and threatened to hurt you. He said Angela didn't want to cooperate with him, so he's got something to do with her disappearance, if not her death."

"He called you?"

"Yes. He's dangerous. He wants me to give him Angela's photos, but I can't. They're gone. Someone stole them. Wait, did you say *people*, as in there's more than one?"

"There are at least three people in the next room."

I dropped my head into my free hand. "Ben, please, if they're not watching you right now, get out. They have a gun."

"Can't, at the moment," he said, and I felt an urge to giggle bubble up inside me. He said he couldn't leave, as if he were in the middle of a television program and didn't want to miss the end. I clamped down on a feeling of panic. "Ellie," Ben said patiently, "I'm not running. This might be the only chance to find out who killed Angela. The police don't even think she was murdered. Don't worry about the photos. I'm going to find out what I can here. Then I'll leave."

"You'll leave? Just like that? If they did kill Angela, they probably won't let you leave. They're *killers*. They'll kill you, too, to keep you quiet."

"Do you really think they could keep me here if I wanted to leave? I've been through SERE. This guy is a total amateur."

SERE was the acronym for the military's Survival, Evasion, Resistance, and Escape training. Pilots and other military members went through the course. I bit my lip. I'd heard about the course in a general way, but Mitch and the guys he worked with were careful not to get into specifics about what it involved. I think they were bound by some sort of confidentiality clause or agreement, but I did know one thing about the course: it was tough. It tested and prepared them, in case the enemy captured them.

"He didn't sound like an amateur on the phone. He pulled a gun on you and knocked you out. That doesn't sound amateurish to me. It sounds dangerous."

"I wasn't expecting either attack, but I'm on my guard now. I won't underestimate anyone from now on. It's no worse than Camp Sunshine," Ben said, referring to the summer camp in the mountains of New Mexico that we'd both attended for a few years when we were in our early teens. It had the usual array of swimming, horseback riding, crafts, and campfires, along with a few more interesting options, including a zip line. "Ellie? Are you there?"

"Yeah, I'm here," I replied, weighing the odds. One young, fit military-trained guy against Mr. Sandpaper Voice, who apparently wore Hawaiian shirts and flip-flops. Yeah, my money was on Ben, and I really didn't have much to tell the police. I didn't know who Mr. Sandpaper Voice was or where Ben was. I had no license number for the sports car or even a make or model. Those things could be found out, though. They probably had video surveillance in the hotel and this call could be traced, but how long would that take? How many hours would it take to sort out that I was telling the truth and that Ben really was missing? Better to find the missing memory card and ensure I had a bargaining chip, in case I needed it. Because, no matter what Ben said, they had a gun and he didn't. "Okay," I said, my voice shaking. "I won't call the police, but you're on a deadline. If you haven't found anything by tonight, I'm calling Detective Jenson."

"Fine. I won't call you back on this line. I'm not

even sure whose phone this is, so don't go all crazy and try and trace the call. There are at least three people in there. It could belong to someone who's not involved in the situation with Angela."

"How did you get it?"

"It was on the table I hit when I collapsed. I palmed it on the way down."

"They're going to realize it's missing at some point," I said, my voice rising.

"Calm down. I'll delete the call in the outgoing call log and then put it under the door. There's at least a half an inch between the door and the carpet. I'll give it a good shove and send it back to where it would have landed if it fell off the table."

"Sounds risky," I said.

"Got to go. I'll figure out a way to stay in touch. I doubt it will be by phone."

"This is crazy," I said, suddenly gripped with second thoughts. "If anything happens to you, Mom is going to kill me."

"Nothing's going to happen to me," Ben said, and I heard a hint of . . . what? Excitement in his tone? He was actually enjoying this.

"Sit tight. Don't do anything stupid," he said. "Talk to you soon."

"Stupid!" I said, but he'd already hung up. "Don't do anything *stupid*? You're the one who got kidnapped," I shouted at the phone. *Sit tight!* The gall of him to tell me to stay put when he was the one in danger—whether he admitted it or not.

I paced around the room huffily, doing a good imitation of the big bad wolf. I couldn't sit around and wait. Ben might think he had everything under control, but they had at least one gun, and, while I knew Ben was competent and well trained by the military, I wasn't going to leave everything to him. I had to do something. I grabbed the tattered fake Leah Marshall purse and headed out the door.

Digital Organizing Tips

Backing Up Files

Few things are more frustrating than a computer crash. Take the time to set up a back-up system and you won't be devastated when you get that awful "blue screen of death." Backing up now will also eliminate worry and expense later.

Back up manually—Use an external hard drive to back up your files. As long as you do it, this system works, but few of us are as consistent as we'd like to be. Computer backups can get pushed down the to-do list or forgotten altogether.

Back up online—Pay a small fee per month or annually and have all your files backed up when you are online. The advantage to this system is that you don't have to remember to do the backup and if there is a catastrophic situation like a hurricane, tornado, or fire, you don't have to worry, because your backup is offsite.

Chapter
Nine

M y computer was gone, but I still had my phone. Sitting in the van in the hotel parking lot, I made a quick call to Summer, asking if she could possibly keep the kids for another day. "Something's come up . . . ," I said, and she jumped into the pause.

"Oh, good. I was going to ask if they could stay an extra day, anyway. Livvy and Nathan are playing with my neighbor's kids and they're having a great time."

I didn't want to impose, but I certainly didn't want to drag the kids into this situation. They were safe where they were, and I wanted them to stay that way. I thanked her profusely and disconnected the call, feeling relieved that the kids were fine, and Summer sounded as if she really was having fun with them.

Next, I listened to Mitch's voice mail. The part for the repair had arrived, and they were "going to step," as soon as they could, which meant they were leaving base ops for the plane. I dialed his number, got his voice mail, and left a message for him to call me when he could.

With my obligations taken care of, I used my phone to search for information on Chase Day. Even though Chase hadn't been the person waiting for the purse in the hotel lobby, I still wondered if he had some connection to the incident. He was Angela's closest relative, and he shared an apartment with her. She might have mentioned the photos, or he might have overheard a phone conversation about them. His proximity to her made it more likely he'd know about the photos. He and Angela probably shared an Internet connection, so it was possible he could access her e-mail account through their Internet provider. He could have sent the e-mails suggesting we meet to exchange purses, then sent the young Magnum look-alike kid to pick up the purse from me so I wouldn't connect Chase with the request. It made sense to start with Chase.

Social networks can be slightly frightening. Well, actually, that's not true. It's not the networks themselves that are scary, but the amount of information people put on the Internet about themselves and their friends. I found Chase listed on Angela's Facebook account. I clicked on his profile and, within a few seconds, I knew he currently worked at The Hideaway, a seafood restaurant. His previous employer was Sandy Beach Sports Medicine Clinic, where he'd been the office manager. He liked movies based on comic book characters, his favorite ice cream came from Cold Stone Creamery, and he'd visited a club the previous night in Tampa, which had been "rocking."

He'd "checked-in," using a mapping feature, which showed his current location was at The Hideaway. There were already a few messages of sympathy about Angela on his news feed, the list of current interactions with all the people in his network.

Even though Honey had said Chase was only going to work to get someone to cover for him, his update on where he was located was sent fifteen minutes ago. I plugged the address of the restaurant into my GPS and turned the minivan in that direction. I stopped at a drug store and bought a tiny sewing kit. Crafts aren't really my thing, but I know the basics of sewing, and I did a passable job of stitching up the lining of the purse.

Five minutes later, I was standing in the cool, dark entry to the restaurant. I'd seen a black BMW with a specialized vanity plate with the name *Chase*, so I figured he was still there. The restaurant's interior was a strange mix of *Gilligan's Island* and Captain Jack Sparrow. Thatched awnings hung over the booths, which ringed the two large rooms. Nautical prints decorated the walls. Nets hung from the bamboo ceiling, draping around antique lanterns. Sailing kitsch ranged along the walls: maps, circular life preservers, compasses, telescopes, and even a ship's wheel. A life-size pirate, complete with dreadlocks, loomed beside me in the entry as I scanned the restaurant looking for Chase.

A prickle of discomfort ran down my spine. I was doing exactly the same thing I hadn't wanted Ben to do—seeking out info on the pictures. I straightened my shoulders and pushed those thoughts away. I had to do this. I didn't have any choice, not with Ben in the situation he was in now. Besides, I was in a busy restaurant. What could happen? *I* certainly wouldn't chase suspicious people into the parking lot.

The entry opened into a waiting area with long, padded benches. It was crowded with several families with small children, college-age kids, and a few people waiting by themselves. A smiling coed with long mahogany hair and a clipboard took my name and gave me a square pager that would light up when my table was ready.

I didn't really want to eat lunch—I didn't think I had the time. Every minute was another minute that Ben spent with Mr. Sandpaper Voice, but the pager gave me an excuse to watch for Chase and get my thoughts together.

I moved to a corner of the waiting area and took up a position by an Ichabod Crane–like man with scraggly brown hair trailing out of his *Phineas and Ferb* baseball cap. I scanned the restaurant but didn't see Chase.

A hefty woman with curly black hair pulled back into a long braid fidgeted in front of me, shifting her pager from hand to hand. She wore booty shorts with a tight yellow tank top and kept cutting into my line of sight as I watched for Chase.

After about ten minutes of waiting, I still hadn't spotted him, so I stepped up to the podium. "I need to talk to your manager," I said to the hostess.

"I'm really sorry about the wait, but it's lunch. We'll get you a table as soon—"

"No, it's nothing like that," I said. "It's about his sister."

"*Oh. My. Gosh*," she said, emphasizing each syllable and leaning closer. "Isn't that terrible? And he's *such* a nice guy. He's not a total jerk like the last manager. I mean, he even came in today—after everything that's happened. He's great," she said with a little stolen glance over her shoulder. "Did you know her? His sister?" she asked.

"Only slightly." I hedged. The woman in the yellow tank bumped into me as she paced in the crowded area.

The skinny scarecrow guy in the *Phineas and Ferb* baseball cap made eye contact with her, gave her a warning shake of the head, then looked away.

"Oh. Well, we're here for him," the hostess said. "We're a family. That's what he keeps telling us. We have to stick together."

"I'm sure he appreciates it. Do you think you could grab him for me? It will only take a second," I said. "I really need to talk to him about his sister."

"Sure, I'll check," she said.

While she was gone, one of the pagers went off with a loud buzz and a flash of red lights. It was the one for the woman in the yellow tank. She all but threw it at the second hostess, who led her away. The brunette hostess returned. "He stepped out, but he'll be back in a minute."

"Do you know where he went?"

"Next door," she said, glancing out the windows in the bar to the strip mall beside the restaurant. "To see his old boss, I bet. They're really close." Sandy Beach Sports Medicine Clinic, which had been listed on his bio page online, was only a few doors away.

"Do you want to wait in his office?"

"That would be great," I said and followed her to a hallway at the back of the bar, which had doors opening off of it to the restrooms, the manager's office, and the parking lot. The woman in the yellow tank scurried around us and exited through the door to the parking lot, as the hostess waved me into the office and said, "Make yourself at home."

The office was a closetlike room and needed some serious organizational help. A mishmash of binders, advertising coupons, kids' paper place mats, and other debris covered every surface in the room: the desk, two metal filing cabinets, even the worn brown carpet. I ignored the piles. I wasn't here to organize.

Besides the rolling chair behind the desk, there was only one other chair in the room and it was piled with binders and files. I stood in the center of the room, not wanting to sit in the rolling chair. I moseyed over to the doorway where I could see through the glass panel in the exit door to the parking lot. No sign of Chase returning from his visit to the clinic. The only person in the parking lot was the woman in the yellow tank. I frowned as I watched her walk along the back of the adjacent strip mall, which was set a little closer to the street than the restaurant, so I had a good view of the area behind the stores. The woman looked up, checking the numbers posted on the back doors. She paused at the third one, pulled it open, and went inside.

That was weird, I thought. While I watched, a teenager in baggy athletic shorts and an oversized sleeveless top emerged from the same door. He ambled across the parking lot and pushed through the restaurant door with a clatter. He noticed me watching him from the office. His gaze narrowed and became challenging. Instinctively, I broke eye contact and moved back into the office. The teen paused, then continued down the hallway. I realized my breath was coming quickly and my heart was pounding. Why was I scared of that kid?

Because he was intimidating.

But why would he be worried about someone watching him walk across the parking lot?

I went to the door again and peeked around it into the corridor in time to see the teenager make his way through the waiting crowds at the front of the restaurant and leave through the front door. Why would he do that? Come through the restaurant to go to the parking lot? There was space between the restaurant and the strip mall. He could have gone to the parking lot from the strip mall. He didn't need to come through here. And he didn't meet anyone or talk to anyone.

The man in the *Phineas and Ferb* hat handed his buzzer to the hostess and moved in my direction. I ducked back into the office and watched as the guy made for the parking lot exit door and followed the same path as the woman in the yellow tank had, to the third door in the back of the strip mall. Another person emerged from the doorway as he opened it, a woman with frizzy gray hair. She hurried in the direction of the restaurant. I slipped out of her line of sight as she came inside, then I leaned out and watched her walk to the waiting area and then out the front door to the parking lot.

A buzz sounded, and I reached for my phone, then realized it wasn't my phone. It was coming from the desk. I shifted closer to the mounds of paper on the desk and lifted a file folder. The phone was vibrating, and the message Unknown number was on the screen. The phone went dark, and I knew the caller had hung up or left a message on voice mail.

I stood there for a few seconds, biting my lip. There was something weird going on at the restaurant. Was it related to what had happened to Ben? Was it all linked somehow to the photos and to Angela's death? I assumed this was Chase's phone since it was on his desk. I glanced at the office door, then picked up the phone quickly. I had to look. If it helped Ben get out of the situation, I had to do it.

The phone didn't have a lock or passcode. I quickly scanned the calls and texts, then looked at the calls listed in his voice mail. If it was his phone, he hadn't talked to Angela for several days. Most of his calls were to someone named Rowley at an 813 area code.

He had a program set up to download his e-mail to his phone. I selected the mailbox icon, quickly shifting through e-mails. They confirmed it was Chase's phone because all the sent mail had his name on it. There was nothing to or from Angela's mailbox. No sent messages or received messages. Angela's mailbox wasn't even loaded on this phone. I double-checked, but there was nothing.

The exit door clicked and I jumped. Footsteps continued by the office door, and I quickly replaced the phone under the file. I contemplated the desktop computer. Maybe that's how he did it?

My hands were trembling so badly that the cursor jumped around the screen when I grabbed the mouse. I blew out a deep breath and reminded myself I was doing this for Ben. To help him. I quickly selected the mail icon. The messages were the same ones that were on his phone. He had all his mail downloaded to his phone, and there were no other e-mail accounts. I opened a Web browser and clicked on the history, which showed a list of websites that involved restaurant supply sales and map searches for Tampa. It seemed Chase hadn't sent those e-mails to me, asking to meet in the lobby.

The exit door from the restaurant to the parking lot clanked open, and a murmur of voices mingled with footsteps in the hall. I stepped away from the computer.

"Chase! I wanna talk to you."

I missed some words as I lunged to the middle of the office, away from the computer. In the hallway, I could see the guy in the *Phineas and Ferb* baseball cap leaning close to Chase, the bill of the cap nearly touching Chase's forehead. ". . . and I didn't come all this way to play your little game of hide-and-seek. If you can't deliver, you should say so—"

"We always deliver," Chase said.

I wished I wasn't in the office, but there was no way to slip out without them seeing me. The atmosphere was so tense between them that they didn't notice me.

"You better." The man shoved by Chase and strode to the front of the restaurant.

There was a pause, then Chase entered the office, running his hands down his tie, smoothing it back into place. He stopped short when he saw me, then his gaze went to the desk. The computer monitor had gone dark while I had eavesdropped on him.

I said, "Hi, Chase. The hostess told me to wait here for you. I'm so sorry about Angela."

"Thank you."

He looked puzzled, so I added, "I'm Ellie. I was with Ben this morning."

"Oh, right." He glanced over his shoulder. "Sorry about that. Complaints," he said with a half-hearted laugh. "They always want to talk to the manager."

"It's fine. I should apologize to you. Barging in on you like this, but I need . . ." I faltered, taking in his haggard face and puffy eyes. He'd changed into a fresh edition of the slightly dressed down corporate look: white dress shirt, yellow tie, black pants, and dress shoes with tassels. His distress combined with his conventional clothes gave him an air of respectability. Could this guy really be involved in the situation with Ben? He looked pitiful.

I held out the fake Leah Marshall purse. "I need to give this to you," I said, and left it at that, watching his reaction.

He looked confused again, so I added, "Angela called me and asked me to bring it by your apartment this morning. That's why I was there."

His face cleared. "Right. The purse mix-up." He took the purse and tossed it on a tilting stack of binders. "I can get you the right one. Maybe later today or tomorrow."

"Sure. That would be fine. No rush. I wanted to get the purse to you because it was important to Angela. She was so worried about it—that I get it back to the apartment."

Chase nodded.

"It seemed a little . . . odd, to be so concerned with a purse," I said, fishing for a response.

"She probably wanted to get the right one to you. She was a fanatic about bad feedback. She wanted to keep her ninety-nine percent positive rating. She was proud of that," Chase said. He closed his eyes and rubbed his fingers over his eyelids. "Sorry," he said, blinking. "It's . . . I can't believe it. I got busy here for a little bit and actually almost forgot what happened, but then, *wham* it hit me that she's gone." He sucked in an unsteady breath.

"I'm sorry," I repeated, but he didn't seem to hear me. He plopped onto the rolling chair. "I can't believe that they think she was on drugs. She'd never do that," he said, rubbing his hand across his forehead.

"So you think that Angela's death wasn't an accident?" I asked.

Surprised, he looked at me as if he'd forgotten I was in the room with him. His phone buzzed, and he pushed the folders around to uncover it. "Sorry, I've got to take this," he said.

"Right." I moved to the door, frustrated that I hadn't figured out how to ask the questions I wanted to ask about the photos. I hesitated in the hallway. If it was a short phone conversation, maybe I could duck back into his office.

There was a framed black and white photograph of a boat moored at a dock on the wall opposite his office. I could see a vague outline of Chase reflected in the glass. "What?" I could hear his sharp question from the hall. He stiffened, his head moving quickly as he scanned the room. He said something else that I didn't catch, then ended the call. He moved quickly back and forth across the room, stuffing files into a leather brief-case. He jerked open a filing cabinet drawer, shoved something small into his pocket, and hurried out of the office without even closing the file drawer or noticing me. He hit the door to the parking lot, it snapped back, and he jogged to his car, then peeled out.

I edged to the office door and looked at the purse sitting forgotten on the stack of binders. I guess he wasn't too concerned about it, after all. I left the restaurant through the front door. On my way to my van, the woman in the yellow tank nearly knocked me over as she hurried to climb into a car. The guy in the *Phineas and Ferb* hat was at the wheel. Their black Camry with Tennessee plates followed me out of The Hideaway's parking lot, and they tailgated me for a few blocks, then turned off.

I tapped the steering wheel, trying to figure out what to do next. I didn't know what to make of Chase. His grief seemed legitimate and deep. And his reaction to the purse had been . . . nothing. No reaction at all. He hadn't shown surprise or eagerness. He hadn't even looked like he was trying to hide some emotion. It seemed he didn't care about the purse at all.

If Chase hadn't been involved in the effort to get the memory card, who else would be interested in it? It could be anyone from Angela's life, I thought miserably, and I didn't really know her that well.

Maybe Honey had seen something. She apparently kept an eye on her neighbors' comings and goings. She'd been the one who told Ben that Angela hadn't made it home last night. I could go back to the apartment complex . . . but Ben was my primary concern. I had to focus on getting that memory card back.

I doubted Honey knew anything about the memory card, but someone who was actually in the pictures, someone like Cara, might know something, I thought suddenly. She had been in the club and a friend of Angela's. She must know the other woman in the picture, the one who was pushed off the balcony. What had happened to her? I hadn't had a spare moment to think about her. Cara would probably know.

I inched along in the creeping traffic, wishing I knew the roads well enough to find a shortcut, but I didn't want to get lost and waste time cruising through the residential areas of condos that interspersed the hotels. I was sure there were plenty of switchbacks and dead-end cul-de-sacs that would eat up more of my time. Finally, I spun the wheel and pulled into the hotel parking lot. The Sea Cottage wasn't far down the street and finding a parking slot on the beach road was about as likely as finding a genie in a bottle on one of the beaches.

I strode down the sidewalk to The Sea Cottage, where I was told that Cara had the afternoon off, but

that she might be at her other part-time job as a lifeguard at the Park Palms Hotel. I retraced my steps toward our hotel, then went a few yards farther and
crossed the street to the luxuriousness of the Park
Palms Hotel. Because Sandy Beach and Costa Bella
were small beach towns, I was able to get there in a few
minutes. The Park Palms was another beachfront hotel
and, even though it was located less than a block from
our hotel, it was obviously a world away from our ac-
commodations. This place had *grounds*.

Instead of a having only a few palms and segos lining the edges of the hotel like many of the moderately
priced hotels, the Park Palms had a curving drive that
separated it from the beach road. I walked up the sidewalk that mirrored the drive. It twisted through bursts
of flowering plants and alongside a stream that trickled
down to the front of the property, where it fed into a
fountain that sent spray as high as the coconut palms.
Space was at a premium on the beach side of the road
and the sheer amount of space the Park Palms covered—almost a block—stated that this was a resort.

I slipped under the portico supported with Doric
columns and into the colonial plantation–style interior
of the hotel. Ceiling fans whispered and dark paneling
covered the lower third of the walls. Above the paneling, the walls were painted a crisp white and lined with
botanical prints and antique maps. Curved, dark wood
armchairs with wicker insets were grouped around
huge pots of elephant ears and ficus. I turned away
from the imposing front desk in rich dark wood and
moved in what I hoped was the direction of the beach.
A set of French doors opened onto a colonnaded veranda with white wicker chairs scattered over its dark
wood. Beyond the wide set of steps leading down to a

pool and garden area was the expanse of the gulf, the water a glittering turquoise.

I followed the brick path to the hotel's pool area and saw Cara swinging a string bag onto her shoulder. She wore a one-piece red swimsuit with the word *Lifeguard* across her chest. She waved to another lifeguard perched in a chair at poolside, then headed in my direction. "Cara," I said, moving toward her. "I don't know if you remember me. I came to The Sea Cottage—"

"Asking about Angela. Yeah, I remember you," she said, moving by me.

I fell into step with her. "Have you heard about Angela?"

She nodded. "I got a text from a friend."

"I'm sorry," I said.

"Yeah, thanks." She shrugged a shoulder. She kept her head down, her gaze focused on her feet as she moved swiftly along the brick path.

Oh boy, this wasn't going to be easy. "Cara, do you have a few minutes? Could I ask you something?"

She shook her head and picked up her pace.

"I'm sorry to bother you, but I think Angela was mixed up in something dangerous—"

"You think?" She spun to me, her thick bangs falling over one eye.

"Yes, I do. And now my brother is caught up in it, too." She was already shaking her head and hurrying forward again, moving down another path that curved around the hotel. "Sorry. Can't help you," she said, pulling a set of car keys from her string bag.

"It's something to do with Club Fifty-two, isn't it? And what you saw there." We came to a side entrance to the hotel's parking garage. Cara pushed through the heavy door. I followed her into the dim interior. "You and Angela and the poor girl who was pushed off the balcony. You were all there."

She jerked to a stop again. "How do you know about that?"

"I saw the pictures."

Her free hand shot out and gripped my wrist. "You have the pictures?"

"No." I stepped back, twisting my wrist free. "But I saw them. You were in them, along with Angela and the girl who fell."

"Ruby. Her name is Ruby."

"What happened that night with you and Angela and Ruby? I need to know so I can help my brother. Please? I don't want anything bad to happen to him."

She looked at me for a long moment before she sighed and said, "Okay, but I don't know what's going on. All I know is that Angela's dead, and Ruby's in the hospital. The doctors say it's amazing she's alive."

"Will she recover?" I asked gently. I wanted to hear the details of what had happened, but she was obviously scared and skittish and more worried about her friend than helping me. Her tone was completely different from the defiant, angry vibe she'd radiated this morning when she was irritated with Angela for not showing up at work. Now, her worried expression scored her forehead with wrinkles, and she had dark half circles under her eyes.

"Yeah. She has a concussion. They were worried about head trauma, but it sounds like she's going to be okay. She's got to have two surgeries on her leg, though. They're doing the first one today, which is terrible, but in a way I'm glad, because it means she's in the hospital. She's safe there, you know?" She glanced along the dim aisles of cars. "No one can get to her."

"So you've talked to her?"

"Only a few minutes on the phone. She's mostly loopy and out of it, which is probably a good thing."

"Surely the police have asked Ruby what happened."

"Yeah, but she says she can't remember anything. I don't know if that's true or not, but I hope she keeps saying it."

"Why? What happened that night at Club Fifty-two?"

Cara pushed her bangs off her face, and I noticed her dark fingernail polish was now chipped. "That's what's so scary—I don't know what happened."

"What do you mean? You were there, too."

"Well, yeah, but I wasn't with them, like, the *whole* time. There was a really cute guy from Jacksonville. We danced a lot. Angela and Ruby hung out. That's how it always was," she said without a trace of bitterness. "They're close. They've known each other for years. Angela invited me to go with them sometimes, you know, if she was heading out after work."

"What exactly did you do that night? Maybe if you went over what happened . . ."

She looked down at her fingers as she picked at the dark polish. "Club Fifty-two is one of our favorites. It was a normal night—we had some drinks, danced, Angela took pictures. She always did that. She liked to post them on Facebook. Ruby usually took pictures, too, but her phone was dead, so she didn't take any that night. Anyway," she sighed heavily, "there was this pulse of excitement that went through the club, and everyone was whisper-yelling that Suzie Quinn was there. We saw her. Angela snapped a few pictures of them in the loft. Later, while I was dancing with the cute guy, Angela and Ruby went to the bathroom. They came back and said they were ready to leave. I wanted to stay, so they left without me."

"So what happened after that? You saw Angela at work later, right?"

"Nothing," she said, frustration vibrating through her voice. "She threw out that comment about getting some big money, but, except for bragging about what she'd buy, she didn't say anything else."

"What about Ruby? What did she say about the night the club?"

"Nothing during the last few days." Cara looked off into the distant corner of the garage. "And now she's not exactly up to talking, you know?"

"I can imagine. So there was nothing else Angela said or did that struck you as odd or out of place?"

"No, except for having a kind of excitement, like, simmering under the surface. I told that police detective who came to the store the same thing. He thought Angela overdosed," she said, the corners of her mouth quirking down in a skeptical twist. "Like Angela ever touched drugs. She was, like, the poster child for 'Say No To Drugs.' Anyway, I told him no way would she do drugs and no way would she commit suicide."

I felt a sinking sensation in my gut. Ben had told Detective Jenson the same thing, and it sounded like Chase would have said the same thing about Angela's firm avoidance of drugs. How long would it be before Jenson widened his investigation beyond accidental death or suicide to possible murder? Maybe he already had.

"Did you tell him about her big find?"

"Yeah, of course," she said.

Her eyebrows shot up as she remembered something. "Oh! I didn't tell him about Angela and Ruby's argument." She deflated again. "It was only something about a bidding war, so it was probably nothing important—something to do with her online auctions, I think."

"What did they say?"

"I don't remember exactly, just that Angela was trying to convince Ruby that a bidding war was a good thing, and Ruby disagreed, I could tell by what Angela said. She was in the back room at work, but I could still hear her since she was, like, shouting into the phone. Do you think it's important?"

"It might be. Did she say anything else?"

She scraped away another flake of dark polish as she said, "Not in exact words, but after she hung up she did mutter something about 'going to the source' like it was the stupidest thing she'd ever heard."

The door to the parking garage swung open with a bang, throwing a swath of blinding light over us. Cara sucked in a breath and grabbed my arm. A man stepped through the door, the long strands of his gray comb-over flittering around his face in the breeze. Cara relaxed and let go of my arm. The man nodded to us as he moved by, giving us a look. I'm sure we did look a bit strange, having a huddled conversation in a dark corner of a parking garage—very Deep Throat.

As his echoing footsteps faded, Cara said, "I'm so freaked right now. I swear, I jump at everything."

"I can see how you'd be nervous."

"I'm off work at both jobs until next week. I'm leaving town—going to see my dad in Charlotte. It's the first time in my life I've actually looked forward to a ten-hour road trip."

"Sounds like a good idea," I said, wishing I could hit the road, too, and escape my troubles. Unfortunately, getting out of town wouldn't help me. There was something I wanted to ask her, a vague thought that formed then slipped away while we were talking, and now I couldn't remember it. I gave up trying to nail down the thought and, instead, got her phone number.

My phone buzzed with a call. It was Mitch. I told Cara I had to take the call, and she left quickly for her car, but by the time I'd said good-bye to her, my call had gone to voice mail. I listened to the message as I walked back to my hotel.

Mitch had landed in Georgia. One of the nice things about military flights is that they're direct. No hubs, no changing planes, and Mitch flew the big jets, so they made great time. His phone was about to die because he'd forgotten his charger, but he'd go home, repack, and hit the road for Florida. He planned to drive straight through and arrive around nine or ten tonight. I had mixed feelings about the message. Mitch's steady personality and levelheadedness were always assets, but I wasn't exactly looking forward to explaining the convoluted situation.

Outside my hotel, a man with a tool belt perched on a ladder, working on a camera mounted discreetly under the eaves of the veranda. "Cameras," I breathed and picked up my pace. I'd thought about them before, but in all the craziness, they'd slipped my mind.

The lobby had the same hushed stillness and murmur of flowing water, but I barely noticed. There was only one couple at the front desk and as soon as they were finished, I asked the clerk if they had video monitoring of the parking lot or hallways.

It was the same woman with the rich southern drawl and she didn't seem to think it was too strange of a request. "Oh sure, honey. We're high tech. You're safe with us here, although," she rotated her torso and leaned one elbow on the counter like she was letting me in on a secret, "we've never had any problems."

"So do you keep the recordings?" I asked, my heartbeat speeding up. If the sports car were on tape I would have a license number and a video of the attack on Ben.

"Recordings?" she said, her voice incredulous. "We don't have any. We just run the cameras to monitor the halls and the parking lots. We don't actually record anything."

"Oh," I said, dejection hitting me. "So no one saw anything . . . out of the ordinary lately? Earlier today?"

"No. Well, except for that kid throwing up in the koi pond," she said with a shiver. "Don't see that every day. And that guy in the exercise room who nearly passed out on the treadmill. Pretty normal day around here."

"Okay. Thanks," I said, turning away from the desk.

I looked at my watch. Nearly two hours had gone by, and I had nothing productive to show for my running around. I *had* to find that memory card. My gaze fell on the poster about the upcoming Fourth of July community celebration. "Take it to the source," I murmured.

Chapter
Ten

Since Suzie Quinn began dating Nick Ryan, she had become a staple of the tabloid press. I hurried across the lobby and took a seat in the business center in front of a computer. A few minutes later, I was logged onto the celebrity news website, In The Know, which was usually shortened to just ITK. "Secret Beach Wedding Plans," read one headline with an accompanying picture of Suzie and Nick walking on the beach. "Has Hollywood's bad boy finally found true love with America's swimming sweetheart?" asked the first line of the story. "A friend close to the couple confirms they are both head over heels in love and a wedding isn't far off." Farther down the page, another story shouted, "Ring Shopping?" with a picture of Nick striding by a jewelry store.

I bit my lip. What would the tabloids—Internet and print—do if they had pictures of "America's swimming sweetheart" doing drugs? The famous person who had it all, but crashes and burns, was a mainstay of the celebrity media. Coverage of Britney and Paris were proof of that. Add the fact that Suzie was seeing a genuine movie star . . . well, that made it a bigger story. I skimmed through the rest of the website, but couldn't find anything specific, except that Suzie had stayed in the luxurious Park Palms Hotel on a previous visit to her hometown.

I shifted to the local paper, which had a short two-paragraph story in the entertainment section, confirming that Suzie had arrived in Sandy Beach and would headline the community fireworks event. The last sentence was exactly what I was looking for: "Today, the gold medal Olympian will talk with children at the Sea Grass YMCA where she learned to swim."

After a quick Google search for an address, I was out the door.

The Sea Grass Y was tucked into an older neighborhood with a worn and tired air, a few blocks inland from the gulf. Narrow driveways led to single car garages attached to modest one-story frame homes painted beige, powder blue, and a chalky yellow color. Mature stands of pines and palms ringed the houses, and mailboxes decorated with reflective circles teetered on unsteady supports near the roads. The sleek hotels and plush beach resorts seemed miles away.

I slowed down and coasted by the cinder block and stucco building that housed the YMCA. The parking lot was full, and cars had parked on both sides of the street. People lined the chain-link fence that enclosed the building. A police officer stationed in the street motioned for me to move on, so I accelerated by the satellite trucks with news logos. I parked several blocks away and walked back. I passed a news reporter standing in front of the crowd, reporting on how Suzie's popular water safety campaign delighted both parents and kids. "Here's a hero who kids—especially girls—can look up to," the reporter gushed. I stopped at the fence beside a mom with a toddler on her hip and her iPhone in her hand.

"Is she in there now?" I asked, thinking about what Cara had said about Ruby and Angela's argument. Had Ruby wanted to offer the pictures to Suzie, hoping that Suzie would be so anxious to keep them out of the tabloids that she would have paid more than the tabloids would? Apparently, Angela hadn't liked the idea. Had Ruby contacted Suzie on her own? Was that why Ruby was pushed off the balcony? But it was a man who pushed Ruby. I thought back to the man on the balcony. He wasn't the Hawaiian-shirted Magnum kid, I was sure of that. The silhouette of the man hadn't shown unruly hair and his build was different, bulkier.

The woman nodded. "I saw her go in about thirty minutes ago." She showed me a picture on her phone of a black Suburban. "That's her. You can just see her head."

"Er—right," I said because the woman seemed to expect a response. All I could see was the back of a woman who was mostly hidden by the SUV.

"I got here an hour early, but it was already full inside," the woman said, her voice swelling with satisfaction. "Of course, I can totally understand it. We're all so pleased, her being from Sandy Beach and all. She's done us proud."

"You're very interested in Suzie?" I asked.

"Oh my, yes. She's just the sweetest thing. I do hope

that Nick Ryan doesn't break her heart. He's never been what you'd call a steady one." Her toddler popped her thumb out of her mouth and leaned to the fence.

The mom shifted the little girl to her other hip as I asked, "Did you know Suzie when she lived here?" She talked about Suzie as if she was an old family friend.

"No." She breathed a sigh of regret. Then she brightened. "I do live six blocks from the house where she grew up, though. I've been following her ever since I saw her interviewed at the Olympics. She's a down-to-earth Florida girl, even with all her fame and money."

The woman turned to talk to someone else, and I checked my phone. No new voice mail, but I did have several e-mail messages. Thank goodness I'd had my e-mail sent to my phone. Even with my laptop gone, I could still read my mail. Most of the e-mails were either junk or things that could wait until I wasn't in the middle of an emergency, but one caught my eye. It was an e-mail notification that I'd received a Facebook friend request.

My thumb hovered over the name, Evan Benworth, a mash-up of Ben's name, Ben Evanworth. I pulled up the message then brought up Facebook. "Evan Benworth" didn't have a profile picture, just an anonymous outline, and he had zero friends. I quickly hit CONFIRM and the page loaded; it was empty except for one status update. Everything fine here at Camp Sunshine, except food not so good—avoiding it. Deserted here. Knot tying course was a breeze. Having a look around the grounds.

I shook my head, amazed at my brother. The sick feeling in my gut eased a bit. He was okay. I checked the time of the status update. At least, as of nine minutes ago, he was okay. How in the world did he do this? I suppose it wouldn't be hard to set up a fake Facebook account, but where did he get the computer to do it? He'd managed it somehow.

It wasn't hard to translate his message. He was okay. "Camp Sunshine" was the hotel. He apparently wasn't eating what they gave him, which seemed like a smart move. He'd used the word "deserted." Did that mean they had left him there alone, and he was looking around the hotel suite? Did the reference to knot tying mean that he'd been tied up, but was able to free himself? I chewed on my lip. I wished he'd get out of there.

I brought up the box to comment on the status update and typed, Are you feeling homesick? I felt I should stay with the spirit of the original message. Surely Ben was being careful and could cover his tracks. He could delete the browsing history or he might even delete the fake Facebook account he'd created, but I wanted to be careful. I continued the comment, Miss you here. Ready for you to come home.

A few seconds later, a comment from Evan Benworth appeared below mine. I'd love to, but must win the scavenger hunt and won't leave until I do.

"Oh, Ben," I murmured. He was just like me—stubborn to the point of unreasonableness.

His message continued, This cabin is a contender for the Dirty Sock Award.

A little laugh escaped, surprising me. At Camp Sunshine, the Dirty Sock Award was an actual dirty sock given to the messiest cabin. The cabin leader had to wear it pinned to his shirt for the whole day. It was a sort of stinky scarlet letter motivation for campers to keep their cabins neat. Don't worry about me, Ben

added in a new comment. Plans already made for midnight escape, if needed. I waited, but no more messages came in.

I felt a prick of worry again. He thought he had
everything under control, and I hoped he did, but I
wasn't about to go back to my hotel and wait for him to
show up. At least I knew he was okay and I was doing
something to help him out.

There was a flurry of movement in the parking lot.
"Here she comes!" The woman beside me hitched her
toddler higher on her hip and raised her phone.

Several people exited the building, all circling
around a central figure. I couldn't really see her until
the cluster reached the line along the fence. A brunette
in a lime green halter top, tight jeans, heels, and dark
sunglasses that obscured the upper half of her face separated from the group and came toward a section of the
fence a few feet from me. Camera shutters whirred,
and people shouted her name. She might not be swimming competitively now, but she still had a swimmer's
physique with strong shoulders and arms. Her taunt
muscles flexed as she reached out a tanned arm to
shake hands and sign autographs. She swirled her
name on several pieces of paper, then stepped back and
waved, pivoting so that everyone gathered could get a
shot of her, then she moved to the black Suburban. I
wouldn't be able to talk to her here.

I abandoned the fence, sprinting back to the van.
The roads were going to be packed once all those people made it back to their cars. I had the van in gear almost before I was buckled in. I gave it some gas, and it
climbed off the grassy verge lined with mailboxes and
onto the road. I didn't turn around. Instead, I drove

straight ahead, away from the throng of people moving slowly across the road. A few blocks and I was out of the neighborhood. When I stopped at a light on a busy intersection, I quickly tapped the screen of the GPS, entering the name of the hotel where Suzie had stayed before and followed the directions back to the Park Palms Hotel, hoping I'd guessed right on her destination. I watched the minutes tick off on the dashboard clock as I waited in the slow traffic on the beach road.

Finally, I pulled into the hotel grounds and navigated the curving drive. I came to the portico where a crowd was converging on a black Suburban. I slowed to take in the scene. The back door opened and cameras flashed. The pack surged toward Suzie, her lime green top and dark glasses making her easy to spot as she climbed out. She pushed through the crowd, head down, arms tucked to her sides, following a burly guy in a suit as he cut through the throng. Once she stepped inside the hotel, the group disbursed.

I eased off the brake, bypassed the valet, and took the ramp to the hotel parking garage, since the swanky drive to the hotel didn't have a turnaround and led straight to the parking garage. I headed there, thinking gloomily that there was no way in the world I would be able to talk to Suzie unless I knew someone in her entourage who could get me in to see her. I circled through the lowest level of the parking garage, intending to pay the minimum charge and go back to my hotel, but the gate attendant came out of his little booth with his hand up and stopped me a few feet back from the bar. He plopped an orange cone in front of my bumper. "Just be a moment, ma'am," he shouted as I rolled down my window.

He said something into his cell phone as he returned to the booth. A few seconds later, a black Suburban nosed up to the bar from the wrong direction. The guard raised the bar and the Suburban whipped by the booth, cut around me, and stopped a few feet away at a corner of the garage. The back door opened, and a figure in lime green hopped out. Her sunglasses were pushed up on her head, and I could see *this* was Suzie Quinn. The other woman and Suburban must have been a decoy. She and several other people disappeared through a door marked SERVICE.

"Ma'am, you can go now." I jumped. I hadn't realized the guard was by my window. He'd removed the cone and was motioning me forward. I paid him, and he said, "You don't see that every day, do you?" As I took my change, he leaned toward me and said in an undertone, "Too bad you weren't quick enough to snap a picture or two. Might have gotten them in a magazine. I can't do that," he said, straightening. "I'd get fired, but guests . . . guests can do what they like."

"No more pictures for me," I murmured as I pulled away. "That's what got me into this mess in the first place."

I exited the parking garage and merged with the slow moving traffic on the beach road. I'd accomplished nothing. The hours were slipping by and I wasn't any closer to finding the memory card. A brown sign indicated the antebellum home and grounds of Green Groves were half a mile away. The grand home built in Southern Colonial style and set in the famous gardens had been on my list of sights to see. Those plans of carefree days with sunscreen, surf, and sightseeing seemed to be a universe away. My world had narrowed to helping Ben, but I'd been running around, flitting off in different directions without any clear plan.

That was my problem, I realized suddenly. I hadn't thought anything through. I'd run off as soon as a thought crossed my mind, letting my worry and fear for Ben drive my actions. I needed to regroup, assess what I'd done, and make a logical plan. I needed to take my emotions out of the situation (as much as I could, at least) and apply my organizational skills.

I drew a deep breath and gathered my thoughts. First, I needed to see if there were any messages for me at my hotel. Ben might have managed to leave one for me or—worst thought—Mr. Sandpaper Voice might have called back. It only took a few minutes to get to the hotel. I hurried to my room. The light on the phone was dark.

I checked my watch and blew out a sigh that sent my bangs flying. Five o'clock. I'd wasted hours and had practically nothing to show for it. I plopped down on the couch and rubbed my temples, ignoring the mess of the hotel room. Only one thing mattered right now. I picked up the hotel-provided notepad and pen and began to make notes.

Angela had been murdered. Only the police thought that Angela's death was an overdose. Ben, Chase, and Cara had all said Angela would never use drugs and even Detective Jenson had said he didn't think she'd slipped, eliminating the possibility of accidental death. If he were interviewing Angela's friends and family, he'd get the same information. He'd have to reassess. But it didn't matter what the police thought, I reminded myself. I had to move forward with the information I had, which indicated that Angela's death had to be linked to the photos.

I supposed there was a small possibility that she'd been killed for some other reason—an unbalanced ex-boyfriend or something along those lines—except that Ruby was in the hospital and quite possibly could have been killed as well, which argued strongly that the photos were at the center of all that had been going on.

The more I thought about it, the more convinced I became that Chase wasn't involved in trying to get the photos. He wouldn't need to snatch Angela, and he didn't even take the purse when he left his office abruptly. No, it had to be someone else, someone like Mr. Sandpaper Voice.

He must have intercepted Angela last night when she was on her way to deliver the purse. Did he know about the photos on the memory card in the fake purse? Is that what he thought he was getting when he snatched Angela? She had to have been taken forcibly. I couldn't believe that she would willingly leave her phone behind. She wouldn't have missed our meeting, either. She didn't show up because she couldn't. He must have either thought she had the photos with her or that he could get her to tell him where they were.

Mr. Sandpaper Voice had said Angela didn't cooperate with him, at first. She must have held out, but by late this morning she'd called me, nervous and distraught, and insisted that I take the fake purse to her apartment right away. Had Mr. Sandpaper Voice killed her after she made the phone call? I felt ill, just thinking of it. I rubbed my eyes, then forced myself to go back to my notes.

The killer must have dumped Angela's body in the apartment complex pool, but things didn't go according to plan after that. I hadn't left the purse on the porch as instructed. I'd kept it with me, walking inside her apartment, then I'd rushed to the parking lot when the woman discovered Angela's body. The killer had miscalculated. He should have made sure he had the purse before he killed Angela. And he probably hadn't expected her body to be discovered so quickly.

But how did Mr. Sandpaper Voice know *I* had the purse? I felt a chill run through me as I realized he must have seen me with the purse and followed me back to the hotel. I let out a shaky breath. No wonder he was so angry when Ben brought the purse without the memory card. He'd already tried to get it once and failed.

Which brought me to the main point. Who had taken the memory card from my hotel room? As awful as Angela's death was, I couldn't focus on that. Ben was my priority. As soon as he was safe, I'd take all the information I had about Angela and her death to the police, but not until I knew Ben was okay. To go near the police before then could endanger him even more.

Who could have known about the photos and taken them from my hotel room? I jotted down a few more names, Honey, Cara, and Ruby, simply because they knew Angela and were involved in the situation. Ruby couldn't have taken the memory card because she was in the hospital when it was stolen. Cara seemed genuinely scared and confused about the whole situation, and Honey seemed to know Angela only in a passing acquaintance sort of way—they said hello at the mailbox and chatted, but she didn't seem to be a close friend who Angela would confide in. I tapped my pen against her name.

Would she know about the memory card and the

purse? It didn't seem like a subject that would come up during a casual chat at the mailbox. And how would she know Angela's e-mail information to send me the request to meet in the lobby?

I stood and paced around the tight confines of the room, running through everything that had happened—Chase's quick exit, Cara's jittery ignorance, the whir of camera shutters aimed at Suzie, the mom holding up her iPhone to take a picture of Suzie.

I stopped pacing. Angela's phone. That's what I'd wanted to ask Cara about. I quickly dialed her number and sighed with relief when she answered.

After we exchanged hellos, I asked, "You said something about Ruby's phone being dead, so Angela was the only one taking pictures. Did she use a camera or her phone?"

"She always used her phone."

I closed my eyes. Angela's phone. The one Ben and I had in our hands this morning, the one we'd given back to Chase. "Would the pictures still be on her phone, do you think?"

"No, she always uploaded them to her computer right away so she could post them on Facebook."

But she hadn't posted these photos. They might still be on her phone or in her broken computer. I thanked Cara for the info, then hung up and headed back to the van.

Digital Organizing Tips

Organizing Pictures

Photo files can be some of the most disorganized files on a computer. Generally, photos are downloaded into folders according to the date the photo was taken, which is a method of organizing, but it's not very effective. Few people remember the exact month or day a particular photo was taken.

To get your photos organized, use the same principles of folder organization. Create broad categories, then, instead of using only the date, name folders with the subject of the photograph. Include dates or years for clarification. For instance, "Joe's Birthday Party 2011" or "Joe's 16th Birthday Party" are specific names and will let you know exactly what is in the folder.

Renaming individual photos can be time consuming but will help you find your photos quickly.

Delete duplicates as well as out-of-focus or unflattering photos.

If your computer isn't backed up online, burn your photos to a disk, then label and store in a cool, dry area.

Chapter
Eleven

Honey invited me inside her apartment, craning her neck, clearly hoping to see Ben behind me. "Where's your cute brother?" she asked.

"He got held up . . . in traffic," I said, which was absolutely true. He had been held up and there was tons of traffic around when it happened. "Thanks for letting me wait for him here." I figured I had a better chance of getting Honey to talk to me if she thought Ben would arrive shortly. I'd told Honey that we were supposed to meet Chase at his apartment. When I'd arrived, a quick scan of the apartment parking lot had shown Chase was out and that Honey was home—so handy to have the parking slots labeled with the apartment numbers.

There was a shiny new deadbolt on Chase's apartment door, which dashed my hopes of sneaking into his apartment or convincing Honey to help me get inside. I'd hoped she might have exchanged keys with

Angela at some point in the past, but since it looked like that wasn't going to be an option, I decided I might as well talk to Honey and hope that Chase came home while I was here. Maybe I could convince him to let me see Angela's phone. It was five-thirty, and I hoped he would return home for the evening.

"That was fast," I said, indicating the new deadbolt.

"The manager called a locksmith earlier today. She is on her toes now, doing everything she can to convince us all that this is a safe complex, despite the police cars and yellow tape. Come on in." Honey waved me through the living room and into the small kitchen area. "This is Bruno," she said, indicating a German shepherd that was ambling toward me. Honey rubbed the dog's ears as he walked by her. "He's sweet, like me," she said with a wink.

I eased forward, the back of my hand extended. I had a big dog myself, so the size of the animal didn't bother me, but it was always good to be cautious. Bruno sauntered closer, giving my hand a sniff, and I could see the gray in his muzzle. He ducked his head under my hand, clearly wanting to be petted. I rubbed his ears and along his back, then he moseyed over to a large cushion in the living room and collapsed with a gusty sigh. I never would have thought Honey would have a German shepherd. Something more along the lines of a fuzzy lap dog with bows and painted toenails would seem to be more her style.

Honey had on a hot pink swimsuit cover-up with spaghetti straps and enough gold chains to rival Mr. T. "I'm just back from the beach," she said, gesturing at a canvas bag and pink sunhat with an enormous brim sitting near the door. It looked like something a glamorous Hollywood starlet would have worn in a black and white film. I apologized for dropping in on her, but she cut me off. "Nonsense. What's going on next door is *so* interesting. Would you like some lemonade? It's homemade," she added as she walked into the kitchen.

"Sure," I said, following her, noticing that the flower arrangement that had been delivered to Angela was now on the bar that separated the kitchen from the living area. I edged down the bar. I'd completely forgotten about the flowers. Hadn't the card said something about a find? Wasn't that the word that Cara said Angela used to describe the photos?

Honey was busy pouring two tall glasses of lemonade and cutting slices of lemon. I craned my neck, looking for the little plastic fork with the card. It was on the far side. Honey arranged the lemon slices on the sides of the glasses along with sprigs of mint, then turned to a cabinet. Without letting myself think about it, I reached out while her back was turned and snatched the card.

"Wasn't that sweet of Chase to give those to me?" she said with a nod of her head in the direction of the flowers as she set a glass on the bar for me. I agreed and slipped the card into my pocket. Honey arranged several shortbread cookies on a plate, put it beside my glass, and shook her head. "Said he didn't want to keep them," she said, obviously perplexed at why anyone wouldn't want to keep a beautiful flower arrangement.

I took a shortbread cookie and asked, "So what is going on next door?"

Honey picked up her glass and motioned for me to follow her to the dining area, which had windows that looked out onto the porch and sidewalk leading to the parking lot. I grabbed my lemonade and joined her as she pulled back a ruffled white curtain and pointed one of her burgundy talons through the slats of the blinds. "See that car right there?" she asked, indicating a brown four-door car parked in one of the visitor slots across from Angela and Chase's apartment. I could see two shadowy figures inside the car.

I nodded as I sipped my lemonade, which was surprisingly good—just the right blend of tart and sweet. "This is terrific lemonade."

"Never use that powdered stuff," she said with a shudder. "You've got to boil water to dissolve the sugar, *then* add the lemon juice."

"Freshly squeezed?"

"Of course," she said, like there was no other way to do it. She turned her attention back to the window. "I've seen that car off and on for the last few days. They come and park for a while, then leave. They arrived," she paused to consult her watch, "around two-thirty, just after the police left. They've been there ever since."

I glanced at my watch. "Three hours is a long time to sit in a car on a hot afternoon."

"Isn't it?" Honey said.

"Have you seen anything else that seemed strange?" I asked. "Did you see anyone at Chase and Angela's apartment yesterday or last night?" It seemed like Honey kept a close watch on her corner of the apartment complex.

"No one. Nothing." Honey retrieved the shortbread cookies. She put them on the table and waved me into a seat. I took another cookie. They were delicious, too. It seemed Honey was a regular Martha Stewart in the kitchen.

"What about Chase? Did you see his car last night?"

"No, his parking slot was empty until he arrived today, shortly after you came to the apartment."

I squashed an internal sigh. I'd been hoping that Honey would have some tidbit of information—like a sighting of someone prowling around the apartment or some little overlooked detail—that would put a whole new spin on everything.

A shadow moved across the curtains from the parking lot toward the apartments. "Oh, there's Chase," Honey said. Before she'd finished speaking, several more figures moved by the window after Chase, their shadows quickly flitting over the curtains.

Muted voices sounded. The words were rapid and there was a strident quality to them that I could hear, despite being inside. Honey and I looked at each other.

"That sounds like an argument," I said, and Honey nodded. We both moved back to the window where we could see two men, one on each side of Chase, marching him down the sidewalk. I was only a few steps behind Honey when she scurried to the front door and threw it open.

We were in time to see one of the men put his hand on Chase's head as he put him in the back seat of the brown car. The sound of a camera shutter clicked rapidly, and I tracked it to an Asian guy standing under the carport a few feet away from the brown car. "He's being arrested," Honey whispered through her fingers, which covered her lips. The shutter continued to whir as one of the guys who put Chase in the car straightened his tie and adjusted the lapels on his suit coat, then joined the other suited man in the front seat of the car, and they drove out of the complex.

The guy with the camera swung toward us, and I automatically backed away, but Honey didn't move. He came over to the sidewalk, the camera around his neck swinging with each step and tangling with a lanyard. When he reached Honey, the lanyard stopped swaying, and I could read the large print beside the photo: PRESS.

"Joe Zoltiff. *Sandy Beach Journal*. Did you have any idea that your neighbor was involved in a pill mill?"

"What?" Honey said, her hand transferring from her lips to her collarbone. "Pill mill?"

"Yes." The man pulled a long narrow notebook out of the breast pocket of his plaid shirt. "There's a coordinated law enforcement sweep going on today involving local police and the DEA."

"But that can't be right. They've got the wrong guy," Honey protested. "He works at a restaurant, The Hideaway, down by the water. He doesn't have anything to do with drugs."

"But he did work at a medical office . . . ," I murmured, more to myself than to Honey, but she heard me and spun around.

"He did?"

"It's on his Facebook page," I said.

"But that doesn't mean anything now. He might have worked there in the past, but he doesn't work there *now*," Honey said to me, then turned back to the guy with the camera. "Chase Day is the best neighbor. He always helps me bring my groceries in and he took Bruno out for me, too," she said, almost defiantly.

The reporter looked slightly confused. "Um, okay. Can I quote you on that—that he helped you with the groceries?"

"Yes, please do. Honey DeStefano," she said as she jabbed at his notepad as she spell her name for him.

Then she grabbed his arm. "Come inside," she said, dragging him toward her door, which was still open. "I'm sure there's a mistake and you—you're a member of the press—you can sort it out. Have a seat," Honey said, gesturing to the dining-room table.

I had followed them back inside because I wanted to hear what was going on. While Honey prepared another glass of lemonade, Bruno wandered over. The reporter must not have noticed the dog, because he suddenly jumped onto the seat of the dining-room chair. The dog applied his nose to the tips of the guy's sneakers, gave a hearty sniff, then moseyed back to his cushion.

Joe glanced at me. I said, "That's Bruno."

We could hear his blustery sigh from across the room as he turned in a half-circle, then dropped down onto his cushion. Joe cleared his throat and adjusted his collar as he stepped down, his face flushed.

"You can never be too careful with dogs," he said.

"I'm sure you've got to watch out for them in your line of work." I slipped into a seat at the table beside the reporter and tried to pretend he hadn't just been standing on a chair. I stuck out my hand. "Hi. I'm Ellie. I don't live here. Just visiting," I said, hoping that would limit his interest in me. It seemed to work because he lowered the pen he'd poised to write down my name and, instead, he shook my hand. "Joe."

"So what's going on? I've heard about these pill mills on the news."

"They've been a big problem in Florida for years. They distribute painkillers, mostly opium-type drugs, to anyone who walks in the door and pays them. The state is cracking down, passing laws and raiding clinics. That's what is happening today, a statewide sting operation. Until recently, it's been easy to get pills here. Florida has become a distribution point for pills going into other states, like Mississippi, Georgia, even Tennessee and up the East Coast."

Honey set a glass in front of Joe and took a seat opposite him. "Joe's telling me about the pill mills," I said to Honey to bring her into the conversation. I turned back to Joe and asked, "And that was going on here in Sandy Beach and Costa Bella?"

"We're strategically located. Drive a couple of hours and you can be in three different states. Pills were moved up here, mostly from Tampa, then distributed through two main locations, a clinic in Spring Heights and another one, Sandy Beach Sports Medicine Clinic, in the shopping center near The Hideaway."

"But like I said earlier, Chase doesn't work at the sports clinic. He works at the restaurant," Honey said, and pushed the plate in Joe's direction. "Have a cookie."

He took one, ate it in one gulp, and said, "I just came from there. The doctor who owns the clinic was arrested a little while ago, too."

"So what?" Honey said. "I used to work for a CPA. That doesn't mean I'm doing people's taxes on the side."

"Well, in Chase Day's case, it seems he was still working for the sports clinic."

Honey looked doubtful, and Joe said, "The state cracked down on these doctors who prescribe pain meds, so the doctors changed up the way they distribute pills. I've been reporting on this for a couple of years, and I've seen how the docs used to have waiting rooms full of patients at all hours of the day and night—even after midnight. It was easy to spot the bogus clinics because there would be so many people in the waiting rooms and lots of cars with out-of- state plates. Those details were red flags that the police and DEA looked for, so the docs switched things up so they wouldn't be so obvious. Instead of waiting at a pain clinic and clogging up the waiting room and parking lot, the doc and Chase set up an elaborate scheme to funnel the patients through the restaurant waiting area and then over to the pain clinic. The patients gave the hostess a code word, and she gave them a special buzzer. When their pager went off, the hostess sent them through the restaurant to the back door. They slipped around the back of the building and into the back door of the clinic, got their drugs, and were on their way."

"That's so elaborate," Honey said.

"But clever," I said, thinking of the woman in the yellow tank and the man in the *Phineas and Ferb* hat. They had been antsy and didn't seem to fit with the rest of the relaxed vacation crowd. The confrontation between the man and Chase must have been about the changes, the elaborate setup to get into the clinic. "The waiting area at a busy restaurant is always packed, especially at lunch and dinner," I said. "A crowd there wouldn't draw any suspicion and neither would a parking lot full of cars with out-of-state plates. It's frequented by tourists, after all." I realized Joe was taking notes, and I quickly put my hand on his arm. "Don't quote me on that. I'm only thinking out loud."

"But how do they know this about Chase? Couldn't it be a coincidence?" Honey asked.

Joe shook his head. "You couldn't set up a relay like

that between two businesses without the knowledge of the managers. Anyway, law enforcement has been watching him and the doc for weeks. I've been shadowing the agents. They want the press coverage, so they've let me in on the story. Two undercover officers, posing as patients, ran through the whole setup yesterday."

While Honey asked more questions, my thoughts ran in another direction. Could the break-in at Chase and Angela's apartment have had something to do with the pill mill? I'd assumed the break-in was someone looking for the photos, but I couldn't make that assumption now.

Honey said, "Well, that's terrible. I hate to hear that. You can quote me on that. And I know you'll want a picture to go with that quote. Let me get my hat, and we can go out on my patio."

I thanked Honey for the refreshments and slipped out. Joe had edged toward the door with me, but resistance was futile. Honey latched onto his wrist and pulled him to the patio, explaining her right side was her most photogenic.

The door to Chase's apartment was open now, and I could see two men in dark shirts with the letters *DEA* moving around inside, collecting evidence. They must have arrived when Honey, Joe, and I were deep in conversation and didn't notice them. There went my chance to get a look at Angela's phone, I thought dismally.

I pulled the card that came with the flowers out of my pocket as I walked back to the car, marveling at how flexible my morals had become. Normally, I wouldn't take anything—even a piece of paper—from someone's home, but I thought of that scratchy voice on the phone threatening Ben. His matter-of-fact tone scared me. It sounded as if violence wouldn't bother him. The hours were slipping by—it was a few minutes after six now—so quickly. I only had one other person who was linked with Angela. I climbed in the van, cranked the air conditioner, and dialed the number on the card.

Chapter
Twelve

The phone went directly to voice mail. "Monica here with *Celeb*. Leave me a message." The voice sounded young, and I had the impression she was around Angela's age.

Celeb? Monica was with the tabloid magazine? It was a national magazine that appeared at grocery store checkout stands across the country. I'd assumed that Monica was someone local because the flowers had been delivered by a florist in Costa Bella—I remembered seeing the name on the deliveryman's shirt—but obviously Angela had taken her "find" to the top of the entertainment food chain.

The phone beeped, and I said, "Hi. My name is Ellie. I'd like to talk to you about Angela and her find." I left my number and hung up.

My phone rang almost immediately. The caller ID showed it was the number I'd just dialed, so I picked up. "Hi. I'm Monica, returning your call about Angela's . . . find," she said in a quiet but hurried tone, as if she didn't want to be overheard and didn't have long to talk. "Do you have them? The pictures of Suzie?"

I closed my eyes for a second. "Yes." First snooping on phones and computers, then taking the florist card that didn't belong to me, and now lying—it was terrible, but I knew if I said no the conversation would be over and I couldn't have that.

"Let's meet," Monica said almost instantly. "I can give you the same deal. Five now, five when it's published."

"Hundred?" I asked, frowning—that wasn't much money for all the trouble the photos had caused.

Monica laughed. "No, five hundred thousand."

"One million? One million *dollars*?" I managed to squeak.

"Yes," Monica said, her tone swift and businesslike, despite her obvious efforts not to be overheard. "You're local, too, right? You're in Sandy Beach?"

I was so stunned by the amount of money she'd named that it took me a minute to process what she'd asked. "Yes, I'm here."

"Good. Can you be at the Park Palms Hotel in thirty minutes?"

"Yes."

"Fine. Go through the hotel onto the beach. I'm in the fifth cabana on your left."

I strode through the cool, dark confines of the Park Palms, thinking that if I'd known I would be spending so much of my time at the exclusive hotel, I would have paid extra to stay here. It would have saved me so much time. I slipped my sunglasses on as I made my way through the wicker furniture on the veranda. I trotted down the steps, following a waiter carrying a tray of drinks with little umbrellas down the winding path toward the beach, counting off the cabanas as I passed them. The waiter turned off at the fourth cabana. I stopped at the next one. The curtains were shut, and I paused, not sure of the protocol. The fabric pulsed with wind as it caught the stiff breeze from the water. There was nowhere to knock and Monica had seemed intent on keeping a low profile on the phone, so I leaned toward the bow holding the curtains closed and said quietly, "Monica?"

Nothing. I called her name again, slightly louder. This time the curtains twitched open an inch and a chocolate brown eye appeared in the slit. "Yes?"

"Monica? I'm Ellie. We talked on the phone."

The curtains parted farther, revealing a woman with a heart-shaped face and a head of white curls wearing a boxy white caftanlike shirt trimmed at the sleeves and neckline with a Greek key pattern. Fluid black pants swished around her ankles as she stepped back and motioned for me to enter, then take a seat in one of the lounge chairs. The garments engulfed her small frame.

She tied the curtains tightly together as I perched on one of the chairs and looked around. It was a luxurious setup. There were four plush lounge chairs, a flat screen TV, a small refrigerator tucked into a corner below shelves of fluffy white towels, and a tray with fresh fruit, nuts, and bottled water. However, it wasn't the cabana of a person on vacation.

There was none of the usual paraphernalia that surrounded someone on the beach—no tubes of sunscreen, no boogie boards or goggles, no discarded paperback or magazine. One of the lounge chairs was positioned beside the curtains that ran along the back of the ca- bana, the side that faced the hotel, not the water. A large canvas tote sat on the wooden floorboards beside the lounge chair, gaping open, revealing a shiny black camera case, a couple of crinkled notebooks, and a computer laptop case. A digital camera with a long lens rested on the lounge cushion.

Monica sat down on the lounge chair, nimbly cross- ing her legs and picking up her camera. She brought the camera to her eye and peered through the slit in the curtains, the lens aimed at the back of the hotel. "Okay, here's the deal," she said with the camera to her face. "We sign a contract. You give us exclusive rights and agree that you won't speak, publish, text, tweet, or even *think* the name Suzie Quinn until the issue is pub- lished. I pay you the first half now; you get the rest when the issue is published." She pulled her face away from the camera for a second, a look of distaste twist- ing her full lips. "You stay with me until next week when the issue hits the newsstands."

I opened my mouth, but she raised a creamy white hand, cutting me off. She pressed her eye to the viewfinder. "I don't like it either, but my editor insists. This is too big a story to risk a leak. From now on, you're my new BFF."

I stared at her for a second, frowning. If she was an old lady, I'd give up chocolate *and* purses. I licked my lips as I thought, *here goes.* "I don't have the photos."

"What?" She pulled away from the camera, and I got a clear look at her face. Despite a layer of heavy powder, I could see smooth skin, no lines around the eyes or creases at her lips. If she was more than twenty-seven, I'd be surprised. She said, "Now, look, you can't—"

"I have seen them. Angela gave them to me, but someone took them."

She frowned at me for a moment, then shifted around, propped the camera up on a bent knee and balanced it there with her right hand while she pulled her phone out of the pocket of her voluminous pants with her left hand. She dialed a number and checked her viewfinder while it rang.

"If you're calling Angela, she won't answer. I'm sorry to tell you, but she's dead."

She swiveled fully toward me, her camera dropping into her lap. "You're lying," she said, her tone accusing. "You're trying to cut her out, get all the money for yourself."

"No. I wish I were. She died earlier today. Drowned in the pool at her apartment complex."

Monica gave me a long look, then put her camera down on the cushion and opened her laptop. Her fingers flew across the keypad. After a pause, she clicked on a link, then her eyelids flickered as she scanned the text. "Oh my God," she breathed, then looked up at me. "How did you know? Were you a friend?"

"I was there."

"But this doesn't say anything . . . it's just a report that a woman drowned. What happened?"

"The police think it was an accidental overdose." Monica grabbed a pen and a notebook. "Hey," I said, "I don't want to be quoted on any of this. I don't want to be in the news."

Monica looked doubtful. "Everybody wants to be famous."

"I don't," I said.

"Then why say you have the photos?"

"Because I need your help." I couldn't think of a clever lie to trick Monica into helping me, so I went with the truth—a slightly edited version of the truth. There was no way I was telling her about Ben if I could help it. She worked for a tabloid, after all. "I think Angela was killed for the photos. She sent them to me by mistake." I hesitated for a second, then decided I wouldn't go into that part of the story now.

"It's a long story. Anyway, she asked me to bring them to her apartment today, but when I got there, the apartment had been broken into, and her body was found in the pool. The police think her death was an overdose, but everyone who knew her says she'd never do drugs. I didn't even know I had the photos, but I found them after she died. When I saw them, I realized how valuable they were. I think she was killed for them. Then someone stole them from my hotel room. Whoever killed Angela knows I had the photos and wants them. I'm afraid if I don't find the photos, I'll end up like Angela. I've got to find them. Your phone number from the flower arrangement is the only lead I've got."

"That's a rather vague story. Lots of unidentified people."

"No kidding. That's why I'm in this situation. Will you help me?"

Monica blew out a sigh. "Don't have much choice, do I? I just told my editor I had the most explosive front page scoop since Brad and Angelina got together, and now I've got absolutely zero." Her eyes narrowed as she said, "I'll help you, but when we find them, I want them. No fee, either."

"You and everyone else," I murmured. "Fine," I said louder, relieved to have her cooperation. My main goal had to be to get the photos. Once I had them, there would be nothing to stop me from giving a copy to Monica. I wanted Ben safe, but the people who were doing this to him were dangerous and if giving a copy of the photos to Monica was what it took to expose them, I'd do it. I had a feeling that when everything was over and Monica knew the whole story she'd jump at the chance to provide all the details. It would be quite a scoop.

Monica noticed a movement through the gap in the curtains. "Crap." She yanked her camera up, hitting the shutter before it was even steady in her hand. She must have turned off the sound of the shutter clicking because the familiar noise was absent, but her finger pulsed steadily on the shutter button as she adjusted the lens with her other hand. "Three days in this stupid cabana and the first time they step out on the balcony, I'm not ready."

"You've been here for three days?"

"I'm on Suzie Watch," she said, continuing to photograph. "Wherever Suzie goes, I go." Abruptly, she pulled the camera away. Squinting, she watched the balcony for a few moments while she removed the memory card from her camera, slipped another one from her pocket, and loaded it into the camera, never looking away from the gap in the curtains. She plugged the first memory card into a slot on her laptop, then divided her attention between the balcony and her laptop. "At least the light was good," she said to herself.

"So you were at the Y today when Suzie visited?"

"Sure. Nothing very interesting there. We all got the same pictures. The name of the game is to get that one picture that no one else has."

"Like Angela's pictures."

"Right. Those photos are unique—no one has seen anything like that out of Suzie—but the real kicker is the scandal. Perfect sport icon Suzie doing drugs? Huge readership boost. And don't forget the worldwide appeal that the Nick Ryan angle adds. It's a tabloid perfect storm. So tell me about the photos. Angela said they show Suzie doing drugs."

"That's what I saw."

"What was the quality? Sharp or grainy?"

"They looked fine to me, but I'm an amateur. I definitely recognized Suzie," I said. I wanted to get the conversation off of the photos and onto Angela, so I asked, "How did Angela contact you?"

"Phone call. Same as you."

"How did she get your number?" I could see the laptop screen and watched the blur of the pictures uploading from the camera memory card. She typed a short e-mail and hit SEND, then repositioned herself with the camera at the ready.

"Wouldn't be hard. My contact info is listed at the end of every story I do for *Celeb,* and the website has a contact page. *Celeb* encourages tips. You'd be surprised how many photos and videos come in from amateurs now. Freaking cell phone cameras. Everybody's a photographer."

"What exactly did she say?"

"She described the photos and asked me how much *Celeb* would pay. I called my editor, got a figure, and called her back."

"When was this?"

"The day before yesterday. I called her back and told her what we were willing to pay, but she said she had to think about it. That's why I sent the flowers, a little reminder."

"Awfully extravagant flower arrangement."

"That was the idea. A reminder of the *other* extravagances she could indulge in if she took my offer."

"You said you're on Suzie Watch. Are there any other tabloids here?"

"Nick and Suzie are here, and rumors are flying that they're planning a secret beach wedding. Are you kidding? *Everyone* is here. All the tabloids, all the entertainment news outlets, and the British press—oh my God, I don't even want to think about what would happen if they knew about the photos." Monica's phone rang. She answered, but kept checking on the view through the gap in the curtains.

I bit my lip. Cara had said Ruby and Angela argued about a bidding war. Had Angela contacted several paparazzi to get the highest possible price? Maybe it was a member of the paparazzi who took the memory card from my room. But how would they know I had it? How would they know it was in the purse? I jumped up and paced over to the side of the cabana, too antsy to sit still.

Monica's voice oozed seductively as she said, "Tony, you are a dear. What would I do without you? No, I'm glad you called. I'm losing light, anyway. It's perfect timing." There was a pause, then Monica said, "Well, I'll try to get back tonight to show you just how appreciative I am." Her voice was soft and breathy. "Bye," she whispered as she looked at me and rolled her eyes. She clicked her phone off. "So impressionable, kids these days," she said in her normal voice. "He's going to be disappointed when he finds out my appreciation comes in cash, not kisses." Monica shut her laptop and began to pack her belongings. "Suzie and Nick have reservations at El Mar. Eight-fifteen. Then," she stopped to consult a page she pulled from her tote, "Suzie is the honorary guest at the city's fireworks display at Green Groves. After that, Tony says they're off to Club Fifty-two."

"Monica, what if Angela contacted other members of the paparazzi—"

"Press," Monica corrected.

"Okay, another member of the *press*. And, instead of sending flowers to persuade her to give them the photos, they staked out her apartment?"

Monica zipped her camera into its case and settled it on her shoulder. "I suppose that could have happened," she said, clearly not happy with the thought.

"But no one would have seen her because she didn't come home last night," I said, thinking aloud.

"How do you know that?"

"Er—just some info I picked up during the day. Anyway, what if this papa—I mean *press* person watching Angela's house decided to take a look inside? That could explain the break-in."

"Okay, if they're breaking and entering, they're paparazzi," Monica said. "It could happen," she admitted. "Those photos would be quite a motivation."

I paced away a few steps, still working out my thoughts. "Then, because the photos weren't in the apartment, the person stuck around, hoping Angela would return. They saw all the commotion—the police, Angela's death, my attempt to give the police the purse."

"Purse? I'm lost," Monica said.

"That's how Angela sent me the photos. They were in a purse she sent me by mistake. But the police didn't want to take the purse. I was standing outside at the apartment complex when the detective gave it back to me. Someone could have overheard the conversation and assumed the purse contained the pictures because . . ." I stopped and peered at the cabana ceiling. "Yes, I'm sure I mentioned Angela's phone call to me when I tried to give the purse back to the detective."

Monica put her hand on her chest. "You almost gave the photos to the police?"

"I didn't know I had them at that point."

"Still!"

"Anyway, he didn't want them, but if someone was watching and listening, they would be able to figure out that there was something about that purse—that Angela thought it was valuable in some way. She'd called me that morning, sounding scared, and wanted me to return the purse to her apartment. Since the police didn't want the purse, I brought it back to the hotel with me."

"So someone could have followed you back to the hotel and taken it from your room," Monica said.

I nodded slowly. "By then, I'd found the photos. I wish there was some way to find out if Angela contacted anyone else in the media."

Monica tilted her head and looked at me thoughtfully. "How well did you know her?"

"She wasn't a close friend," I said, and Monica's lips turned down in disappointment. "I knew her mostly through online things—e-mail, Facebook, that sort of thing," I added.

Monica cheered up. "That's just what we need. Quick, give me her social media accounts," she said as she dialed a number. "And her cell phone number."

"What? Why?"

Monica made a circular, hurry-up motion at me with her hand as she said into the phone, "Freddie, honey! Of course I haven't forgotten you. No, I'd love to drop by next time I'm in Atlanta. I haven't been home in *ages*. Listen, I need a favor."

By this time, I'd found Angela's e-mail and phone number. I read them off to Monica. She tilted the phone away from her chin and raised her eyebrows as she asked, "Social media?"

"Facebook under her name, probably Twitter, too. I don't know what else she had."

"You get that?" Monica asked Freddie. "Right. In Sandy Beach, Florida." She smiled. "I know, darling. I'm practically on your doorstep, but I'm stuck here until Suzie and Nick make a move. Think of some way to lure them up to Atlanta, and I'll be there."

She kept flirting, but I tuned her out. I'd set my account to send me alerts when I received Facebook messages, and I had a new one from "Evan Benworth." I turned away from Monica and quickly brought the message up. All fine here. Confined to my cabin, but should have a chance to explore soon.

I quickly sent a message to him. Be careful.

"What are you doing?" Monica asked as she attempted to look over my shoulder.

"Keeping in touch with a friend."

She gave me a long look, then said, "Those photos are mine. I'll help you find them, but don't think you can double-cross me."

"Wouldn't dream of it."

"Good," she said, briskly. "Freddie will call us back when he finds something."

"And Freddie is?"

"Excellent at digging up what people have been doing online."

"You trust him?" I asked, wary of what I was getting myself involved in.

"Known him for years. Used to push me off the swings when we were in grade school. Don't worry. He's discreet—and smitten with me—so he won't do anything that will put us in danger."

"How long will it take?"

"Couple of hours."

I bit the inside of my lip. I didn't have a couple of hours. It was after six-thirty. The media angle was all I had. "Monica," I said as a thought struck me, "when you're photographing Suzie, you probably catch other media people in your photos, right?"

"Sure. Especially somewhere like a restaurant or the hotel, where everyone knows she'll be."

"And you know most of the media people who follow Suzie around?"

"Yes," Monica said.

"I need to look at your photos of Suzie."

She narrowed her eyes as she watched me for a moment. "You think you might recognize someone who you saw hanging around Angela's apartment today—in my photos? That the person might be media?"

"It's the only possibility I can think of right now."

"Worth a shot," she said. "We'll have to do it on the fly, because I need to get to that restaurant, and my photos don't leave my sight. You'll have to go with me."

"Fine," I said, glad she agreed so quickly. "What about photos of Suzie and Nick leaving the hotel?"

She made a face. "No. Security is too good around here—that's why they stay here. The hotel shuttles them through different entrances and exits. The details are very hush-hush. Not even my contact can get them for me. I never know where they'll be, so it's not worth my time to stick around here. Better to be in place where they're going. Now, I need somewhere to change. I don't think I can get by the attendant in the hotel's restaurant again. Guess it will have to be the Burger King on the main drag."

"You're not staying in the hotel?" I asked, pointing with my phone in the direction of the Park Palms.

"Are you kidding? *Way* too expensive. My boss sprung for the cabana because I can't sit on the beach and take photos of the hotel without drawing attention, but a room here? No way. I'm at a Holiday Inn Express out on the Interstate."

"You can change in my hotel room," I said, thinking it would be better to keep her close. "I'm just down the street."

Digital Organizing Tips

Social Media Organizing

Social media websites like Facebook and Twitter are great ways to catch up and keep up with friends and family, but it can be difficult to stay current with all those interactions. If you're spending too much time on your social media accounts, here are a few tips to reduce your time online without cutting your social media connections.

Use the grouping or list features to make sure you highlight updates from the people you want to keep up with.

Use social media managers like Hootsuite or Tweet-deck to consolidate social media interactions. You can track interactions, post to multiple social media accounts simultaneously, and schedule future posts.

Chapter Thirteen

We drove separately back to my hotel, with me in the lead and her following in her black Jetta. Not wanting to waste a minute of time, I'd driven directly to the Park Palms earlier, instead of going to my hotel and walking over. I kept an eye on her in my rearview mirror. As soon as we were off the Park Palms property, she pulled off a wig and shook out her shoulder-length black hair. When we arrived at my hotel, I parked and walked over to her car. She was bent over the trunk, digging through several canvas tote bags. "Where is my party girl bag? I know I put it in here," she murmured.

"So you're not a grandma. I didn't think so," I said, picking up the wig of tight white curls. The bright sunlight showed the heavy layer of powder on Monica's skin, but even without any mascara or lipstick, she was striking with dark arched brows, high cheekbones, a slim nose, and full lips. As she pawed through the clothes in her trunk, I saw a flash of a brown shirt with the UPS logo, as well as a white lab coat.

"All that grandma disguise has to do is fool some- one for a few minutes. It's not supposed to stand up to close inspection. It's one of my best disguises, too. No one looks twice at an old woman. Agatha Christie knew exactly what she was doing when she created Miss Marple." She latched onto a blue canvas tote and said, "Ah, here we go. Party Girl, the blond edition." She quickly checked the bag. "What about you? Want to borrow something so you're not recognized at the restaurant or the club? Might be a good idea. I've got boho chic and goth girl."

"Ah—I've got something upstairs that I can wear."

She ran a glance over me and said doubtfully, "Are you sure? It's always better to have the element of sur- prise."

I quickly ran through the possibilities in my suit- case. I hadn't planned to party at nightclubs during this vacation. The closest thing I had to a night-on-the- town outfit was a floral print sundress. "Boho chic," I said reluctantly.

"Not goth?" Monica said with a teasing tone. "I have a very nice studded collar in there and lots of leather."

"Please, this is Florida in July. I'm not crazy." I took the bag. "Well, not completely insane," I amended as we walked across the parking lot. "I'm only halfway around the bend."

I let Monica have the bathroom first when we got to the room, calling out that there were towels and wash- cloths in the cabinets under the vanity. She had set me up with her laptop, and I began scrolling through her photos. They were all time stamped, which gave me an idea. Before looking at each one in detail, I went to the photos with the time stamp around eleven today. I quickly skimmed through the pictures during the window of time between eleven and two o'clock.

There were several photos of Suzie and Nick arriving at a restaurant around eleven-thirty. They dined on the terrace facing the beach, and Monica had caught them eating appetizers, feeding each other bites of their entrées, and spooning up some sort of chocolate dessert, which made me want some chocolate. I plucked a Hershey's kiss from the floor where they'd rolled when the coffee table was upended.

I removed the silver wrapping, popped the chocolate into my mouth, and let it dissolve as I flipped through the photos, taking in the time stamps. They hadn't walked out the door until almost one. I felt a sense of relief mixed with disappointment. At least I knew Monica had nothing to do with Angela's death. She'd been busy photographing Nick and Suzie, who were also in the clear.

"When did Suzie arrive in Sandy Beach?" I called out.

Monica's head, now with straight, honey blond hair framing her face, popped around the doorframe. She'd washed off the layer of powder and now had full makeup on: eye shadow and liner, blush and lipstick. She looked stunning. "Three days ago, same as me. They've been holed up in the Park Palms most of the time, except for going out to eat and going to clubs at night. Tony said they did check on a deep-sea fishing trip but haven't booked anything." She unscrewed the mascara tube she held in her hand. "God, I hope they don't do that. I'd have to rent a boat and follow them out there. I'd probably puke over the side the whole time."

She disappeared back into the bathroom but called out, "So how did you find me?"

"I saw the flower arrangement you sent Angela with your name on the card. Another friend of Angela's told me she'd said she had a 'big find.' Your card used the same word, 'find,' which I figured couldn't be a coincidence."

"And then you played me on the phone to find out where I was," she said, her head bobbing out of the doorframe again as she shot me an appraising glance. "Not bad. I'm usually not that gullible."

"Well, I didn't have anything else," I said as I clicked through the photos. She went back into the bathroom, and I ate some more chocolate. Finally, photos with the exterior of Club Fifty-two came up. I checked the date. Yep, three days ago. The photos had to be from the night Angela got her pictures of Suzie. "Did you get any pictures inside Club Fifty-two?" I asked.

Monica reappeared. "No." She pouted. "Nick recognized me and told the doorman specifically not to let me in. I was busted, even when I tried to get in using a disguise. Didn't work," she said, shaking her head as she clipped a gold bracelet on her wrist. "Thus, the new disguise," she said, waving her hand from her blond hair to her shimmery, short green dress and high black heels.

"Your turn." She hooked her thumb toward the bathroom. "You can look at the photos in the car while we wait. I know just the spot. I scoped it out earlier today on my way back from the Y because I had a hint about where they'd be dining."

"Help yourself to some chocolate," I said on my way into the bathroom.

"No way."

"You don't like chocolate?"

"Love it. It's my hips that don't like it," she said.

I changed into my own cranberry tank, then slipped Monica's gauzy printed top, with a lace border edging the scooped neckline, over my head. I pulled on a pair of dark jeans, glad for all those miles I'd put in with the stroller brigade. I didn't look too bad. I'd never be as skinny as Monica—just like I'd never be twenty again, but I thought I'd be able to get into the club. "Here," Monica said when I came out of the bathroom. She dropped several long necklaces over my head. "Perfect. Now, shoes. Do you have some boots with heels?"

"No," I said, and Monica gave me a look. "Florida, remember? Hot. Muggy. No boots. I do have some espadrille wedges."

"I suppose they'll have to do," Monica said, packing her laptop. I pulled the shoes out of my suitcase and slipped them on, then returned to the bathroom and swept my hair up with a clip, but left a few strands floating around my face. I leaned over the large vanity and added a few swipes of eye shadow, mascara, and lip gloss, then stepped back. On the whole, I thought my best friend and go-to fashion guru, Abby, would approve. Thinking of her made me want to call her and tell her everything that had happened, but there wasn't time, and she was busy with her son's first Cub Scout campout this week. I'd have to fill her in later and, boy, would that be a conversation—just like the one I'd have when Mitch got here. I had no idea what I would say, but I didn't have time to worry about it right then. I'd have to figure it out when the time came, which was still hours away.

Monica was standing by the door impatient to go when I came out. I shoved the room keycard into my purse and was on the way to the door when the room phone rang. My breathing went funny as I changed course and picked up the phone. "Hello." It came out as a whisper.

"Ah, Mrs. Avery, you're a hard woman to catch."

I recognized the voice immediately—gravelly, abrasive with a layer of maliciousness that made my stomach clench.

"Perhaps I should give you my cell phone number," I said.

"That won't be necessary. Don't like them, myself. Too easy to track and record things on cell phones. This old-fashioned connection will do fine for us. Now, why haven't you been in to take my calls?"

"I've been busy, trying to get what you asked for." Monica picked up on the tension radiating from me. She went still and watched me with wide eyes.

"Good. Glad to hear you're so dedicated," the scratchy voice continued. "I'm not sure your brother appreciates what a loyal sister he has. He's holding up remarkably well. How is your little quest going?"

"I almost have it," I lied, and tried to put as much conviction into my voice as I could.

"Excellent. Well, that is good news. Bring it to Green Groves. Do you know where that is?"

"Yes," I said. The grand plantation was one of the places I'd intended to take the kids. I reached for the pen and notepad on the desk and scribbled the words down.

He continued, "Park in the lot at the gate and walk around the left-hand side of the house to the back gardens. Go down the terrace steps and continue to the fountain with the dolphins. I will meet you there at midnight."

"But won't it be closed then?"

"Midnight," he repeated wearily, as if he barely had the patience to deal with my stupid questions.

I tried another tack. "I want to speak to Ben. Put him on the phone."

"I'm afraid he can't speak to you right now. Nothing to worry about," he said quickly, cutting off my protest. "He's resting, that's all."

I sputtered, trying to regroup my thoughts. Did he mean that Ben was drugged? Ben had said he was avoiding the food in one of his messages. Did that mean he knew they were trying to drug him and he'd outsmarted them? Was he faking unconsciousness again to fool them?

The rough voice continued before I formed another question, his tone turning contemplative as he said, "Tomorrow is supposed to be a beautiful day. There's nothing like watching the sunrise. I hope your brother will be able to see it. 'Course, that depends on you." He hung up.

It took me a few minutes to recover from that one-sided conversation. Monica asked if I needed to sit down or if she could get me a glass of water.

"No. No time. Let's go," I said, cutting off her questions. I led the way out the door, but when I stepped into the hallway, I saw a man knocking on Ben's door and jerked to a stop. Monica plowed into me, sending me forward half a step.

My room was on the long side of the rectangle that

formed the atrium. Ben's door was around the corner on the short side of the rectangle, so Jenson had his back to us, but I recognized his thin, sandy hair and cream-colored guayabera shirt. Jenson knocked again. He braced his hands on his hips and put his head down, listening for movement inside the room.

"What the—," Monica said before I could shove her back into the room.

"It's the police," I hissed, trying to press the door closed, but it had one of those pneumatic hinges, and I saw Jenson turning my way before it closed completely.

"The police?"

"Yes. Probably something to do with Angela's death." I had Monica by the shoulder and pushed her backward as I spoke. "Stay in the bathroom. If he sees you, it'll slow us down."

She'd been about to argue, but that shut her up. She nodded and disappeared into the bathroom. The shower curtain rings clattered as the sharp rhythm of a knock sounded.

I blew out a deep breath and closed my eyes for a second to calm my fluttery heartbeat before opening the door.

Jenson stood relaxed, his hands in the pockets of his black pants. "Ah, Mrs. Avery, I thought I saw you. Going out?"

"Dinner." I couldn't really deny I was leaving since I had my purse in my hand.

Without being invited, he strolled in, angling his head to look into the back of the room. "Ben around?"

"Ah, no. Afraid not," I said, hoping that Mr. Sandpaper Voice wasn't keeping an eye on me. At least Jenson was in plain clothes, not a police uniform.

"Where is he?"

"I'm not sure," I said, being completely honest.

Jenson raised his sandy eyebrows, and I shrugged. "We aren't spending every minute of our vacation together."

"I only ask because no one in the hotel has seen him since this afternoon. He hasn't returned my phone calls. It's almost like he's avoiding me."

"I'm sure that's not what's going on. In fact, I know it isn't."

"Well, what do you know?" Jenson moseyed closer to the bathroom for a glimpse in there. I made a little movement toward him, which drew his gaze back to me.

"Not a lot, actually. I haven't talked to him since this afternoon. We've—ah, kind of gone our separate ways today. Would you like to sit down?" I asked, moving over to the couch.

"Nah, I'm good," he said and, with his hands still in his pockets, ambled a few steps closer to the bathroom. "Oh, I'll take that purse now, Mrs. Avery."

"I don't have it. I gave it back to Chase this afternoon."

"Ah, I see," he said.

I considered telling him everything. It would be such a relief to turn everything over to him, but I hesitated. The scratchy voice seemed to ring in my head, repeating *no police*. If I told Jenson, would they be able to find Ben before the deadline? Would Mr. Sandpaper Voice know I'd spoken to the police? Would it endanger Ben more?

I felt my chest rising and falling with my quickened heart rate, and I realized I had one hand clenched around my purse strap. I released my death grip and tried to slow my breathing. "Why do you want to talk to him? Has something come up? Something to do with Angela?" And why was I asking so many questions?

He didn't move from the little hallway by the bathroom door. He rocked back and forth on his heels as he said, "Yes, quite a lot has changed. We've got a new tech. Gung-ho kid. This is something like his second case, and he spotted an unusual thing, a light dusting of particles on Miss Day's belongings, the ones that were found by the pool. Well, this kid isn't like some jaded, worn-out tech who's been around for years. This guy is enthusiastic. Keen to prove himself. So instead of writing the particles off, this kid analyzed them right away and brought the report directly to me. Do you know what they were, Mrs. Avery?"

"No," I said, sure that I wouldn't like the answer.

"Scopolamine. Ever heard of it?" I shook my head, and he continued. "It's called Devil's Breath, a powder that turns people into zombies, basically. We haven't seen it much here in the States, but it's very popular in Colombia, especially with thieves, rapists, and prostitutes. The criminal element," he summarized. "Not surprising, really, because it blocks the formation of memory. A few puffs of the powder in someone's face and they're docile. They do whatever you want. Empty bank accounts, open homes and let robbers inside, pretty much anything they're asked, they'll do. Too much is fatal."

I leaned against the arm of the couch. "You're saying that this drug was used on Angela?" My thoughts were racing, thinking of Ben and the possibility that he could be in danger of having the same drug used on him. How could he possibly defend himself from a powder? I felt myself breaking out in a cold sweat.

"It certainly appears that way."

"But when I talked to her, she wasn't docile at all. She was scared and"—I searched for the right words—"animated, passionate even. She really wanted me to bring the purse to her."

"The powder works within minutes."

"So you're saying someone had Angela call me, then gave her this drug?"

"That's a possibility. There is an autopsy underway at the moment—it's such an unusual case, we were bumped to the front of the line. We'll know as soon as the tox screen results come back. In the meantime, I need to speak to your brother. As you can imagine, this has changed the direction of our investigation."

"So now you don't think Angela took this drug on purpose? That seemed to be your theory earlier—that she overdosed."

"We've discovered that Miss Day had a strong moral resolve when it came to drugs. All her friends and family agree that she wouldn't willingly take drugs. That fact, combined with the scopolamine powder, argues for other causes of death."

Like murder, I thought, but kept that to myself.

"So you can see why I need to talk to Ben."

"But he didn't do that to her. He was with me all morning."

"All morning? Didn't you state that you left to pick up your children, and he went to the apartment to return Angela's phone?"

A wave of panic rippled through me. He really thought Ben was involved? That was crazy. "Yes, we were apart, but that was only a few minutes, and Ben would never do anything like that. Never," I said adamantly. "Look, I know that it might seem like Ben is involved in this, but he's not. He may have been by himself, but he had no reason to hurt Angela."

"I've always regarded motive as the weakest aspect of a case. Motives are so . . . unpredictable. Much easier to nail down means and opportunity."

"Even if he had the opportunity, that doesn't mean he did it," I said.

"Of course not." Jenson studied me for a moment, then nodded. "Okay, I understand you, Mrs. Avery. You're in your brother's corner. I got that, but things will go a lot better for him if he talks to me. Not returning my calls and lying low doesn't make him look good. I do need to speak to him, if only to mark him off my list, so to speak."

"Yes, I understand. The minute I hear from him, I'll tell him you want to talk to him."

"Thank you," he said with a nod, then he darted for the bathroom, calling, "I'll just grab a drink of water, if you don't mind."

I hopped up from the couch. The game was up. I'd have even more explaining to do once he discovered Monica. Now there would be no keeping the Ben angle quiet from Monica, either, I thought. The shower curtains clanked. I tensed. There was a pause, then Jenson stepped out of the bathroom, a small crease between his eyebrows. He walked to the closet, edged the sliding door open with a finger, then with a shake of his head said, "Have your brother call me as soon as possible, Mrs. Avery." He let himself out.

I hurried over to the bathroom. The shower curtain

was pushed back. The rest of the tiny room was empty.
I scurried to the closet and pushed back the door. It
slammed into the wall with a thump. Empty.

Monica hadn't had time to make it to the balcony
and she wasn't under the bed, either.

Chapter
Fourteen

I spun back to the bathroom and opened the door on the vanity. Monica was folded like an accordion, her knees under her head, which was shoved up next to the underside of the sink bowl.

"I get the feeling there's more to your story than you're letting on," she said, working one leg out of the tight space.

I helped her extract herself from the cabinet. She basically fell out in a cascade of towels, her laptop gripped to her chest. "Why did you hide in there?"

She stretched her legs and rotated her neck before reaching out a hand. As I pulled her up, she said, "He's the police. Like you said, if he saw me, there'd be more questions, more delay. He'd want to know who I was and how I'm connected to you. No time for that," she said, checking her watch. "We've got to get to the restaurant before eight. Come on. You can explain what all that was about on the way."

I was cramming the towels back into the cabinet when she reappeared in the doorway. "What are you doing? We've got to go."

I closed the door and stood up. "Sorry. Sometimes I can't fight my instinct to keep things neat—a by-product of my nature. I'm a professional organizer, and clutter and mess bother me. But that's the least of my worries right now."

"Then this situation must be driving you crazy," she said as we crossed the hotel room.

"Pretty much." I took the lead and opened the door a crack to peer out. "Don't see him."

"Okay, let's take the stairs. Those glass elevators are too out in the open for me."

"Good idea," I agreed.

We reached the parking lot without seeing Jenson. "My car," Monica said, waving for me to follow her. After racing down ten flights of stairs, I didn't argue.

"Now, about your brother," Monica said in a leading tone as she pulled out of the parking lot.

"Okay, I'll tell you, but this is not for print. It can't be in your magazine."

She agreed, and I took a deep breath, then said, "He's missing." I rubbed my temples. The situation was stretching beyond what Ben or I could handle. I'd avoided telling Jenson about it. That would have been the moment to dump it all in his lap and walk away. If only I thought he'd be able to move on it quickly and actually get to Ben before midnight. However, my up-close-and-personal experience with government bureaucracy via the military hadn't given me much faith in either their efficiency or speed. I doubted the bureaucracy of a city police department would move any faster. I checked my watch and groaned. So little time.

"What?" She shot me a quick glance.

"I don't know where my brother is. It all has to do with Angela's pictures." I didn't see how I could do anything but tell her everything. I had to keep her on my side. She knew enough about me that she could cause me some real problems if she went to the police. I realized she probably wouldn't do that—she was a reporter, but I didn't doubt she would do whatever she could to get her story. And, she had the contact who was researching Angela's e-mails. I needed that information.

"My brother, Ben, was with me when Angela's body was found. They had dated, and he had broken up with her. At first, the detective thought Angela had overdosed, possibly because she was depressed over the breakup, but everyone I've talked to agrees that's not something Angela would do. So Ben and I thought murder was a possibility even before we found the photos. When we saw those . . . well, I figured those were the reason she died." I blew out a sigh. Monica listened intently. I had a feeling she was itching to park and get it all down on paper, despite her agreement not to print anything.

"Anyway, after her body was found, we got an e-mail from Angela's e-mail account, asking us to bring the purse to the lobby of the hotel. We figured whoever sent it probably had something to do with Angela's death. I didn't think it was a good idea, but Ben went down with the purse—minus the memory card that had the pictures. The guy waiting for him took the purse. Ben followed him to the parking lot and tried to take his picture. When the guy realized the memory card was gone and saw Ben taking his picture, he attacked Ben. He knocked him down, then pulled a gun and made Ben get in his car. They drove away before I could get to them."

Monica threw the car into PARK with such force that her blond pageboy swung forward. She stared at me. "Wow. Just, wow. Talk about a backstory." She reached into the back seat for her notebook and pen, biting down on the cap and pulling the pen out, the cap still in her mouth. "This could be a sidebar to the pictures, if not an entire article," she said around the cap.

I gripped her wrist and stilled her hand. "You agreed. You can't print this, at least not until my brother is safe. Once he's with us, then you can run with it." She recapped the pen a bit sulkily as I continued. "I got a call demanding the pictures in exchange for Ben. Since I didn't have them anymore, I bargained for time and have," I looked at my watch, "about four hours or my brother won't have twenty-twenty vision, at the very least."

"Okay," she said, drawing out the word. "That does change things. And you're sure you don't want to go to the police?" She spoke the words as if they pained her.

"And tell them what? That Ben got into a car which I can't describe and that I don't have the license plate for? That a strange man, who I can't identify, is calling me, threatening my brother? And then there are the photos, which I don't have, either. Add in the fact that Ben is a grown man and he's been missing for only a little over"—I consulted my watch—"six hours."

"Okay, I see how that might be an uphill battle."

I slumped back against the seat, glad to hear the tone of concern in her words. At least, it appeared that she wasn't so totally focused on her scoop that she would sacrifice Ben for it. "But don't think that I didn't notice you planned to stiff-arm me on the photos," she added.

"No, I planned to give you a copy and let you have the exclusive story—every tiny detail—once Ben was safe. I figured you wouldn't be too upset with that."

She rolled her eyes and grinned. "Yeah, you're right. Can't argue with that." She pulled her laptop out. "Better get busy."

While she powered it up, I looked around. I'd been so focused on telling her what had happened and ensuring her cooperation that I hadn't taken in our surroundings. "I thought we were going to a restaurant?"

We were in an outlet mall parking lot with the Jetta tucked beside an island of landscaping, a group of hedges that surrounded a trio of palm trees set at angles so their trunks crossed a few feet in the air. Monica pointed straight ahead, across a road to the back of a building. "That's the back door to El Mar. I guarantee that is where Nick and Suzie will arrive and depart."

As if on cue, a black SUV lumbered over a set of speed bumps and halted not far from a door set into the back of the building. "Time to go to work," Monica said, almost tossing the laptop at me as she picked up her camera. She leapt out of the car and squeezed between the hedges, looping the camera cord around her neck. I sat up straight to get a better look. The hefty guy in the suit that I'd seen earlier escorting the "decoy" Suzie into the hotel emerged first and went to open the back door of the SUV. We were parked in the perfect position to see both the SUV and the restaurant's back door.

Monica grabbed one of the palm tree trunks and boosted herself up into the V created by the crossing of the trunks. She braced her feet against one tree, leaned her hip against the other, and moved the camera to her face. By this time, the SUV door was open. Nick, in a white jacket over a white shirt with a mandarin collar, stepped out of the SUV and turned back to hand out Suzie. Between cars whooshing by on the road, I saw Suzie had changed to a royal blue halter dress and had her hair up in a loose ponytail. With a whirl of color, she exited the SUV and disappeared into the blackness of the doorway in a few seconds. Monica climbed down from the trees much more slowly than she'd climbed up and made her way back to the car.

"A curse on prickly hedges. They should be banded from landscaping," she said, dropping back into the car and examining the scrapes on her bare legs.

"Did you get anything?" I asked. "They moved so fast."

"Of course I got something," she said, as if I'd questioned her ability to do something as simple as add two plus two. She tilted the screen on the camera toward me and flicked through the pictures. The first one was a little blurry, but the next one jumped into focus. It captured Nick reaching for Suzie's hand. Like stop-action animation, the next photos showed Suzie stepping out of the car, all with clear shots of her face.

"Impressive."

"It's what I do. I'm good at it," she said with a tiny shrug.

While Monica examined the photos on her camera, I went back to the photos on the laptop. The same faces showed up again and again, hovering around Suzie and Nick. "Who are all these people who are always around Suzie and Nick? Don't they go anywhere by themselves?"

"That, my dear, is their entourage. If you're an A-list

celebrity like Nick, you don't do *anything* alone. I doubt some celebrities can even pee by themselves."

"That's absurd," I said.

"You'd think so, but I've heard stories about stars asking their assistants to come in the bathroom and take down e-mails or make phone calls for them."

"Gross. And weird."

"Yep, celebrities are strange birds. No matter how many pictures there are of them buying groceries or working out at the gym, they're not like us. Suzie has learned quickly the ways of the star. I went on Suzie Watch right after the Olympics. She only had her mom and her coach with her then, but within two weeks she had the whole complement of attendants. It's like a royal court. Here, I'll show you." She pulled the laptop toward her. "Okay, this is Hobbs," she said, tapping a burly guy with a shaved head and dark glasses in a black suit. "He's head of Nick's security."

"Nick needs security?"

"Sure. He had that crazy stalker girl following him around L.A. last year with his name tattooed on the back of her neck under a barcode. She tried to break into his house. She wanted to take a bath in his tub," Monica said with a one-shoulder shrug as if the scenario was weird, but not the craziest thing she'd heard of. "So he's got Hobbs and a few other guys. I know them all," she said. "Of course, Suzie needs security, too. Big athlete like that, she hasn't totally ruled out going to the next Olympics, and she doesn't want someone going all Tonya Harding on her, so she's got Jerry and his retinue." Monica tapped another burly, dark-suited guy in shades, this one with a full head of curly brown hair.

She took a deep breath. "Then, you have the managers." Her finger traced back and forth in the air over the photo. "There's Dwight," she said, pointing to a tall man with a wrinkled face wearing a white shirt, jeans, and cowboy boots. "He's with Suzie. There's Nick's manager, the bald guy who's sweating so much. That's Suzie's stylist, Marie." She pointed out a woman with spiked purple hair. "And her publicist," she added. The publicist looked especially harried, her short brown hair hanging limp against her damp forehead, her bangs dipping over the frames of her glasses. "Then you've got the PA," she said, tapping the head of a skinny girl with long blond hair who looked scared. "Poor Nell, she spends her whole day halfway to a heart attack."

"PA?"

"Personal assistant. Basically a gofer, the lowest strata of the entourage. Anything the celeb wants done, they do it—e-mail, grocery shopping, cleaning out the litter box, you name it. Nothing is too menial. People will do anything to get and stay close to a star."

"How do you know all these people?"

"Oh, the big ones with the official positions are easy to keep straight. I see them all the time. Going back to the royal court analogy, they're the star's ministers or cabinet. They are officially connected to the celebrity, and I have to know who they are. They're my 'in.' They either keep me informed or try to keep information *from* me, depending on what it is. It's the other people who are harder to keep track of. There is always a group of hangers-on around a star, like minor celebrities or old school chums. It's like an ecosystem, actually. All these people circulate around the star, living off of them in many cases. The hanger-on people get quite paranoid and protective of their position."

"Hey, who's this?" I asked sharply, spotting a guy in a blue Hawaiian shirt, turned away from the camera. He stood slightly apart from the group around Suzie and Nick. "Is he part of the entourage?"

"I don't know. I haven't seen him before. I think I'd remember someone who wears shirts like that. He might be a new PA, or he might be someone who was on the sidewalk at that moment."

"Hmm," I said, going back to the photos and looking specifically for that Hawaiian shirt. Could the guy who snatched Ben work for Suzie or Nick? I found two more pictures with the guy, but one only showed his sleeve, and, in the other, he stood in the shade, his face obscured by the change in the light. I couldn't tell if he was part of the group around Suzie and Nick, a careful fan, or a possible stalker. The security guys didn't seem worried about him, though. Interestingly, he didn't show up in any photos after about noon. Had Suzie or Nick sent one of their minions to obtain the memory card with its compromising pictures? It seemed possible. Had he snatched Ben, then made the scratchy-voiced threatening phone call when he didn't get the photos?

Monica's voice cut into my thoughts. "I'll be back. There's my source," Monica said as she spotted a guy in a white shirt and black pants stepping out of the back door of the restaurant.

While she was gone, I scrolled through the pictures on the laptop, thinking of what a strange, altered world Nick and Suzie lived in. Never alone, always surrounded by a court of people who had to be anxious to keep their jobs, and who would probably tell them whatever they wanted to hear.

I browsed through the pictures with new eyes. After

their long lunch, Nick and Suzie had window shopped while eating ice cream cones. Their entourage strayed into the shots occasionally. The time stamps on the pictures indicated they were nowhere near the hotel when the guy in the Hawaiian shirt took the purse and then snatched Ben. I went on to the next set of photos, which were of Suzie's event at the Y. I focused on the people at the fringes of the photos, looking for anyone who I might have caught a glimpse of at Angela's apartment complex or in the hotel.

I went through the next two hundred photos and didn't see anyone who looked even slightly familiar. I hoped Monica's contact called back soon because it looked like my photo idea was a bust.

Monica returned with a bag from Subway. "I got you a ham and cheese on whole wheat. Recognize anyone?"

"No," I said, and rubbed my eyes, then put the sandwich on the dashboard.

"You need to eat," Monica said, and held out the sandwich. "Now. I live on the fly like this, and you need some food." She raised her eyebrows, and I took the sandwich from her.

I unwrapped it and took a bite. I hadn't realized how hungry I was until I had food in my hands. I ate several bites, then said, "Yeah, you're right. I do need to eat."

"I can channel my Italian grandmother. No one leaves her presence without eating at least one meal."

"What's going on in there?" I asked, nodding toward the back of the restaurant.

"Not much. All the other photogs are camped out in the front. They think they can't get a good shot from the back because of the road," she said with a little smile. "Of course, with palm trees that's not a problem." She set her phone on the dashboard. "I've got a busboy who'll call me when they're leaving."

"Do you have any sources who aren't guys?" I went back to the beginning of the pictures and began looking at them again. Suzie and Nick were always the centerpiece of the pictures, so the crowds around them tended to be a bit blurry and out of focus.

She looked at the palm trees. "Um, not really. Women are usually hard to work with. So catty and jealous. I don't have time for that. They're not like you. You're cool."

I'd been hitting the PAGE DOWN button rhythmically every second as I glanced at the photos, but stopped abruptly and leaned forward to make sure I wasn't imagining things.

"What is it?" Monica asked, tilting her head to the computer screen.

"One of the men in this photo—one of the photographers—is wearing a pair of sunglasses that looks like the ones I found under the couch in my hotel room after the memory card was stolen."

Digital Organizing Tips

E-mail Cleanup

Just as your mailbox at home attracts junk mail, your e-mail inbox is also a magnet for clutter. Here are a few ways to keep it organized.

Unsubscribe to e-mail newsletters from companies that you are not interested in. Avoid signing up for e-mail newsletters or updates in the first place. Most companies have a box that you can uncheck if you don't want to receive e-mail communication from them.

Sort the e-mails you need to save into folders. Be selective. If you've had an e-mail conversation with e-mails bouncing back and forth between you and another person, you don't need to save all of them. Only save the last one, which will have a summary of your prior e-mails below the current message.

Many e-mail programs have an automatic e-mail cleanup feature, which you can set to delete old e-mail. Just make sure to check the settings so that you don't lose e-mail you need.

Chapter
Fifteen

I found the zoom and enlarged the picture, then quickly rewrapped my sandwich and tossed it on the dashboard before scrambling for my purse. I pulled out the sunglasses. Yes! They had the same unusual silver and green earpieces, which where discernible even in the pixelated blowup of the photo. The zoom made the man's face even fuzzier, and I couldn't distinguish much because the video camera he carried on his shoulder obscured half of his face. But I could see that he had a beaky nose and washed-out yellow hair, which was short around his tanned face, but hung long and wavy to his collar in the back.

"That's Pete Gutin," Monica said slowly as if trying out the idea that he might be the thief. "He's a dinosaur, one of the oldest guys in celebrity news. I call him Gramps. He started on *Entertainment Tonight* back when it was the only game in town, way back before celebrity news exploded. Little gruff, but he's a fairly nice guy. I've never thought of him as incredibly competitive. He's on Nick Watch for *Exposé,*" she said, naming a half-hour entertainment news show that specialized in showing short video clips of celebrities, usually on their way into or out of restaurants or the airport. "He's always there, gets the shots, but he's a beach bum, loves surfing and the water. He told me he became a photog because he could live in Southern Cal and go to the beach every day. He does have a pair of sunglasses like that. I remember the frames."

I fingered the sunglasses. "I suppose there could be some gift shop on the beach road that sells these, except I've never seen sunglasses with a big nosepiece like this," I said.

"Let me see," Monica said, and I handed them over. She ran her finger over the heavy squared-off nosepiece. "Do you know what kind of sunglasses these are?" she asked, her voice quickening. "They're for surfers. My old boyfriend had some. The nosepiece keeps them from slipping off in the water."

"So they could have belonged to Pete. He might have the memory card," I breathed, feeling a tiny portion of the anxiety that was hanging over me ease. If we'd slightly narrowed the field . . . well, that was progress.

I went back to the photos with renewed vigor, checking to see if I could find Pete in any of the peripheries of the photos taken earlier today when Angela was killed and when the memory card was stolen. After looking through them, I leaned back. "I found him in a picture outside the restaurant where Suzie and Nick had lunch. I can't find one picture of him after that. Do you think he got a shot or two of Suzie and Nick at the restaurant, then left?"

Suzie chewed a bite of her sandwich thoughtfully. "I haven't seen him this afternoon. He's not with the pack at the front door of the restaurant right now, either."

"Is that like him?"

"No. I mean, he likes to surf, but he'd never sneak off. Not now, not when the rumors are flying about a secret wedding. If he missed that, he'd be done."

"Unless he found something even bigger than a secret wedding," I said, and Monica groaned.

"Don't say it. Don't even *think* it. If *Exposé* has those photos . . . *I'm* the one who's done," she said.

I checked my watch. "There's an easy way to find out." I tapped at the screen on my phone to bring up the Internet. "Wouldn't *Exposé* post the pictures as soon as they had them?"

"Maybe," Monica said, her voice small. "They'd have to check them, make sure they weren't doctored, but if they've had them since early afternoon . . . it's possible they'd be up by now. At *Celeb,* we'd have to keep everything quiet until the magazine went to print and was shipped, but *Exposé* could run with them right away online, then put them on their show tonight."

"Well, you're in luck. Nothing on the website," I said, and Monica sagged against the seat for a second, then snatched up her phone from the dash. She dialed a number. I could hear it ringing in the quiet of the car. After the voice-mail message came on, she said, "Pete, where are you? I haven't seen you since lunch, and I'm worried about you. You're not sick, are you? I can bring you some chicken soup, if you need it. Oh, and I heard Nick and Suzie are going to a new club tonight. Call me, so I can gloat."

She hit the END button, then stared at the phone. "If his phone is on, he'll call back. He wouldn't be able to resist trying to get me to slip up and tell him where Nick and Suzie will go."

"But you said they're going to Club Fifty-two. They've been there before. That's where the photos were taken."

Monica gave me a look that I'd already seen on Livvy's face—the *Mom, I can't believe you're so clueless* look. "I said that to get him to call me back," she said.

"Oh."

"You're not good at subterfuge, are you?"

"Let's just say I'm not comfortable with it."

After five minutes, Monica shifted in her seat. "He's not going to call."

"I wonder where he's staying."

"At the Park Palms. If we're near a beach, he upgrades to stay right on the water and pays the difference himself. I heard him talking the other day, telling two other photogs to meet him at his room before dinner." She squeezed her eyes shut in thought. "Room five-o-five," she said, her eyes popping open. "I'm sure that was it," she said, reaching for the ignition.

"You can drop me there and probably be back here before Suzie and Nick leave," I said.

"Forget about them. I've already got exclusive pictures of them tonight. Those pictures on the memory card are worth more than anything else I'll get tonight tagging along behind the lovey-dovey couple to a restaurant or club." She pressed the accelerator to the floor. I grabbed the laptop with one hand to keep it from sliding to the floor and braced my other hand on the window as Monica whipped the car around and headed for the hotel.

* * *

"Back again," I said as we stepped onto the dark wood floor of the Park Palms lobby. "I'm getting a distinct *Groundhog Day* vibe."

"I know the feeling," Monica said as we walked through the scattered chairs and potted plants. "He's not in the lobby," Monica said, giving the room a quick sweep. We knew he wasn't in his room, either, because I'd called the hotel from the car, which was quite a feat because Monica drove like she was in the Indianapolis 500. It wasn't easy to surf the Web, find phone numbers, and dial while alternately gripping the dashboard and pressing my foot to the floor, but I'd managed to make the call. It was after eight-thirty by the time we made it to the Park Palms lobby, and I felt as if the minutes were rushing by.

We paused at the bar's entrance, and I bounced on my toes. I wanted to hurry through the room, checking each table, but that would cause a scene. It wasn't the sort of place where you rushed; it was the sort of place where you sipped your drink and chatted while waiting for your table in the very expensive restaurant next door. Dark paneling, gold sconces, and plenty of plush green armchairs gave the place the feel of an exclusive country club. "Is that him at the bar?" I asked, spotting a guy with wavy pale blond hair.

"That's Pete," Monica said. We moved to a table in a back corner. The room was dimly lit, and I hoped that if he turned around, Monica's disguise would keep him from recognizing her.

"So he's not sick or hurt," I said, then leaned to the side to get a better view, and added, "but he is sipping champagne."

"That is not a good sign," Monica said in a tight voice. "Let me try something." She quickly pulled out her phone and tapped a text message. "I'll send him a message, tell him I heard a rumor . . ."

Pete's phone was on the bar. After a few seconds, he pulled it to him, read the message, then pushed it away and took another long sip of champagne.

"Oh, that's bad," Monica said, and twisted a strand of her blond wig around her finger. "If he's not going after a tip about Brangelina suddenly showing up in town, he's not going anywhere."

"You think that means he's got the memory card?" I asked.

"I'm afraid so. I can't imagine why he's not with the rest of the photographers unless he's got something much better."

"Well, since it hasn't shown up on *Exposé's* website yet, do you think he has it on him?" I asked doubtfully. I could see his reflection in the mirror behind the bar. He wore a loose linen shirt without pockets. "Are those swim trunks?" I asked, squinting in the low light.

"I think they are," Monica said. "He does look like he came from the beach, doesn't he?"

"He's wearing flip-flops." His feet were propped up on the rung of the bar stool, and I could see the soles. "I'll be right back," I said, and made my way through the tables to the bar, where I dropped my purse and picked it up. As I stood up, I jostled Pete's elbow, which was hooked over the back of the bar stool. "So sorry," I said, my gaze sweeping over his flushed face to the high counter in front of him.

I took a circuitous route back to the table where Monica waited. "He's got sand on the soles of his flip-flops and there's a dusting of it on his heels and calves, too."

"So, he probably just got back from the beach," Monica said. "I doubt he'd take the memory card with him there. He wouldn't want to risk it getting wet or losing it."

I nodded. "And, he doesn't have anything on the bar in front of him except a keycard, his phone, and the champagne flute."

"Impressive," Monica said. "You might have a future in journalism."

"I don't think so," I said, pressing my hand to my stomach and taking a few deep breaths. "I feel jittery and a bit like I might throw up."

Monica laughed. "Reporter's high. I live for that. Okay, I'll hit his room, see if I can get a maid or someone to let me in. If he doesn't have the memory card with him, it's got to be in his room."

A terrible thought struck me. "What if he's e-mailed the pictures?"

Monica instantly replied, "Don't say that. I'm sure he's hanging on to it. He'd have to. We have to verify all our photos, show that they're original and haven't been tampered with or doctored. That's probably why they're not up on *Exposé's* website right now. They want to verify them, see the actual memory card. No one wants to get sued, and this is going to be a doozy of a story. They're probably being careful."

Monica twisted the loop of hair a bit tighter around her finger as she said, "Besides, even if he's e-mailed the pictures, as long as you get the memory card back, you can swap it for your brother. I'm the only one who's screwed if he's e-mailed the photos."

Pete motioned at the bartender for a refill on his champagne as Monica continued. "The fact that they're still unpublished argues that he's keeping them under wraps. He's probably booked on the first flight out of here tomorrow. Maybe they want him to hand-carry them back to *Exposé's* L.A. offices or . . . he's waiting for a courier."

"Wouldn't he FedEx them?"

"Not those photos. An editor wouldn't take a chance of an envelope being misplaced or delayed. No, those photos will have a personal escort to the newsroom." She released the strand of hair and shook out her hands, reminding me of an athlete preparing to run a race. "Okay, I'll check his room. You stay here, keep an eye on Pete, and call me if he leaves."

I stood up. "No, I'll check his room."

"You?"

I gave her a long look. "I think you're on the level with me, but if you were me, would you trust someone like yourself to search that room alone? How do I know that if you find the memory card you won't leave me sitting here in the bar?"

"I would never do that."

"You're overdoing the injured tone," I said.

Her lips twisted to the side. "Okay, so I'm never going to win any awards for being the most dependable person around, but how do I know I can trust *you*?"

"Because every time I break a promise it absolutely kills me. I don't like any of this deception and you thrive on it—am I right?" She raised one shoulder half an inch, which I took to be agreement. "So, I've promised you'll get the photos. I just want to copy to make sure Ben is safe."

"Okay, fine," she said with a roll of her eyes. "You can go. How will you get in?"

"I'll find a way," I said, and left before she could ask any more questions.

I paused in the lobby, considering if I might be able to con a maid into opening the door to Room 505 for me, but I thought the likelihood of finding one at this hour of the night was probably low to nonexistent. If it had been eight in the morning with lots of people checking out, that ploy might have worked, but at eight-thirty at night it wasn't a good idea.

I turned away from the elevators toward the front desk. "I'd like a room," I told the fiftyish clerk. "Fifth floor, please."

He looked at me over the rims of his half-glasses and asked in a snide tone, "Any particular room?"

"Yes. I'd like five-o-three or five-o-seven," I said, praying that one of the rooms was unoccupied.

"I see," he said, his tone conveying that he thought I was a loon. But I was past caring what a stuck-up desk clerk thought about me. I had to get into the room and find out if Pete had the memory card. Even if I couldn't find the memory card, if he had my laptop, that would let me know he had been the person in my room.

"You're in luck, ma'am. Room five-o-three is available," he said, and I handed over my credit card.

"Wonderful." The clerk raised a finger, and a bellboy trundled my way, pulling a baggage cart. "Oh, no luggage," I said, which drew a sharp glance from the clerk.

"At the moment," I quickly amended. "My husband dropped me off. He'll be along shortly." I scribbled my name on the paperwork, trying not to look at the total at the bottom. One night at the Park Palms Hotel wouldn't break the budget, but there were other things I could have spent that money on. Like a new designer bag. All leather, too. I handed the paper back to the desk clerk as the bellhop reversed course.

"Is there any reason you requested Room five-o-three in particular?" the clerk asked as he pushed the little folded envelope with the keycards across the counter. "We like to meet all our guests expectations . . . so if there is something specific . . ."

"Oh . . . I—ah, I just love the view."

He frowned. "But it faces the street, away from the beach." He leaned toward the computer keyboard. "I'm sure we have a room available on the other side of the hotel—"

"No! I mean, no thanks. It's fine. I can't look at all that water," I said, improvising. "It makes me a little seasick. Besides, I love the traffic and movement on the beach road. Sandy Beach is such a quaint little town. Who wouldn't like to look at it?" *Stop babbling*, I commanded myself and pocketed the keycards. I could feel him watching me as I walked to the elevators. He was probably making a note for security to keep an eye on the weird woman who doesn't like the water, but checked into a beach hotel without luggage.

I emerged into the hush of deep carpet on the fifth floor. It was deserted. I hurried to 503, let myself in, put out the DO NOT DISTURB sign, and went straight to the sliding glass doors. Like the rooms that faced the beach, these rooms also had a balcony. I examined the lock. It was a simple lever, and there was no bar or brace in the frame to hold the door closed in case the lock in the handle broke. I guess the hotel figured at five floors up, there wasn't much need for extra security. I dumped the contents of my purse onto the bed and sorted through my options. A ballpoint pen and several credit cards were the only things that seemed like they would work. Why didn't I carry a nail file—a good metal one, at that?

I replaced everything in my purse, slipped it across my body and, after poking my head out the window to check distances, went back into the room and stripped a sheet off one of the double beds. I looped it over my shoulder and headed for the balcony.

Chapter
Sixteen

I had one leg draped over the edge of my balcony, and I was straining to reach Pete's balcony when my phone rang. The noise, even though muted inside my purse, seemed unusually loud. I glanced down at the entrance to the hotel below me where the glow of car headlights cut through the night and voices of people walking to the hotel from the parking garage floated up. I pulled my leg back, hooked my foot into the curly wrought iron surrounding the balcony, and perched there on the balustrade as I dug my phone out. The last thing I needed was for someone to glance up and see my bad impression of John Robie, the "Cat." I checked over the railing and didn't see anyone with their heads craned back. The people continued to stroll while the palm fronds clattered in the soft breeze.

My phone glowed with Mitch's picture. I closed my eyes for a moment, debating whether or not to answer. If you're about to break into a hotel room, should you tell your spouse? Probably not, I decided. Especially if you're already halfway over the railing. I bit my lip, and, in that moment of hesitation, my decision was made for me. The picture disappeared, and the call went to voice mail. I did some mental math and realized Mitch must be close to arriving. I'd been so swept up in searching for Pete that I'd forgotten Mitch's arrival time. Well, I'd just have to finish here and get back to the hotel.

A quick check of my voice mail confirmed that Mitch was about an hour out and would call when he arrived. I also had a second voice mail. I must have missed the call when we were in the noisy bar. It was from Detective Jenson. He got right to the point. "Still waiting on that call from your brother, Mrs. Avery."

"Okay, okay," I muttered. "I'm working on it." I put the phone on vibrate and loosened by foot from the wrought iron. The balconies were spaced about four and a half feet apart, slightly beyond the length of a "giant step," which I figured was intentional. It was designed to discourage exactly what I was doing. The gap was wide enough to give a sense of privacy to each balcony and also caused me to break out in a cold sweat at the thought of crossing the space. I'd tied the bed sheet tightly to the balustrade on my balcony. I wiped my forehead, tried to ignore the fact that I was actually above the coconut palms, and gripped the sheet tight. I leaned, using it to extend my reach a few more inches.

My fingertips brushed the wrought iron balustrade on the other balcony. I breathed deeply and lengthened my stretch, thinking of the stroller brigade workout— just like a cool-down stretch for the oblique muscles. My fingers connected with the iron again, and this time I was able to get my fingers all the way around the balustrade. I didn't stop to think. I shifted my weight and was across, my heartbeat thundering in my ears. "Okay. Good," I muttered, and swung my shaky legs over the railing. I'd kept hold of the sheet as I came across and looped it around the balustrade, in case I had to go back this way. I actually intended to go out the door, if at all possible.

My phone buzzed against my hip. It was Monica. "Is he leaving?" I asked.

"No, he's still here. Are you in yet?"

"I would be if people would stop calling me."

"Testy. Testy. Maybe I should have done it, after all."

"No, I'm almost there," I said as I cradled the phone on my shoulder and wiped my palms on my jeans. "I'll call you back if I find anything."

I'd experimented a few times on the latch on Room 503's sliding glass door before I'd set out and, surprisingly, found that my Kroger club card fit best into the sliver of space between the frame and the sliding glass door. I hoped it worked as well from the outside as it did from the inside. I worked the card into the tiny space and moved it up firmly. It stuck. I bit my lip and tried again. There was a metallic click, and I couldn't help smiling. The glass door moved smoothly down the track when I pushed on the handle. My Kroger card was a bit mangled, but I figured paying full price for milk was the least of my worries right now.

As soon as I was in the room, I moved to the door to put on the interior deadbolt, then I closed the curtains and hit the lights.

"Oh, no," I whispered, looking around.

I'd broken into the wrong room. No one was staying here. I turned in a circle, taking in the immaculate room. Not a single wrinkle marred the smooth lines of the comforters on the double beds. Nothing on the desk or the nightstands. Even the remote was tidily lined up in front of the television. I checked the tab on the phone, and it listed this as Room 505. It was the right room. Had Pete already checked out? Or was he just extremely—maybe compulsively—neat? I hurried into the bathroom and let out a relieved breath. There was a toothbrush, a wrinkled tube of Crest, and a shaving kit.

Okay, he hadn't checked out. I quickly looked through the shaving kit and only found typical toiletries, like shaving cream, razors, and deodorant. There was nothing else in the bathroom besides the hotel's thick bathrobe on the back of the door. I hurried back into the room, moved to the closet. A small hard-sided rolling suitcase and a duffle bag were tucked into the closet along with his video camera.

Pete Gutin was packed and ready to go at a moment's notice. I hauled the suitcase out and opened it on the floor. I worked as carefully as I could, looking through it, trying to keep everything exactly as it was. Lots of clothes—lightweight collared shirts, several pairs of pants and shorts, underwear, sandals, sneakers and socks, a waterproof jacket, and more swim trunks— exactly how the experts tell you to pack for travel. Everything was wash-and-wear, made of fabrics that would dry quickly without wrinkling, and all were either white, tan, or black. I found a few receipts in the small pockets of the suitcase along with two cherry LifeSavers and a stubby pencil.

I zipped the suitcase closed and switched it for the duffle. The duffle held snorkeling gear, a really nice digital camera, a bag of trail mix, a whole package of LifeSavers, two paperback thrillers, a laptop computer, and a spiral notebook with wrinkled edges and coffee-ring stains on the front. I quickly checked the smaller exterior pockets but didn't find the memory card. It wasn't plugged into any of the slots on the laptop or the digital camera, either.

I sat back on my heels and rubbed my forehead. Had I been completely wrong? Was Pete the wrong person? I left the duffle bag and went back to the closet to double-check. Maybe there was something else . . . some other bag I'd missed, I thought. I was getting desperate and the closet was tiny. There wasn't another bag in there, but I looked anyway, patting the top shelf. Nothing.

Then I picked up the video camera and saw my laptop. I recognized the diagonal scratch that Nathan had put in it when he'd run his front loader over the top. *Thank goodness*, I thought. I carefully put the video camera down and picked up my laptop. Nothing in the ports, but at least I knew Pete had been in my hotel room. I was on the right track.

I put the laptop down on the carpet with the other things I'd removed from the closet. I was afraid to put anything on the smooth comforters and leave an impression that would show I had been here. With my hands on my hips, I turned in a half circle, looking at each item, then scanning the room. The memory card was tiny . . . it could be anywhere. I was searching for something roughly the size of a paper clip.

Be methodical, I told myself. Don't get overwhelmed. I needed to approach this like an organizing job. Okay, then. I'd finish the personal stuff first, then search the room. I replaced everything in the duffle except Pete's laptop and the notebook, then I looked over the video camera, but I didn't see anywhere he'd be able to hide a memory card. I moved quickly through the room, checking drawers and trash cans, then under the bed, but didn't find anything.

It isn't here. I dropped down on the carpet. I was exhausted and scared. What was I going to do? Call Jenson and tell him everything? Would he believe me? Would he be able to help me now? Could I get Mr. Sandpaper Voice to give me more time? But that wouldn't help me if I couldn't find the photos.

I didn't have time to panic right now. I wiped my hands down over my face and took a deep breath. I had to put everything back and get out of here. Then I could have a meltdown in my very own expensive room next door.

I picked up the spiral notebook and flipped through the pages as I moved to replace it in the duffle. Most of the notes looked like travel information, hotel names and flight numbers. I opened a set of papers folded in half and shoved in the middle of the notebook.

The paper was a printed boarding pass. I blinked. Pete Gutin was going to the Cayman Islands tomorrow morning. My mouth felt dry as I flipped to the next page. It was a two-page document, a legal contract. I skimmed the text, whispering, "No, no, no."

Pete had sold the photos to the British tabloid, *The Daily Bulletin*, in a seven-figure deal.

My phone buzzed. I jumped, dropping the notebook and the papers. I pulled my phone out and saw it was Monica.

"He's left," she said.

"What?" I bent down and picked up the papers automatically. I felt dazed. The memory card was gone. The photos had been sold.

There was nothing I could do. Absolutely nothing. I

could send Ben a message, but I had no idea if he'd get it. He didn't understand how much trouble he was in. What would Mr. Sandpaper Voice do when I had to finally admit that I didn't have the photos? And then, if that wasn't enough, there was Detective Jenson waiting in the wings, who thought Ben had something to do with Angela's death, which he now believed was murder.

"Pete. He left the bar. He's heading for the elevators. Did you get in his room?"

It felt like a splash of cold water had hit me. "Yes, and it's not good. There's no memory card here, and he's sold the photos."

"What? To who?"

"*The Daily Bulletin*," I said, spreading the papers on the floor.

"He went to the British tabloids with them? Oh my God. They'd pay a fortune."

"They did," I said, grimly.

"What do you mean?"

"Two million dollars. There's a signed contract, and since I can't find the memory card, Pete must have already sent them to *The Daily Bulletin*. Will they put them online right away?"

"Probably as soon as they can," she said, her voice miserable. "Once they've examined them, and they're sure the photos aren't doctored, they'll run them. Probably either tomorrow or the next day." Her voice changed. "Oh, his elevator is here. He's definitely going up to his room."

"I've got to go."

I quickly snapped photos of all the pages with the camera in my phone, then stuffed the pages back in the notebook, and replaced it with the laptop in the duffle.

My phone vibrated with another call from Monica. I ignored it, shoving it in my pocket.

How long did it take to ride five floors in an elevator? I heaved the duffle back in the closet, then hesitated a moment over my own laptop. I wanted to take it with me, but if I did, Pete would know for sure someone had been in his room. I quickly replaced it in the closet and set the video camera on top of it. There was no way I could get it back across the balcony with me, anyway. I needed both hands for that maneuver.

I closed the closet door and sprinted for the sliding glass door. I hoped he had to stop on every floor. My phone buzzed again, causing me to do a little leap in the air. I was as tense and quivery as a poodle waiting for the mailman. I let the phone continue to buzz.

I'd have to leave the sliding glass door unlocked and hope Pete didn't notice it. Maybe he'd think he left it unlocked.

I gripped the sheet and was about to lunge for my balcony, mentally giving myself a quick pep talk, when I remembered I'd flipped the interior deadbolt. I shoved the sliding glass door back open, rocketed to the door, flicked the deadbolt to the open position, then took a few steps and halted in my tracks. The lights! They'd been off.

I quickly reversed course, slammed my hand down on the switch plate to douse the lights, and dashed back to the balcony. As I pushed the sliding glass door closed, I heard the familiar click of the door lock releasing. I let out a whimper as I inched the glass door closed. Thank goodness the curtains were closed.

I threw my legs over the railing, grabbed the sheet, and jumped across the gap without even thinking about it. Fear and adrenaline are amazing things. Safe on the other side, I shifted my legs over the railing and untied the knot in the bed sheet with trembling fingers. Then I darted into my room and crumpled onto the bed.

After a few minutes, when I felt that I could walk without my legs collapsing, I got up, left my room, and made my way to the elevator. Monica was dialing my phone nonstop, and I figured she needed to see the photo of the contract to actually believe it. She met me in the lobby.

"Glad to see you made it out," she said, removing her phone from her ear.

I shrugged. I was too drained to talk. I brought up the pictures of the contract on my phone and handed it to her. "We're sunk," I said, dropping down into one of the chairs scattered throughout the lobby.

She skimmed the document, shaking her head. "Do you know what this means?"

"It means we have nothing. No photos. No memory card. No bargaining power. Nothing."

Monica paced across the dark wood floor, not listening to me. "It means Pete is done. He saw the opportunity for a big payoff, and he took it. Instead of handing the photos off to *Exposé*, he decided to keep them. He negotiated his own deal with the British tabloids. He'll never work again in celebrity media."

"I'll say. Look at the next picture."

Monica scrolled to it and shook her head again as she said, "The Caymans! I never would have thought it of Pete, but he is getting up there. He's said a few things about retiring. This probably seemed like too good a deal to pass up. He snatches the photos from you, sells them to the Brits, and disappears to the

Caribbean where he can catch waves until he can't get out of his wheelchair."

Monica sat down in a chair beside me. "Clever idea, getting the room next to his. I'll have to remember that in the future."

"Thanks," I said listlessly.

"I wonder how long I can put off calling my editor. At least until the morning, right?" Monica sounded as apathetic as me. She didn't seem to expect an answer, and we both sat in silence. Laughter mixed with music floated from the bar. People moved through the lobby, snatches of their conversations drifting through the air. I felt too tired to move and let the music and words flow around me for a few moments.

"I told you, that's not good enough." I stiffened as the speaker, a man, passed right behind me, his voice carrying through the lobby. "I'll never let her sign," he continued, "until you get rid of that exclusivity clause. Not going to happen."

I felt the hairs on the back of my neck stand up. I knew that abrasive voice. I wanted to swivel around. Instead, I gripped the arms of the chair and slowly turned my head. In a white shirt and jeans, he stood out from several pudgy tourists in floral prints and pastels. He was striding away from me, his cowboy boots ringing out with each step, a phone pressed to his ear. When he turned his head, I could see his face was furrowed with wrinkles.

Monica picked up on my altered posture. "What is it?"

"It's Mr. Sandpaper Voice," I said, staring at the man, who was repeatedly punching the elevator button. "That's who threatened Ben. He's the one who wants the memory card."

"Dwight? Dwight Fellows?" she asked, her forehead wrinkling. "Suzie's manager?"

"Yes. That's him. I'd recognize his voice anywhere."

"It is distinctive," she said, but there was doubt in her tone. "You think Dwight kidnapped your brother and . . . what? Has him tied up in the penthouse?"

"I don't know. Ben could be somewhere else, but he did say he was in a nice hotel on the beach, but . . ." I frowned. "That's not the guy who pulled a gun on Ben in the parking lot."

The elevator dinged, and Dwight stepped inside. The air stirred around me as a young man jogged by, his flip-flops slapping the floor as his blue Hawaiian shirt fluttered. "Mr. Fellows, wait," he called, and Dwight reluctantly held the button to keep the door open. The younger guy stepped inside and pushed his gold-rimmed glasses up his nose. Dwight Fellows sent him a look that, even at a distance, I could interpret as distaste. The younger guy held out a set of car keys, and the elevator door slid closed as Dwight took the keys.

"They're together," I said, sitting back in the chair, trying to work it out. "That younger guy, I saw him in some of the photos today. Do you know who he is?"

"No . . . but I suppose I could ask Tony. He'd probably know."

"Who's Tony again?"

"One of my contacts here. Works for the concierge," she said. "He got off at eight, thank goodness, or he'd be trying to buy us drinks."

"You should be nicer to your contacts," I said in an aside.

"He's seventeen!"

"Oh, in that case, you need older contacts. Who aren't smitten with you."

"But then they're not nearly so cooperative," she said with a little pout as she dialed a number on her phone. "Tony, honey. Me, again. Yes, I know, I have to talk to you every few hours. So who's the scruffy guy with brown hair and glasses with Suzie's entourage? Hawaiian shirt, young guy . . ." She listened for a moment, then thanked him effusively. Turning to me, she said, "He's Lee Fitch, a new PA."

"They both work for Suzie," I said, lowering my voice as a woman joined us, taking a seat in the third chair in the conversational grouping. The woman opened her laptop and began typing. She had the same brand laptop that I had and, as I watched her out of the corner of my eye, something stirred in my mind, a thought that I couldn't quite nail down. I turned back to Monica and focused on her, trying to work out what had happened.

"Suzie must have found out about the pictures somehow. Maybe Angela did contact her and offered to sell her the pictures instead of selling them to the paparazzi."

"Press," Monica said automatically. She looked through her messages on her phone. "Nothing from my tech guy. I'd call him, but it would only slow him down."

"Suzie sent someone to meet . . . or *intercept* Angela. Maybe Suzie hoped Angela would have the photos with her. When she didn't, the person forced Angela to go with them. After a night in the company of Lee and possibly Mr. Sandpaper Voice—I mean, Dwight Fellows—Angela called me and asked me to bring the purse. That's why Lee tore the lining out of the purse. Angela must have told him where the memory card was."

The woman shot us a look and heaved an irritated sigh. We ignored her. Monica said, "And when Lee realized he didn't have the memory card, he took Ben, brought him to Dwight, and Dwight called you." She nodded again. "It does make sense, that Dwight would take over at some point. If anyone bungles something, he's the one who would clean it up."

I said, "Even if we know who has Ben, I still don't have the memory card."

The woman in the other chair gave a little huff of disapproval, slapped her laptop closed, then strutted away to another chair.

"What does she think this is, a library?" Monica said, but I didn't respond because I was staring at the woman's laptop.

"I'm an idiot." The wisp of an idea that had nagged at me crystallized into a coherent thought, and I grabbed Monica's arm. "My laptop. Pete still has my laptop," I said, my voice growing stronger and more excited as I spoke. "Upstairs in his room."

"That's irritating, but I don't think you need to worry about that right now," Monica said.

"I looked at the photos on the laptop and didn't close any of the windows. My laptop is password protected. If Pete closed the laptop, it would go into hibernation, and he wouldn't be able to open any programs or documents without the password. The photos could still be on the laptop."

"Did you save them?" Monica breathed. "If you didn't save them, I don't think you'll be able to view them without the memory card. You'd get that error message about the missing drive or disk or whatever it is."

I closed my eyes, trying to remember. I shook my head. "I don't know. Everything happened so fast. I might have hit SAVE FILE when I opened the documents, out of habit. I usually do that, but I might have just hit the OPEN instead."

Monica's eyes sparkled as she said, "But, either way, those photos have to be on there. Even if you didn't save them specifically, you opened them. That had to create some kind of temporary file. I'm no computer expert, but I bet the files are there. It might take a specialist to find them, but I bet you the biggest Hershey bar they've got in that gift shop that the photos are on that laptop."

"We've got to get that laptop."

Chapter
Seventeen

Since I didn't want to repeat my "giant step" maneuver between the balconies, I convinced Monica to call Pete and invite him down to the bar for another drink. Her cover story was that she was celebrating her exclusive shots of Suzie and Nick at the back door of the El Mar restaurant.

"Weak," she'd muttered when I suggested it.

"But it should be a piece of cake for you, right? Don't you do this all the time?" I'd countered.

Now I was standing in Room 503 with my cell phone pressed to my ear, holding the ice bucket as I talked to Monica. I had my door cracked the teeniest bit so that I could see Pete the minute he left his room. "He didn't want to come back down," Monica said, "but I convinced him. Told him he had to see my current disguise. I'll probably have to buy him more champagne."

"Put it on my tab."

The distinctive metal clank of the door lock releasing sounded through the wall. "There he is," I whispered, and ended the call, my heart immediately zooming into the aerobic workout range as he stepped over the threshold and headed for the elevators.

I waited a beat, then stepped into the hall, half a step behind him. *No balcony, if you pull this off*, I mentally repeated as I dipped down, propping the lid from the ice bucket against the doorframe of his room to keep his door from closing completely. The elevator was about ten steps away. I resumed pacing behind him, my door clicking closed behind us with a solid *thunk*.

Don't look back at your door, I tried to mentally telegraph to him. He stopped at the elevators, and I continued by him, ducking my head, as if I was going to the ice machine at the end of the corridor. I kept walking a few steps after the elevator dinged. I glanced over my shoulder. The doors were closing with Pete inside.

I sprinted back down the hall and into Room 505. I flipped the interior deadbolt and went to the closet. The room looked the same as when I left it earlier, except the television was on, tuned to a baseball game with the sound muted. Nothing had changed in the closet. I moved the video camera and blew out a breath that sent my bangs fluttering. The thought that the laptop might not be where I left it had crossed my mind, but I hadn't let myself dwell on it. I grabbed it, then replaced the video camera. On the way to the door, I picked up the ice bucket and lid. Juggling everything, I opened the door a sliver. The corridor was empty so I slipped out the door and back into my room as quickly as I could.

I ditched the ice bucket and set the laptop on the desk. I'd never been so glad I'd used a password in my life. As soon as I typed in the password, my initials followed by a string of numbers and letters—a combo of Livvy's and Nathan's birth dates—the screen loaded and all the photos popped up, just as I'd left them. I dropped into the chair. I had them. I had saved them to the computer when I'd opened them.

I dialed Monica's number. "I've got them," I whispered, feeling like I'd finished a triathlon.

"Hello, Ed," Monica said in a formal voice. "Just give me a moment." She tilted the phone away from her mouth, and I could hear her say something about her editor, that she had to take the call.

"Back in a moment," I heard her say faintly. After a few seconds, she came back on the line. "Okay, I'm out of the bar. You got them?"

"Yes," I said. "And they're saved to my computer." I leaned back in the chair. "Now all we have to do is get them to Mr. Sandpaper Voice. I mean Dwight."

"And get me a copy."

"Of course. You've earned it."

"I've got plenty of memory cards. I'll bring one up to you."

"What about Pete?" I asked.

"He's fine. He's got a bottle of champagne on me, er, on you, actually. I charged it to your room. I'll call him and tell him I had to go. My editor had an assignment for me."

A small window popped open on the computer, informing me I needed to switch to outlet power. "Oh . . . low battery." I let out a groan. "Just when I let myself think things might be coming together. I don't have the power cord. Pete didn't take it when he took the laptop," I said, looking around as if I might find a spare power cord in the hotel room. "I have to go back to my hotel room. My *other* hotel room."

"Okay. I'll meet you in the lobby," she said.

I reached to close the laptop, but another small window opened with the information that Ben Evanworth was calling. I had a program that let me send and receive video calls via the Internet. I'd used it a few times to call friends or family, but I mostly used it to talk with Mitch when he was deployed or away on short trips. Ben was also in my contact list.

I still had 15 percent battery life. I hit the ACCEPT button, and his face filled the screen. I hit the button to start my camera so he could see me as well.

"Ben!" I said. "I'm so glad to see you. Are you okay? Where are you?" He looked haggard.

"I'm fine. Still in the hotel. I don't have long," he said as he glanced quickly to his left. I couldn't see much behind him, just a wall papered in thin stripes and the edge of some dark drapes.

"I don't have long, either. Low battery." I glanced at the percentage of power remaining. Fourteen percent.

Ben asked, "Is there any way you can get to the front desk of the Park Palms Hotel quickly? There's a package of documents for you with hardcopies of everything I've found."

"Yeah, I can be there in about two minutes."

He'd been drawing a breath to continue speaking, but my words threw him off. "What?"

"I'm in the hotel now. It's where I found the photos of Angela. I've got them," I said a bit smugly.

Ben closed his eyes and gave a little laugh. "Right. Of course you looked for them. I should have known you wouldn't curl up in your hotel room and stay put. I forgot how stubborn you can be."

"Runs in the family," I retorted. "Besides, I like to think of it as persistence. I wasn't going to leave your fate solely in your hands. I'm down to thirteen percent battery life. So you are in the Park Palms?"

"Yes, but I can't leave right now." His face turned serious as he said, "Good thing you went after the photos. These people we're dealing with . . . well, it pains me to say this, but you were right. They're not quite as amateurish as I thought. I haven't seen the bumbling kid since he brought me here. Another guy has taken over."

"Dwight Fellows, Suzie Quinn's manager?" I asked.

Ben's forehead wrinkled. "Yes. How did you know that? Never mind. You can tell me later. Are the kids still with Summer?"

The quick swerve in the conversation brought me up short. "Yes," I said cautiously. "Why?"

Ben paused, obviously reluctant to tell me something. "Ben, what is it? Why are you asking about the kids? What do you know?" I asked, my heart already thudding.

"They're fine as long as you hand over the photos tonight," he said, his voice heavy. "I overheard that guy, Dwight. He called someone and told him to get a friend and sit on Summer's condo, to watch her and the kids. If Dwight doesn't get the photos tonight, he'll call that guy. He and 'the friend' are supposed to get the kids."

I dropped my head into my hands, "No, no, no. That can't happen. They should be safe." I raised my head, reached for my phone. "I'll call Summer and tell her to leave, right now. Then I'm calling the police."

"Ellie," Ben said sharply. "If Summer and the kids suddenly leave her condo during the night, the guy will know something is up, and he'll call Dwight. Dwight will realize I've been listening at doors and searching their rooms instead of sleeping off their drugs."

I shook my head as I flicked through the contact list on my phone. "These are my kids. It's one thing to let you do your thing. You're a grown man. Livvy and Nathan are kids. They don't have your sophisticated training. Summer doesn't even know they could be in danger."

"Think about it, Ellie," Ben pressed. "Any unexpected change will alert Dwight and then, not only will the kids be in danger, I'll be in worse shape. If either you or I tip our hand, the situation gets worse. The best play is for us to make sure the exchange happens. Once I'm out of here, we can take the documents I found and go to the police."

I found Summer's name in the contact list, but paused, my finger hovering over the DIAL button. "I don't like it."

"I don't, either, but it's the best thing to do in this situation."

"How does Dwight even know about the kids?"

Ben rubbed his hand over his mouth, then said, "He's into details and finding out everything he can about the people he comes into contact with. It's all leverage to him. I promise you, Ellie, handing over the photos is the best thing to do."

I closed my eyes briefly, then said, "Maybe. What's in the envelope waiting for me downstairs?"

"Everything I've found. E-mails, text messages, Web histories, phone logs. These people killed Angela so the photos wouldn't be published. Ruby contacted them—told them about the photos."

"It was Ruby, not Angela," I said, realizing I'd forgotten about her when I'd tried to work out Dwight's involvement earlier. Ruby was the one arguing for "going to the source."

Ben continued. "It's all there. She e-mailed them, they replied back, said they were interested. Ruby met with Dwight at the hotel across the street from your hotel. He must have picked it because it was close, and he didn't want to meet with her in public, in case she didn't want to do things his way. I'm assuming she didn't have the photos because Dwight replied to a text from Suzie that night, saying that he'd taken care of Ruby and had the information he needed to get the pictures."

I said, "When Dwight realized Ruby didn't have the pictures, he probably held her over the balcony to make her tell him who had them."

"I think that's what happened," Ben agreed. "He sent the kid to get the photos from Angela, but he bungled it—a regular occurrence, apparently."

"Lee," I said.

"What?"

"His name is Lee. Lee Fitch. He's Suzie Quinn's newest PA. That's short for personal assistant," I said quickly. My battery was down to 11 percent.

"When he realized Angela didn't have the photos, he decided to bring Angela back here. After a couple of hours with Dwight, he convinced her to give him her login information for her e-mail account. It wasn't Chase sending you e-mails, requesting an exchange of the purses, it was Dwight. It's all there in the e-mails. He sent the kid, Lee, to pick up the correct purse, but . . ."

"The purse we gave him didn't have the photos, so he took you."

"Yeah. Didn't learn, I guess. When he brought me in

the door, Suzie freaked. She shouted, 'You brought another one?' I didn't get a good look at her until tonight, so I didn't know who she was until a few hours ago."

"It's still hard to believe this is Suzie Quinn we're talking about—America's perky swimming sweetheart."

Ben paused. "She's nothing like she appears on television. It seems all she's interested in is yoga and the calorie count of every food that room service sends up. But then, she'll have a burst of screaming. Quite the diva. I have a feeling she's aware of everything that's going on, but is intentionally not asking for specifics. She keeps asking Dwight if the issue has been 'handled.' The walls here are surprisingly thin for the amount of money they're paying for this place. It's easy to keep track of when I'll have it to myself."

"So there is definite proof in those papers that Angela was murdered?" I asked.

He tilted his head from side to side. "It's not a signed confession. There's motive—Suzie's got a huge endorsement deal with a soft drink company. Her first appearance for them is tonight at Green Groves. She's frantic to keep anything out of the news that could jeopardize it. Either Suzie, or Suzie and Dwight, set Angela up and planned to do whatever it took to get the photos, whether it was legal or illegal. Either way, the hardcopies prove we're not lying."

"Or insane," I said. "My battery is almost gone and you need to get back to wherever you're supposed to be tucked away," I said.

"Yep. They'd be quite disappointed to know I was using the penthouse suite's business center for myself. And the concierge is so obliging, too. They'll deliver packages, like the one I have waiting for you. It's just a phone call away."

"Don't eat any of the food they give you. And watch out for a powder—I don't know how you'd do that, but be careful. Detective Jenson told me Angela's things had a coating of a powder, a drug that causes the person who inhales it to become docile and do whatever they're told. Breathing in too much can be fatal."

"That's what they think happened to Angela?"

"Jenson is still working on it, but he really, *really* wants to talk to you about it."

"Another thing to look forward to," Ben said.

My battery was on 2 percent, and Ben was getting more fidgety by the moment, so we signed off. "See you at midnight?" he asked.

"Yes," I said reluctantly.

Carrying the laptop, I hurried down to the lobby where Monica was pacing impatiently. "What took you so long?"

"In a second," I said, and stopped at the front desk and requested the package they were holding for me. The same snotty clerk handed me a thick, oversized envelope.

I gripped it so tightly that I wrinkled the paper.

"What's that?" Monica asked.

"Evidence," I said in an undertone. "Let's get out of here." I stepped away from the desk and led the way across the lobby. I didn't see Pete until he stepped directly in front of me, and we collided.

"Sorry," he said, his voice slightly slurred. He put out his hands to steady me, but I got the feeling he was using my shoulders to keep himself upright. He blinked, focusing on my face. His gaze sharped. He'd recognized me and noticed the laptop. "Hey, that's mine." He reached for the laptop in my arms.

I tightened my grip and stepped back a pace, leaving him weaving uncertainly.

"Hey!" He squinted at the desk clerk, raised a hand, and waved to get his attention. "She stole that from my room," he called.

Chapter Eighteen

I glanced at the desk clerk, who narrowed his eyes and quickly picked up a phone. Clearly, the desk clerk had taken a dislike to me and relished the thought of calling security.

"Wait!" I said. "This is *my* laptop."

"That's true," Monica said, coming forward. She gave Pete a scorching look and pointed to him. "*He* stole it from *her.*"

A ring of people watched us. The desk clerk glanced around the lobby, then put down the phone and marched over to us. "Is this true, Mrs. Avery? Is this indeed your laptop?" he asked.

He remembered my name? That was inconvenient. Not only could he describe me to the police, he could give them my name, too. I felt my breathing shorten and a dampness breaking out at my armpits and across my forehead. I didn't think he'd take my word about the scratch Nathan's truck had left on the laptop.

"She's lying," Pete said, angling his shoulder so that he cut Monica out of the conversation as he leaned in to try to grab the laptop again.

I shifted it to the other side and stepped back. "This is my laptop. He's the liar," I said, then had a thought. "I can prove it. I can unlock it with the password. Something this man can't do." I flipped the laptop open, praying there was enough juice in the battery to start the computer. It took a few moments to bring up the login screen. When it was up, I turned it toward Pete. "Care to give it a try?"

He lowered his head, staring at me from under his eyebrows. "No," he barked.

I sat down in a chair, placed the laptop on a table facing away from Pete, and quickly typed in the password. A chime sounded and programs began loading. "See. There you are. It's mine," I said, waving a hand at the computer screen. "I don't think there's any problem here, is there?" I asked, looking at Pete.

His mouth was set as he shook his head. The desk clerk slowly said, "Very well, but please, no more disturbances."

"Not a problem." With a blip and a gusty burst of the laptop's fan, which almost sounded like a sigh, it went dark. The battery was totally dead. I closed the lid and stood. "We were on our way out."

Monica fell into step with me, and we quickly crossed to the exit and stepped into the thick air of the still warm night. Pete stumbled along behind us. "That was a dirty trick," he said.

I ignored him and kept walking to the parking garage, but Monica whirled to face him. "No, Pete. It wasn't a dirty trick. It was the truth, which is a word you seem to have forgotten the meaning of. I can't believe you'd stoop so low as to break into a hotel room and steal."

"You'd do it, too," he said, poking a finger at her. I think he was aiming for her shoulder but missed completely, his finger shooting off into the air beside Monica, which set him wavering. "You were after the photos. You wanted them, too."

Monica grabbed his shoulder and steadied him. "Sure I wanted them, but I was going to buy them, not steal them. And I would have given them to my editor instead of selling them myself."

Pete pulled back. "I didn't—"

"Don't bother," Monica interrupted him. "I know you sold them to the Brits, and you're skipping town." Pete's face went wary. "I hope you enjoy running," Monica continued, "because the photos are connected to what looks like murder, so you better hit the road fast, but keep looking over your shoulder. If you'd just stolen a laptop, the police might not get around to looking for you, but with a possible murder involved, I'm sure they'll look a lot harder."

Pete took a few unsteady steps backward and stumbled. "Oh, and look for my by-line," Monica called out as Pete turned and tottered back to the hotel. "I'll have the whole story. You know what they say, it's not the crime, it's the cover-up. I'll have the murder *and* the cover-up story. You could have had an even bigger story, if you hadn't been so greedy."

"Come on," I said, pulling at her arm. "We don't have time for this."

"Sure we do. There's always time to gloat," she said, but her abandon at the steering wheel more than made up for our little tête-à-tête with Pete. We made it to the other hotel in a few minutes. There were plenty of angry drivers on the beach road, but they didn't bother Monica at all. She'd said, "Please. I drive the L.A. freeways. This is like kindergarten."

During the drive, I only had time to look through the first few pages of the documents, but what I saw confirmed what Ben had said. The first e-mails were between Angela's friend Ruby and Dwight. He'd e-mailed her, assuring her that "an arrangement satisfactory to both parties could be negotiated." I quickly read the line aloud to Monica, and she whistled.

"This next one is from Dwight, too, setting up a meeting at the hotel where Ruby was pushed off the balcony."

"I heard about that. She's part of the story, too?" Monica asked as she pulled into a parking space.

"Yes. She's been in the hospital since last night and isn't talking to anyone. Says she can't remember anything."

We exchanged glances, and Monica said, "That's what I'd say if someone tried to kill me and wasn't successful. You wouldn't want to give anyone a reason to complete the job."

We shot through the lobby, up the elevator, and into the corridor. I checked my watch. It was nine forty-five. Plenty of time. Monica wanted to see the papers, too. She was like the persistent no-see-ums, the little gnats that come out every year in middle Georgia and pester you until you go mad or go indoors. I was handing her the first e-mails as I threw open the door to my room, then jerked to a stop.

"Mitch! I completely forgot about you."

He stood in the doorway of the bathroom. He had on

khaki cargo shorts and was pulling a polo shirt over his head. His hair was damp, and steamy air drifted out of the bathroom.

"Obviously," he said, but there wasn't any censure in his voice, only a bit of teasing. He worked the shirt over his head and came forward to kiss me. "I fly thousands of miles, drive through the night to get here, and how am I greeted? With an empty hotel room," he said, sweeping his arm around the room. "Sight of a massive party, apparently," he said, indicating the open suitcases and the general disarray of the room. "I was on my way over to Summer's. I figured you'd be there. You look nice," he said, taking in my gauzy top, jeans, and espadrilles.

"Oh, Mitch." The stack of papers crumpled as I leaned into the solidity of his shoulder, relaxing into the curve of his arm. Everything went misty. Most of the time I didn't mind being on my own, which was a good quality to have, considering that Mitch's job took him away at frequent intervals, but there was an enormous relief to know I didn't have to handle *this* situation alone anymore.

"Ah, I'll wait for you downstairs," Monica said in a small voice.

"No, it's okay," I said as I pulled away from Mitch, blinking rapidly. "Sit down." I waved Monica to the couch and smiled reassuringly at Mitch. His face had gone from slightly teasing to concerned. "I'm okay. I just need to tell you what's happened." I took a deep breath as I put the papers and the laptop down on the coffee table. "It's about Ben."

I introduced Monica, then recapped everything as best I could. As I talked, I handed off the laptop to Monica. She connected the power cord, then I typed my password. She went to work, copying photos to the memory cards, one for her and one for me to give to Dwight Fellows.

As I caught Mitch up on what had happened, I skimmed over a few tiny things, like the balcony stunt. I noticed Monica shot me a raised eyebrow when I seamlessly avoided that in my narrative, but I kept going until I wound up with the description of how I'd remembered the photos were on the laptop.

When I finished, Mitch ran his hand over his mouth. "So, the deadline to get that memory card to this Dwight Fellows guy is midnight?" he asked, checking his watch.

"Yes," I said.

"Then we better get going."

"I love you, you know that," I said, giving him a solid kiss on the lips. No questions, no recriminations. He just focused on what needed to be done.

He smiled and pulled me close enough so that only I could hear him say, "Yeah, you can tell me all the parts you left out later."

When he released me and went to get his shoes and wallet, Monica handed me the memory card and raised her eyebrows. "He's delish. And a man of action. Do you know how lucky you are?"

"I think I do," I said.

Monica got a phone call, listened for a moment, and motioned that she would be in the corridor. She stepped out the door, and I gathered up the papers. I paused with my hand on the laptop. To bring it or not? I quickly logged into my e-mail account and attached the photos to an e-mail, then sent it to my own e-mail address. Now the photos were out there zipping through cyber-space. In fact, they'd probably already come to rest at a server farm in some anonymous warehouse in Nevada or Arizona. The sent e-mail popped into my inbox, and I felt better. I really did need to look into an online back-up service, I decided.

"Ready?" Mitch asked.

"I have to be, don't I?" I said, shifting the memory card from one hand to the other so I could wipe my sweaty palms on my jeans.

"Where's Monica?"

"In the hall," I said, heading for the door. "The cell phone reception is terrible in here." I stepped out the door, but there wasn't anyone hovering near our room. I did a quick scan of the whole floor and the elevators. No blond pageboy. No shimmering green dress. "Where is she?" I asked, hurrying to the end of the hall and throwing open the door to the stairwell. No one.

"Looks like she took off."

"I can't believe she'd do that."

"You said she's a tabloid reporter, right?"

"Yes, but this is a huge story. She's got the best angle, the inside track, if she sticks with us. Why would she go it alone? I hope nothing happened to her," I said, thinking of the ominous Dwight Fellows and his back-up plan involving the kids. "If Dwight figured out who she is—that she's a reporter—who knows what he'd do."

"I think she can take care of herself."

I turned down the hotel hallway. "There are three other emergency stairwells—"

Mitch cut in. "We need to go. The earlier we get to Green Groves, the better," he said with a quick look at his watch.

"You're right," I said, reluctantly. "The elevator will be faster than the stairs."

I was still scanning the lobby for Monica as we hurried through it, but there were plenty of places to hide. All she had to do was step behind one of the oversized elephant ear plants and I wouldn't be able to see her.

As we passed the business center, I grabbed Mitch's elbow and changed course. "Copies! We need copies of these," I said, patting the package from Ben. I'd been careful to make sure I had digital copies of the photos. I needed copies of the papers as well. I was sure that if Dwight or anyone in the Suzie/Nick orbit figured out what Ben had done, the files would vanish off hard drives faster than Nathan could make a scoop of chocolate ice cream disappear.

I stopped short in the door of the business center. Monica was hovering over the printer, eagerly pulling each sheet out as it printed. "Monica, what are you doing?" I asked.

She jumped. My voice had come out a bit sharper than I intended. It had the same accusatory tone that I used when I found the kids doing something they weren't supposed to do, like digging in my purse or playing on the computer long after I'd told them to quit their game.

My thoughts switched from thinking, oh-no-Monica-might-be-in-danger to oh-no-what-double-cross-has-she-pulled? I couldn't help thinking of how she'd told Pete she had a phone call from her editor and slipped out of the bar. Had she sold us out? Had she sent the photos to her editor before we'd even had a chance to trade them? I suddenly had the weirdest sensation that the walls were tilting, closing in on me, and I couldn't breathe properly.

Monica pressed a hand to her chest. "God, you

scared me," she said. "Look!" She shoved some paper at me. "Freddie came through!"

"Freddie?" I asked.

"My contact, remember? My tech guy? Angela's texts."

"So you really did get a call?" I asked, gripping the back of a rolling chair to steady myself and breathe now that my lungs seemed to be working again.

"Yes," she said, her forehead wrinkled. Then her face cleared. "Oh. You thought . . . I see," she said, and then it was her turn to look imposing. "You really think I'd ditch you? *Now?* When everything is about to come together?"

"Well, you did skip out on Pete . . ."

"Because Pete is an idiot. I'm a reporter. These," she slapped the papers with the back of her hand, "are collaboration. Text messages between Angela and Ruby about the photos. Angela told Ruby that she contacted Pete. She told Ruby that she'd taken care of everything and they'd have their money soon." As another paper emerged from the printer, she said, "We have my texts with Angela on my phone and her texts with Pete. Angela wanted a bidding war, but Pete offered more than I did. Two million. I guess she figured that was high enough. She gave him her name and address, and told him to meet her there at noon today."

"Pete could have arrived early and searched her apartment for the photos," I said.

Monica's eyes narrowed. "I wonder if he planned to swipe them all along."

"Could be, but whether or not that was his plan, when he saw Angela was dead and he heard me talking to Jenson about the purse and how Angela wanted me to deliver it to her apartment, he must have figured out the photos were in it. Then, he followed me back to the hotel and stole the memory card along with my computer."

Monica slapped the papers against her hand. "These are a second source, which we need to prove what happened. Just because I work for *Celeb* doesn't mean I don't do my homework," she said.

"Sorry," I said.

"Forget it," she said easily, her attention already on the pages. "This is just what we need."

"We need to get out of here," Mitch said. He'd been waiting silently in the doorway.

"Last one," Monica said as she pulled the page from the printer.

"Let's go, then," Mitch said.

"Copies! We need copies," I said, gathering the two stacks of paper.

We ran two copies of all the documents while Mitch tapped his foot, jiggled his keys, and made other nonverbal gestures to communicate his impatience. I left one copy of the documents at the front desk in a sealed envelope with Detective Jenson's name on it. I seized the stack of originals and the second set, then we sprinted through the lobby and into the parking lot.

"How are we getting inside Green Groves?" Mitch asked.

"I don't know," I said, jogging along beside him. I handed the second copy of the papers to Monica, eyeing her night-out-on-the-town dress. "I hope we don't have to climb over a wall."

Digital Organizing Tips

Use Online Helpers

Take advantage of some of these free digital organizing tools:

Dropbox is a free online digital storage service. It's handy because you can drop files into your account from your computer, then access them on another computer.

Note-It lets you create sticky notes for your computer.

Create your own list at PrintableCheckList.org. Super simple and easy to use.

You can find generic grocery lists at many sites online or customize one at grocerylistmaker.com.

Store and share your photos with online photo sharing sites like Flickr, Photobucket, and Shutterfly.

Chapter
Nineteen

Mitch drove as Monica and I scanned the pages. The van was silent except for the rustle of paper and the posh voice coming from the GPS as it navigated us to Green Groves. I was shuffling the most important papers into a smaller stack when the GPS announced that we had arrived at our destination. I frowned in confusion at the mass of cars clogging the entrance and the bright glow of lights illuminating the sky beyond the imposing gates.

I'd expected Green Groves to be closed, and the gates locked tight. I'd researched the place online and knew the extensive grounds were enclosed on three sides by a high wrought iron fence. The fourth side of the property abutted Sandy Bay. Although Green Groves wasn't a working plantation and had been built more as a showcase of the owner's wealth, it still followed the usual pattern of locating the plantation home near water. Water had been the main highway of the day, and Green Groves's location on Sandy Bay meant easy travel to and from the plantation for the owners.

"The Festival of Fireworks," I read aloud as I saw a sign. "I'd forgotten about that. There was an advertisement for it in the lobby," I said to Mitch. He followed the line of cars to the parking area, and we stepped out of the van. Night had brought some relief from the stifling humidity, but it was still warm. I knew the grounds surrounding the home were famous for being spacious but hadn't grasped how large the estate was. Majestic live oaks, their twisted branches draped with Spanish moss, stretched out in every direction, seeming to go on for miles. Even at night, the whole landscape was tinged with various shades of green, from the emerald green of the grass underfoot to the gray-green of the Spanish moss.

I looked around at the kids jumping excitedly and tugging on parents' arms. I wished we were here with Livvy and Nathan, with nothing more to do than fight the crowds for a pretzel and admire the fireworks.

"The kids wanted to come," I said as we crunched along the path of crushed shells through the entrance, which cut straight through the forest of live oaks to the white pillars of the antebellum house in the distance. Lights had been threaded through the tree branches, which met overhead and created a tunnel-like corridor that was lined with vendors offering arcade games, T-shirts, and food.

"I can see why," Mitch said. "It's a carnival."

Aromas of grilled meat and fried foods wafted toward us. I saw signs for pretzels, hot dogs, hamburgers, ice cream, funnel cakes, and cotton candy. And, it seemed anything from ice cream to Oreos could be deep-fried. "Deep-fried Oreos," I murmured. "Sounds repulsively good. I think I might have to try those."

"They're to die for," Monica said, and I gave her a surprised look. "What?" she asked.

"You turn down a Hershey's kiss, but you'll eat deep-fried Oreos?"

"It was a long time ago," she said wistfully. "I grew up in Atlanta, one of the fried-food capitals of the world." We moved down the aisle between booths of food, games, and souvenirs.

We emerged from the tunnel of live oak branches into an open, grassy area. Ahead of us, still about half a mile away, stood the two-story plantation house, its pristine white pillars and portico rising above the circular sweep of the shell drive. A large stage had been set up to our right.

I gripped Mitch's arm. "Look at the banner," I said, and Monica pulled her camera out of her bag. She clicked off a few shots of an enormous banner with a picture of Suzie Quinn tilting a can with a familiar soft drink logo to her smiling lips.

Suzie herself sat at a table on the stage, signing autographs for a line of fans that snaked down the stairs from the stage. On the ground, the line twisted between elastic dividers. It doubled back, winding back and forth across the grass, making me think of my last trip through airport security. A few people sat with Suzie on the stage, including two of the security guys I'd seen in Monica's photos. There were also a few more normal, less bodybuilder, types in business suits, whose job seemed to be hurrying people through the line and preventing anyone from saying more than one sentence to Suzie.

Monica hissed, "There's Dwight." She nodded toward a cluster of people on the edge of the stage. I pointed out his Western shirt and cowboy boots to Mitch. Everyone else was either in a business suit or beach casual. We all shuffled across the grass to the cover of the trees. Once we were positioned behind the wide girth of one of the oak trunks, Monica propped her camera on a gnarled branch and began clicking away.

"Do you see Ben?" I asked. I knew it was unlikely that he'd be up on stage, even in the wings, but I couldn't help asking.

"Don't know what he looks like," she said.

"Here, let me check," I said, and she handed over the camera somewhat hesitantly. "I won't drop it." I quickly found the group and zoomed in on them. "No, he's not there." No tall, dark-haired, lanky guy in his mid-twenties stood with them.

There was a distant whistling sound, then a loud crack. I jumped, and Monica quickly pulled the camera out of my hands. "What was that?" I asked.

"Fireworks," Mitch said. He glanced at his watch. "They must be running late. The sign said fireworks over Sandy Bay are from ten until eleven." Another whine split the air followed by a boom, this one louder than the last. The tree branches were thick, and I couldn't see any sparks of color when I glanced overhead.

"The fireworks viewing is down there," Mitch said, pointing to a group of people who were headed toward the house, following the signs that led them around the right-hand side of the plantation to the path that dropped down to the bay. The area where we were didn't clear out completely. Plenty of people still circulated along the drive. Some people had spread blankets in the grassy area and were feasting on their deep-fried goodies while others stayed in line for an autograph.

Mitch checked the stage and said, "Since Dwight is up there, I'm going to check out the place he told you to meet him. See if I can watch from a distance."

"I'll go, too. I'll need to find the best place to get photos," Monica said.

"I don't know if that's a good idea," Mitch said.

"The more evidence we have for Jenson, the better," I said. "If Monica can get a shot of Ben being brought to us and get the exchange on film, then we've got proof for Jenson. Do you have a video option on that camera?"

"Of course," she said, but she didn't look excited about the idea of shooting video.

"You'll be able to get some stills from the video, right?" I asked, but in a slightly distracted way as I glanced around. I had that funny feeling you get when someone is watching you.

Monica said, "Yeah. Don't worry. I'll make sure I get it."

I swept my gaze over the crowd of people. Most were moving at a lazy pace, taking in the scenery or eating as they walked.

"What is it?" Mitch asked.

"I don't know. I feel like someone is watching us." I shifted so I could see around the rough trunk of the oak. "It's Jenson," I said as our gazes locked. He'd changed into a new guayabera shirt, this one black with white stitching, and wore jean shorts with a pair of sturdy sandals. His hands were in his pockets and he was staring in my direction intently, his sandy eyebrows lowered. A slim, dark-headed woman in a sleeveless shirt and linen shorts had paused beside him, her attention on a brochure. A teenaged girl in short-shorts and a T-shirt with the same dark hair as the woman trailed behind the couple, making her discontent with the situation clear though her body language of sloped shoulders and a mulish expression.

"Who?" Mitch asked.

"The detective," I said. "Looks like he's here with his family. He wants to talk to Ben about Angela's death."

"Great," Mitch muttered.

"I know." I clenched my hands into fists as Jenson said something to the woman, then strolled toward me. "No. Go away. We don't have time for this."

Mitch glanced around. "Has he seen me?"

"I don't think so. You and Monica are both hidden by the tree, I think," I said.

Mitch looked back at the lighted tunnel of tree branches.

I knew what he was thinking. "You and Monica go on. I'll get rid of Jenson and meet you . . . somewhere," I said, looking for a place that would be easy to get to, but that wouldn't leave us in the open.

Mitch said, "Let's meet at the van. It's too open here." I agreed, and he and Monica left at a quick clip. "Left side, down the terrace steps to a fountain with dolphins," I whispered, and then immediately felt silly because it wasn't like Jenson would hear me. He was still several yards away. Without looking back, Mitch raised a hand in acknowledgment as he and Monica reached the main drive and blended in with the people moving under the archway of lights.

"Evening, Mrs. Avery," Jenson said. "Friends of yours?" he asked, looking in the direction Mitch and Monica had gone.

"My husband and a friend," I said. "They've gone to get . . . something to eat. Deep-fried Oreos, I think."

"I see. They're excellent."

Had everyone but me eaten fried Oreos? How had I missed out on this culinary experience?

Jenson pivoted on his heels, taking in the crowd. "Your brother here, Mrs. Avery?"

I licked my lips. "He'll be . . . arriving later."

"How much later?"

"Around midnight."

"So you're saying your brother is meeting you here—at midnight?"

"Yes. That's the plan, anyway," I murmured under my breath.

"This event shuts down at midnight."

"Oh."

"Tell you what," Jenson said as he checked his watch. "That's not too long from now. I'll just stick with you until then." Several explosions thundered through the air.

Before I could protest, Jenson waved his wife and daughter over, introduced them, and told them he had to stay and they should go ahead to the fireworks without him. His wife gave him a slightly exasperated look, but it seemed she wasn't really upset.

"I don't want to spoil your evening," I said. "You don't have to stay with me. I'll have Ben call you the minute I see him."

"It's fine. Happens all the time," his wife said with a wrinkle of her nose at him. "It's why we take two cars everywhere we go. See you at home, babe." She gave him a quick kiss on the cheek, then tapped his arm as she added, "I expect it to be before six a.m. Come on, Kayla," she said to the teen, who had been texting during our exchange. She dragged her gaze away from her phone long enough to wave at her dad, then went back to her phone as she followed her mom.

Jenson had his hands in his pockets as he rocked back on his heels and said, "Well, looks like you're stuck with me. How about we get in line for those fried Oreos?"

I blew out a breath, coming to a decision. "As much as I'd like to try one, there's something I need to show you."

Chapter
Twenty

"Circumstantial," Jenson said, replacing the last paper back in the stack I'd handed him. We were sitting in the minivan. I was in the driver's seat, and Jenson was in the passenger seat. It was the most out of the way place I could think of to take him. I didn't want Dwight to see me chatting with Jenson. Jenson wasn't in a uniform and there wasn't any sign of a badge, but I still wanted to be careful. Faintly, I could still hear the fireworks whistling skyward and the dull thud as they exploded.

On the walk to the van, I'd tried to summarize what had happened from the purse mix-up to the news that Dwight had someone poised to take my kids. Since Jenson was sticking with me, I figured my only option was to tell him everything. It was actually a relief. Well, it had been a relief until he'd thrown out the "circumstantial" word.

"But it's all there . . . Dwight and Suzie's e-mails,

setting up Angela, the texts between Angela and the tabloids, even Ruby's contact with Dwight before she was pushed off the balcony.

Jenson tapped the edges of the pages, lining them up. "I'm sorry, Mrs. Avery, but this doesn't prove anything. It could be supporting evidence, but it's not a smoking gun. Anyone can set up an e-mail address and name it whatever they want. Anyone could set up an e-mail account as," he paused to consult the top paper, "dfellows@gmail.com."

"But the e-mails can be traced, right? If you trace them to the Park Palms suite where Nick and Suzie are staying . . ."

"Even if we can trace the e-mail, that doesn't pinpoint one person."

"Well, what about the fact that he's holding my brother?"

"Do you have any record of his calls? How did he contact you? Cell phone?"

"No. The hotel phone," I said miserably. "And I wasn't smart enough or quick enough to try and record it. I could have done that with my cell phone. But he did call. The hotel will have a record of incoming calls, but that would probably take time to track down."

"Yes, and you're sure that time is of the essence here?"

"Yes. Absolutely sure," I said. A series of explosions rumbled, and we both tensed.

"It's the finale," Jenson said as the air filled with pops, whines, and explosions.

The clock on the dashboard read eleven o'clock. Jenson shifted position in the seat, propped an ankle on one knee, and said, "Now, back to your brother . . . you said he told you he could leave at any time?"

"Yes," I said with an internal groan, knowing where this conversation was going. "But that was in the beginning. The last time I talked to him, he said he'd underestimated the people he was dealing with. He outsmarted them into thinking they'd drugged him, but I don't know what they'd do to him if they knew what he'd been doing . . . sneaking around, looking at their computers and phones."

Jenson stared at me for a long moment, then blew out a long sigh. "Clearly, you are distraught and worried about your brother," he said, as if running through a mental pro and con list. "There is nothing in your brother's past that would indicate he'd concoct such an elaborate scheme or participate in a murder, but—"

My heart, which had ballooned with a bit of hope during the first part of his speech, immediately deflated. The fireworks continued, each explosion seeming to further decimate my hopes. All Jenson had to do was make a call, and the place would be swarming with police. He could probably even take me into custody and come up with a dozen charges . . . withholding evidence being the first one.

"You understand, I have to error on the side of caution," Jenson concluded.

"Yes, I understand," I said quickly. I had to try and convince him to help. I leaned over the armrest as I said, "But we don't have a lot of time. Look, I didn't call you when Ben was . . . taken, snatched . . . whatever you want to call it, because I had no proof. There weren't any witnesses in the parking lot. No video. I didn't have the laptop or the memory card, only the purse that you hadn't wanted. Ben is a grown man. You wouldn't be able to do much until he'd been gone for twenty-four hours, right?"

I hurried on before he could answer. "And then there was the Angela component. At that time, you didn't think she'd been murdered, but Ben and I did. We didn't know for sure, but her death seemed suspicious. I didn't know if I'd get any help if I came to you. Later, when you reversed course and began investigating Angela's death as a possible murder, I couldn't come to you because . . . well, I didn't know for sure where Ben was. Since he was MIA, that would make him look even more guilty."

I paused for a breath, hoping I wasn't muddling the situation even more. "All I'm asking is that you wait until midnight, let me make the exchange with Dwight. Watch it—from a discreet distance without going all *Die Hard* and calling in a ton of police. If Dwight shows up with Ben and hands him over for the memory card, that will prove Dwight is involved. You can take it from there. I just want to make sure Ben is safe and that my kids don't get hurt."

His fingers had been tapping out a quick beat on his ankle as I spoke. When I finished, he considered me for a moment, then said, "Let me make a call." I opened my mouth, and he held up his hand. "Not for reinforcements," he said. "This is a . . . delicate situation and, as much as I hate to say this, I think it may fall outside our normal procedure."

I jumped at the tap on the window beside me. It was Mitch. "This is my husband, Mitch," I said quickly because Jenson was reaching for something; his gun, I presumed. I opened the door and stepped out quickly, saying to Mitch, "This is Detective Jenson."

Mitch and the detective nodded at each other. Detective Jenson's call went through, and he pulled his phone closer to his ear as he spoke quietly.

"Couldn't ditch him?" Mitch asked under his breath.

"Had to bring him on board," I said just as quietly. "I *think* he's going to help us."

"That's good, because we don't have time for anything else. But don't you think Dwight will notice you're bringing a rather large party, considering he only expected one person?"

"This place is crawling with people. Like you said, it's a carnival. If it was deserted and there was no one here but us and Dwight, I'd be worried, but I think even Jenson can blend in here. And, I'd rather have him close in case something goes wrong . . ."

"Nothing will go wrong," Mitch said, and I nodded. Despite the conviction in his tone, I still had a sick feeling in the pit of my stomach. It was probably a good thing I hadn't indulged in any deep-fried food. I ignored the churning in my stomach and said, "So, the fountain. What does it look like?"

"Dwight won't see me or Monica. There's a gazebo not too far from the fountain."

I looked around. "Where is Monica?"

"On the roof of the gazebo."

"Oh."

"Okay, Mrs. Avery. You get your wish," Detective Jenson said as he put away his phone and leaned down so he could see out the door. "If I'm to be a part of this affair, you better bring me up to speed."

I hit the button to unlock the other doors, and we climbed into the van, Mitch taking the seat behind me. He picked up the kids' Etch-A-Sketch from the floorboard and drew several lines. "Here's the plantation," he said, leaning forward between the seats and pointing to a long line on the right. "The fountain is here," he said, transferring the pen tip to a circle in the center of the Etch-A-Sketch.

"There's a gazebo to the northwest," he said, adding an octagon to the upper left-hand side of the screen. "That's where Monica is. The sidewalks have pathway lighting every two feet or so. There are spotlights on the fountains. There is an interior light inside the gazebo and two spotlights on the lower portion of the gazebo, but no light up around the roof. There are two other fountains," Mitch said, drawing additional circles near the top and bottom of the screen. "They're illuminated, but there's no other lighting."

Mitch put an *x* on the octagon. "I'll be on the roof here with Monica. It's a good vantage point. The darkness will hide us."

I looked from the sketch to the grove of oaks brooding beyond the fence. "Where do you think Ben is? He's probably already here, right?"

Mitch ran his hand over his jaw, then added another square to his drawing up near the plantation house. "There's a building here behind a screen of bushes, a storage or equipment shed. They might stash him there, or somewhere around the stage, or he could be in a car out here."

"Or in the crowds," Jenson said, eyeing the gate, "but people are already leaving, and it will thin out even more since the fireworks are over."

"Will we be able to get out?" I asked, because as nice as the grounds of Green Groves were, I didn't want to hang out any longer than we had to.

"I think so. It will take at least an hour for everyone to leave, and then they'll have to shut everything down. I doubt these gates will close before one a.m."

He leaned toward the drawing and tapped the square that Mitch had drawn to represent the outbuilding. "Any place to wait around there, besides the building?"

Mitch nodded slowly. "Yes. There's a large tree and one of those arch things with flowers growing over it," Mitch said, looking to me for the exact wording.

"An arbor?"

"That's it. It's not one of those wobbly ones. This one is made of iron and about six feet tall."

"Okay, that's where I'll be," Jenson said. He reached for the door handle, but his phone buzzed. He took the call, grunted, then said, "Okay, can you stay on it?" There was a pause, and then he said, "Yeah, I know. I owe you another one."

He carefully put his phone on SILENT, then said, "That was a colleague of mine who lives close to your sister-in-law."

Earlier, when I'd run down everything that had happened, he'd asked for Summer's address and nodded like he was familiar with the area.

"I asked my colleague to drive by the condo," Jenson continued, and my hands curled into fists. What had he done? Had he tipped our hand?

"Don't worry, Mrs. Avery. She's one of the best on the force. She was careful but says that there is a car parked outside the condo with two men in it who seem to have nothing better to do than wait in the parking lot on a muggy night."

"So it is true," I said, realizing that I'd hoped Ben had been mistaken. I felt like I did during my bouts with morning sickness.

"Afraid so, which is both a good and bad thing,"

Jenson said. "Bad, because it shows that Dwight means business."

"How can it be good?" I asked, my fingernails digging into my palms.

"It's good because it confirms one part of your story. So I think we can move ahead with these plans," he said, pointing to the Etch-A-Sketch. "I'll watch the exchange, and then take Mr. Fellows aside, let him know I'm anxious to chat with him about day's events."

"But the kids," I said quickly.

"My friend won't let them out of her sight. If those guys in the car make a move, she'll take care of it."

"Are you sure?" I asked, glancing at Mitch.

"Oh, she'll be fine. She's an aikido instructor," Jenson said.

"I don't know . . ."

"And she's got her gun. No one will get through that condo door without her . . . approval, let's say."

"Okay, I guess that will have to do," I said. "Not that I don't appreciate you calling her, but I'd rather the kids weren't involved in any way."

"I understand," Jenson said.

"Any questions, any concerns?" Mitch asked as he checked his cell phone, making sure it was on SILENT as well. Jenson took the Etch-A-Sketch and looked over it one more time.

"Nope. I'm good." I was sure the absurdity of using a kid's toy to plan a swap with a kidnapper would have struck me as funny if I hadn't been so nervous.

"One thing," Mitch said, taking the toy back and tossing it on the seat. "Why are you being so cooperative?" he asked Jenson.

Jenson gave Mitch an assessing look, then said, "I've

got as much at stake as you do. I let your wife walk away with evidence that she'd offered to turn over to me. I told her it wasn't important. If I don't want this situation to blow up in my face, my best play is to make sure Ben is safe, your kids stay safe, and that Dwight Fellows is in my custody. That's the only way for me to salvage this. And," he added with a bit of a grin, "you may have noticed I'm not exactly a by-the-book kind of guy. I'm okay with dabbling outside the lines as long as it gets results."

"Understood," Mitch said with a nod.

They both made moves to leave the van, and I said, "Isn't it a little early?" It was only eleven-ten.

"You can never arrive too early at the drop site," Jenson said with a wink. "That's my motto."

I waited until the van's dashboard clock read eleven-thirty. I couldn't stand it any longer and climbed out of the van. If Jenson, Mitch, and Monica could be early, I could, too. I'd spent the last twenty minutes imagining every possible thing that could go wrong.

I slammed the door, clicked the lock on the key fob, and tightened my grip around the memory card in my palm. It felt good to be moving around, doing something.

I walked briskly down the drive, threading through the thinning crowd under the lights. The celebration was winding down. People were moving toward the parking area and vendors were cleaning booths. Pushing against the trickle of people, I emerged into the grassy area. The stage was empty except for two people collapsing chairs. I wondered where Suzie and

Nick were. Would they watch the exchange? I doubted it. They'd probably stay as far away as possible.

The pillars of the antebellum house glowed brightly against the surrounding darkness. People were walking back from the fireworks display, moving at a leisurely pace up the path that ran around the right side of the house. I slowed and moved around the left side toward the gardens, which seemed deserted.

I crossed the bricked terrace and paused at the top of the steps that descended to the gardens, getting my bearings and searching the pockets of darkness. The dolphin fountain was at the center of the gardens. It was well lit and I could hear the burble of water even at a distance. If I stayed close to the fountain, Monica should be able to get everything on video.

Outside the circle of light enclosing the fountain, I spotted the gazebo with its interior lights and spotlights on the flowers mounded around its base. I squinted at the roof, but couldn't pick out any familiar shapes against the black of the sky. I moved down the steps and let my gaze drift to the outbuilding and the arbor, which were clumps of deeper darkness.

The gardens were classic French style with scroll-shaped beds bordered with low boxwood hedges. Crushed shell paths ran in curving lines that converged on the center fountain. I crunched to the fountain. I certainly wouldn't be sneaking up on anyone.

I circled the fountain once, feeling the strain of not knowing how many people were out there hidden in the dark. I felt jittery and wanted to hang back in the darkness outside of the lights, but I didn't want to delay the process any longer, either, so I took a seat on one of the benches that encircled the fountain. I chose the one facing the gazebo and hoped that Monica would be able to get a clear shot. I checked my watch. Eleven-forty.

The water sprayed through the air, sending off little rainbow refractions. Sweat gathered along my hairline and at my armpits, and it wasn't just because of the sultry night air. I carefully switched the memory card from one hand to the other as I wiped my palms on my jeans. I tried to envision a calm and serene place . . . like the beach, I decided, conjuring up the image of the water flowing in and receding. I focused on that image for a while, then checked my watch.

Eleven forty-one.

One minute? Good grief. This must be what a time-out felt like for Livvy and Nathan. I shifted on the bench and tried to look like I spent the midnight hours in the gardens of antebellum homes all the time. Except for the faint sound of voices coming from the people leaving the event, the garden was quiet. The only other sound was the tumble of water shooting out of the dolphins' mouths. After a few more minutes, that noise combined with my nervousness had me wishing I'd made a pit stop at one of the porta-potties that had been lined up at the rear of the parking area. I crossed my legs and thought of deserts and cactus and sandstorms.

I tensed as footsteps crunched sharply through the shell walkway. I turned in the direction of the sound, the direction of the house. "Ah, Mrs. Avery, you're early," Dwight said as he emerged from the darkness, like an actor walking into the spotlight on a stage. "Thank you so much for coming." His voice was jovial, and for a second I felt as if I should thank him for the invitation, but I jerked that thought process to a halt. This wasn't a social occasion.

I stood and said, "There are other places I'd rather be."

"My thoughts as well. Shall we get on with it?" He held out his hand.

"I want to see Ben."

He sighed elaborately. "Really? You insist on that old trope?"

"Yes. I don't care about the photos or selling them . . . all I care about is Ben."

"You think I don't know that? Do you know what I used to do? Before I went to Hollywood? I started in politics. 'Opposition research,' they call it now. Nice name for digging up the dirt on someone. I know all about you. I know you're on vacation. I know you brought your kids to the beach, that you've never been to Sandy Beach before. I know your husband is on his way, but he's been delayed. In short, I know that you're a woman alone, a woman without resources, without help. For all those reasons, we're playing this by my rules. You'll show me the photos first, then I'll show you Ben. Because I heard a nasty rumor that you've been running all over town . . . that you didn't really know where they were. I need to see that there's actually something on that memory card besides pictures of your adorable children at the beach."

"The photos are here. I'd be glad to show you, but I don't have a computer or camera."

"Here you are," he said, and unfastened the pearl snap on the breast pocket of his Western shirt. He pulled out a small camera and tossed it to me.

I loaded the memory card and found the buttons to shift the camera into REVIEW mode. I brought up the first picture of Suzie and turned the camera screen toward him. "There they are," I said, quickly scrolling through the photos.

"Very good," he said, then called over his shoulder, "Lee, you can bring him out now."

There was a shuffling sound along the path near the outbuilding, and then a circle of light thrown from a flashlight danced around the ground.

"His face, you idiot," Dwight shouted, and threw me an exasperated glance as if to say, *you see what I have to deal with?*

The light bobbed erratically for a few seconds across the boxwood hedges, then came to rest on Ben's face. He turned away from the glare. He looked so annoyed that I knew he was okay.

I nodded at Dwight, and he nodded back, extending his hand. "Give me the camera."

"As soon as Ben starts walking."

"Gawd, you watch too many movies," he said, frustration lacing his tone. "Okay." Dwight waved his hand at Ben. "Come on down here. Lee, you stay there." Under his breath, he added, "where you can't muck things up."

I swallowed and slowly began extending my hand as Ben crunched down the path. When he entered the circle of light around the fountain, I fully extended my arm, and Dwight snatched the camera. I turned to Ben and gave him what I'm sure he would classify as a smothering hug.

"I'm so glad to see you," I said, then rushed on as I pulled back to look at him. "What were you thinking at the hotel parking lot? Going off alone like that? If I hadn't followed you . . ." I trailed off because Ben had gone tense and suddenly had a strange look on his face.

My back was to the fountain, but Ben was staring over my shoulder in that direction.

"Folks, we're not finished here," Dwight said.

I turned and sucked in a breath. Dwight had added one accessory to his Western wear. If only it had been one of those clichés, like a bolo tie or cowboy hat.

He held a gun, a sleek black model.

Chapter
Twenty-one

"Where did he get that?" I asked. His jeans were way too tight for him to have had that gun hidden away in a pocket.

"Waistband at the small of his back," Ben whispered.

Dwight slipped the camera into his breast pocket, then used the same hand to remove a phone from a clip at his waist. "I have something I know you'll want to see."

He tapped the screen a few times with his thumb, then turned it toward us. "Recognize that?"

"Yes," I said, my heart beginning to thud. It was Summer's front door at her condo. The lilac door and sea-foam blue trim were distinctive. I recognized it from pictures Summer had sent us.

"This here is a handy thing," Dwight said, his voice billowing with smugness. "It's a live video, coming from a car parked in front of your sister-in-law's condo.

I have two men there who will break in and take your kids, if you don't do as I say. Now, let's finish this up. You're going to do what mothers always do—the noble thing. You're going to sacrifice yourself for your kids."

"What? What are you talking about? I gave you the photos. You have them. We're done," I said.

"Oh, I think not. I can't let you go, not when there's the possibility of you selling your story to the tabloids."

"But I don't want to sell my story. I won't—we won't—say anything," I said with a quick glance at Ben. He nodded, but his face was grim, as if he knew my arguments wouldn't change Dwight's mind.

"Sure. That's what everyone says. I've been around Hollywood long enough to know that everyone sells out eventually. But I'm not unreasonable or unduly cruel. I'm letting your children live," he said with a cocky grin.

I stood there motionless, not believing this was happening. Where were our reinforcements? Why didn't Mitch and Jenson do something?

"They'll have your husband," Dwight continued. "Your children will be fine, I'm sure." His tone changed as he said briskly, "Down to the dock with both of you. Once you and your brother take your tragic little boat ride, I'll call off my friends, and your kids will be safe." He stepped close to us and motioned with the gun for us to move around the fountain.

I glanced at Ben, and he nodded. I raised my eyebrows. Ben wanted us to go along with this scenario? I wasn't walking calmly down to the dock at the bottom of the gardens and stepping into a boat, gun or no gun.

Before I could think too much about it, I swatted at Dwight's hand, the one with the phone.

The phone flew through the air and landed in the fountain with a plop. No one moved for a beat. Dwight's face was a mixture of shock and disbelief. He looked like I'd pushed his firstborn over a cliff.

Then, in the next second, everything happened at once, and the whole scene descended into chaos. Ben lunged for Dwight, knocking his hand with the gun up into the air. The gun sailed off into the darkness. There was a thud and scrambling of feet on the shell path as Mitch and Jenson joined the melee on the ground. I stepped back as Ben landed a punch that knocked Dwight out, then fell back onto his knees, shaking out his hand. Jenson tossed a pair of handcuffs to Mitch, who snapped them on Dwight's wrists while Jenson located the gun in one of the flowerbeds.

Ben looked back at me. "The phone? You go for the *phone* when he's got a gun in his other hand?"

I shrugged. "I was thinking of the kids. If he didn't have his phone, he couldn't call his guys."

I sagged down onto a bench as Monica clambered down a trellis attached to the gazebo. "I got it all," she said, a smile splitting her face.

Jenson shifted the gun toward Monica, but I quickly said, "That's Monica, the reporter."

"I'm going to need to see that tape," Jenson said, and Monica's face fell.

"Hey," I said, sitting up straight and peering into the darkness of the gardens. "Where's Lee?"

"Probably ran at the first sign things were falling apart. We'll pick him up when we round up Suzie Quinn and Nick Ryan. I need to question them all," Jenson said as he pulled Dwight, who was blinking and coming around, into a sitting position. "Including you," he said, nodding at Ben.

Ben leaned close to Jenson and said, "You need to ask Suzie about an envelope of powder in her bathroom."

"Why would I do that?"

"Ellie told me about the powder that you found on Angela's things. I saw that envelope when I searched the hotel room. The envelope is small, like the little envelopes that come with flowers from florists. It's propped up behind her makeup and perfume on the bathroom counter."

"Did you touch it, smell it?"

"No. Sounds like it's potent stuff. I opened the flap with a pair of tweezers, saw it was a powder, and put it back exactly like it was. I didn't want to mess with it."

"We'll check it out," Jenson said, then pulled Dwight to his feet. As he marched him out of the gardens, he called, "I'll need to talk to each of you, too."

The police didn't find Suzie or Nick at the hotel or at Club Fifty-two, which is where they actually were when the whole scene in the gardens went down. Since it was after midnight, Jenson had sent officers to their hotel room first, assuming that they'd be there. He'd forgotten they were twentysomething celebrities who had a slightly different schedule than normal people.

After a few inquiries, the police had tracked them to Club Fifty-two, where it was reported that a harried man in a Hawaiian shirt had rushed into the club and dashed upstairs to their table. After a few moments of intense conversation, Suzie, Nick, and the man—who had to be Lee—had departed. They didn't return to their hotel. The police were still looking for them.

Mitch and I had talked about it this morning and de-

cided they were probably holed up in a hotel somewhere, waiting for the publicity storm to blow over.
After giving Jenson a copy of the video, Monica had
filed her story. Instead of waiting for the print edition
of the magazine to come out, *Celeb* had posted some of
the photos online, a teaser for the full article that would
be out next week. By late this morning, the soft drink
company issued a statement saying that they were "re-
thinking" Suzie's endorsement deal. The Park Palms
was awash in police and paparazzi alike.

I patted the sand on my corner of the castle, rein-
forcing my tower, then dusted my hands and sat back
to watch my kids. Livvy was laboring over the moat.
She was determined that we'd have a complete circle of
water enclosing our castle. The wind, blowing steadily
in from the ocean, pushed her hair up and tossed it in
the air, exposing her thin, delicate neck. I shivered
when I thought about how close Dwight's "friends"
had been to my kids.

About fifteen minutes after marching Dwight away
in handcuffs last night, Jenson had returned and told us
the two men at Summer's condo were in custody and
being brought in for questioning. I hadn't slept much
in the few hours left of the night after Mitch and I finally returned to our hotel. We had spent several hours
with Jenson, then returned to our hotel because we didn't
want to show up on Summer's doorstep at three in the
morning. Mitch convinced me to wait until ten o'clock
this morning to pick up the kids.

We'd updated Summer on everything that had happened, which took quite awhile, then decided to dive
back into our vacation plans. We'd taken a boat tour of
the coast and seen dolphins swimming alongside the
boat. The kids were excited to see the dolphins, but

they enjoyed sitting in the captain's seat and "steering" the boat even more than they enjoyed the wildlife. We'd decided to round out the afternoon with a few hours at the beach before the sun went down.

"Are we going to the fireworks tonight?" Livvy asked.

Mitch and I exchanged glances. "I don't know. We've had a big day. Maybe tomorrow. They have fireworks every night, all week. But I don't think Suzie Quinn will be there."

Livvy shrugged one shoulder. "That's okay. I really want to see the fireworks, though."

"We'll see how we feel after dinner," I said. I had too much parenting time under my belt to make any specific promises.

"Here, Mom," Nathan said, handing me a bucket. "We need more sand."

"Back to work, huh?" I asked, giving him a quick hug, drawing his gritty shoulders close for a second and inhaling the scent of sunscreen.

"You're squishing me," he complained.

"Better get used to it, bud," Mitch said as he formed a tower on the other side of the castle. "I think Mom is going to be hugging you a lot for no reason."

"She always hugs me for no reason," Nathan said in a matter-of-fact tone. "When will Uncle Ben come out? He's been asleep forever."

"Later. He had a big day yesterday and needs to catch up on his rest," I said, then screeched as a rogue wave surged up around us like a tsunami and deflated our sand castle.

"Come on, let's swim," Mitch said quickly, catching the kids' hands before they could get too upset about the destruction of their sand masterpiece.

We grabbed boogie boards for the kids and made

our way through the crowd of athletes gathering for a Twilight Triathlon that began on a cordoned-off section of the beach near us. The triathletes looked so serious with their game faces on, their numbers inked on their arms and legs. They were quite a contrast to the lazy sunbathers on the rest of the beach. "They look like bugs," Livvy said with a giggle, studying several women with swim caps and goggles.

We splashed through the see-through shallows into the deeper, waist-high turquoise water. We floated awhile, watching the kids ride the waves to the shore on their boogie boards, then swim back out to us. The beach was thick with people today, but I could easily pick out Nathan and Livvy in their bright swimsuits.

"What are you worrying about?" Mitch asked.

I sighed. "There are so many things," I said as lightly as I could. Worry was my specialty. I did it often, and I did it well.

Mitch drifted closer. "There's something specific that's bothering you. I can tell. You've got that crinkle between your eyebrows. I can see it even with your sunglasses on."

I pushed my sunglasses higher on my nose and tried to unwrinkle my brow. "Dwight was in Monica's pictures, the ones she took when Nick and Suzie were having lunch yesterday." I kicked lazily and floated into the curve of Mitch's arm. I waited until a woman on an inflatable raft bobbed by, then said, "Which means that neither Dwight, Suzie, nor Nick killed Angela. All three of them had a lot to loose if those pictures went public, but I think they all have an alibi, a very public alibi."

"I'm sure Jenson will sort it out," Mitch said, pulling me closer into his side. "He's got the traces of powder from Suzie's bathroom, and he said her prints were on the envelope. That will link her to the crime."

"Not if she's got an alibi. I thought she and Dwight were in it together, but I guess I was wrong," I said, barely noticing that Mitch had begun to drop kisses on my neck.

"Mom! Dad!" Livvy yelled. "Come see!"

I waved and shouted, "In a second" to her. "Could it have been Lee?" I muttered to Mitch. "He seemed too inept to do anything as complicated as murder someone, but he's certainly devoted to Suzie."

Between kisses, Mitch said, "True, but not our problem."

"Devoted enough to pull a gun on Ben, knock him out, and drag him up to the hotel room," I said, working it out as I spoke.

"Mom, Dad," Livvy and Nathan called in unison.

Mitch sighed and said, "I'll go, since *someone* is too preoccupied with their thoughts to enjoy . . . the beach." He kicked away, sending a shower of water over me that drenched my face.

"I'll get you for that," I called.

"Looking forward to it," he shouted back.

I watched Mitch emerge from the water and stoop to look at the kids' sand castle. Something looped around my ankle. I kicked out hard to shake the tendril of seaweed off, but instead of loosening and falling away, it tightened and yanked me down.

The world disappeared in a swarm of bubbles. I kicked out, flailed around, and managed to get my face above the surface of the water. I gulped in air, but a heavy weight settled on my shoulders and levered me under. The water distorted and deadened sound as it closed over me. I twisted and writhed, panicking as my lungs burned.

I needed to breathe. I needed air.

I thrashed in the muted underwater world, fighting toward the light. I bobbed up for a second. Sound and light assaulted me.

Noises came rushing back—kids yelling, gulls crying, water surging. I blinked the stinging saltwater out of my eyes as I kicked and clawed at water, trying to get away from whatever was behind me.

My foot connected with something. Something solid. The touch spurred a fresh wave of adrenaline.

I splashed, crashing through the water to the beach. I caught a glimpse of Mitch and the kids, still bent over the sand, and of several people, fully clothed in dark uniforms, moving around the beach, before an arm slid around my neck and hauled me backward.

I was on my back, being towed away from the beach. Part of my brain registered that it was a person who held me, that it was an arm around my neck, but I wasn't relieved that it wasn't some sea creature intent on dragging me underwater for an early dinner. I was too focused on trying to break away, raking my fingers over the slippery skin of the arm. When that didn't work, I arched my back and grabbed, straining to twist around. I connected with a slick plastic material and pulled with all my strength.

A silver swim cap and set of goggles came away in my hand as a voice said, "Agh. Stop that." We'd slowed, and I struggled to break the grip on my neck, which was so tight that I couldn't breathe. I twisted and saw Suzie Quinn's face.

"Stop moving," she said, squeezing my neck harder.

I stopped and the pressure lessened enough that I could get a shallow breath. "Let me go," I managed to wheeze.

"I don't think so." Suzie clamped her arm tighter across my throat and ripped her cap and goggles out of my hand. She tossed them away, then resumed her one-armed crawl. She was a powerful swimmer. Even using only one arm, the water was rushing over us as she cut through it. We were on the outer edge of the moderately deep water. The crowds were thinner here. The nearest people were several feet away, two teenagers, their bodies so entwined that they looked like some exotic sea creature. No help there. I doubted they'd notice if Moby Dick swam by them. The mass of triathletes was too far away to call to, and they were focusing intently on their own swims.

Suzie's breathing wasn't labored as she said, "Everything will be so much easier with you out of the way."

I was exhausted from all the fighting and twisting. There was no way I would get away from her. Her grip was too tight and, even if I did manage to break her hold, she was a much stronger swimmer. I couldn't even get enough air to shout for help. I could barely whimper, her choke hold was so strong.

Even in my panic I could hear the satisfaction in her voice. I managed to choke out a few words. "You sound pleased with yourself." I thought I saw a swimmer out of the corner of my eye. He—or she, I couldn't tell which—was several feet away, drifting in our direction. Suzie either wasn't concerned about the person or didn't see them.

"Oh, I am pleased. It's all going to work out fine. In fact, I don't know why I didn't think of it before. I'm smearing you. I'll call a press conference this afternoon and release e-mails showing that you stole the photos from Angela and tried to blackmail me."

I tried to protest, but no sound came out.

"What's that? You didn't e-mail me? Oh, yes, I know. But by the time it all gets sorted out, there will be a cloud over you. It's one of the first things I learned from Dwight—character assassination. Of course, you'll be dead so you won't be able to deny it. I'll also announce I'm going into rehab. You know how much America loves to watch a train wreck, right? Well, they love a comeback story almost as much. I'll emerge clean and sober in a few months, ready to tell my story. God, I can't believe I didn't think of this before. I'll be on the cover of every tabloid for *months*."

The swimmer was closer, but I had to wait. A few more strokes. I could still see the beach where Mitch was looking around now, searching the water, but we were farther out, much farther than where he was looking for me.

I managed to get out Dwight's name.

Suzie said offhandedly, "Oh, Dwight." She paused to tread water as she spoke. "He'll do anything, say anything, if the price is right. He'll back up my story that Lee gave Angela the drugs and put her in the pool. Fortunately, I have enough money to pay Dwight whatever he asks. Lee, on the other hand, will be cheap. He's so in love with me that I don't have to pay him anything. He's going to commit suicide after writing a full confession of how he murdered Angela, which, of course, will leave Nick and me in the clear. Oh, except for your troubling brother, but Nick and Lee are taking care of him right now."

The swimmer startled Suzie, and she forgot to keep her viselike hold around my neck.

I sucked in a breath and screamed, "Shark!"

The swimmer was a woman. She'd been doing the traditional side-to-side breathing, her strokes steady and smooth, but at my voice, her head popped up. "Shark," she echoed, catching sight of Suzie's discarded gray swim cap, floating on the water. The swimmer let out a second, stronger scream that carried to the beach. "Shark!"

The word spread along the beach, accompanied by flailing and splashing as everyone surged for the sand. Suzie cursed and pushed me underwater again. I'd had a rest, floating along being towed, and I struggled with everything I had. Her grip on my shoulders and neck slipped. I kicked hard, angling away from her.

I broke the surface and swam sloppily, sending cascades of water in every direction.

"Out of the water," a voice called through a bullhorn.

Trying! Believe me, I'm trying.

I put my head down and made for the beach, all the while expecting to feel Suzie's hand clamp on my ankle or shoulders and pull me under, but after a few clear strokes, I risked a look and saw I was surrounded by the triathletes, who were sprinting for the beach.

I limped along with the athletes until I felt Mitch's arm come around me and support me into the beach. I crumpled onto the sand as Livvy, her eyes huge, said, "Did you hear that, Mom? You were swimming with a shark."

"That's one way to put it."

Chapter Twenty-two

"How much longer?" Nathan asked, wiggling on the blanket in an effort to stay awake. Ten o'-clock at night was pretty late for him, but he was making a valiant effort to stay awake to see the fireworks, which had involved running in circles around our picnic blanket and eating as much sugar as he could con his Uncle Ben into buying for him from the food vendors.

"Should be any minute now," Ben said, which seemed to satisfy Nathan. Uncle Ben's word carried more weight than mine did. Nathan nodded and settled down, crossed his legs, and looked at the dark sky expectantly.

"Thanks for coming to the fireworks with us tonight," I said to Ben.

"Wouldn't miss it."

"I'm sure there are other places—trendier, more exciting places—you could be."

"I've had my fill of excitement on this vacation, thank you very much," Ben said.

The whine of a rocket cutting through the air signaled the beginning of the show. Both Livvy and Nathan dropped onto their backs to watch the fireworks, oohing and aahing.

I'd had a day to recover from my watery encounter with Suzie. I was sporting a bright red stripe of skin around my neck where Suzie had throttled me. Ben was also fine. Nick and Lee hadn't even made it to Ben's hotel room.

The police had been on the lookout for Suzie, Nick, and Lee. They'd spotted them on the beach road when they dropped Suzie at the beach. Some of the police followed Suzie to the beach and the others followed Nick and Lee. The police caught up with Nick and Lee in the hotel atrium. They'd lost Suzie in the mass of swimsuits and bathing caps of the triathletes. It was their dark uniforms I'd seen moving up and down the beach as they looked for Suzie. They'd nabbed her as soon as she stepped out of the water. She was an excellent swimmer, but even she had to come ashore eventually. With the water clear of swimmers after the "shark scare," she was a pretty easy target to track since she was the only person still in the water.

A burst of white flowered in the sky above us. The bright explosion lit up a leggy young woman with jet-black hair moving around the blankets. Several smaller explosions went off in a series of staccato bursts as green and blue fireworks bloomed overhead. In the flashes of light, I waved, and Monica caught sight of me. She picked her way through the crowd, then dropped down onto our blanket.

"So, is this the real you?" I asked, taking in her shorts, chambray shirt, and flat sandals.

"Yep, this is plain old me," she said.

I introduced her to Ben, whose attention was no longer on the fireworks.

"I brought you something." She handed me a white paper bag. "Deep-fried Oreos."

"You shouldn't have," I said as I opened the bag and pulled out one of the still warm, crispy circles. I handed the bag around so that Mitch, Ben, and the kids could sample them, too.

I took a bite as she said, "Those are Triple Double Stuff—the absolute best."

Ben ate a bite and said, "That is amazing . . .."

"Amazingly bad, but in a good way," I added, savoring the crispy shell and the chocolate. "So you're not on Suzie Watch tonight?"

"No, there's not much to watch. She, Nick, and Lee are in police custody. They'll be charged tomorrow."

"With what?" Ben asked, leaning forward.

"That is the question, isn't it? There are so many possibilities," Monica said, drawing her knees to her chest and wrapping her arms around them. "I've heard through a source that only Suzie's fingerprints were on the envelope of powder, so that's pretty incriminating."

"But she was at lunch with Nick when Angela was killed. Dwight was there, too. It's in your photos."

"Yes, but apparently, the thought of going to jail for murder has broken the spell Suzie had over Lee. I managed to recruit a source close to the police, who says Lee is talking, giving them all the inside details so he can get a deal and avoid jail. Lee says that before Susie left for her lunch date with Nick, she waited for Angela to make the call to you asking for the purse, then Suzie administered a puff of the powder—a special gift from her dealer—to Angela, which put her in a compliant, suggestive state. Suzie told her it was a nice day for a swim. Lee said he didn't think about it at the time, he was so freaked out about the job he'd been tasked with—getting Angela back to her apartment and picking up the purse. Lee says he parked in front of the apartment's swimming pool and left Angela in the car. She was groggy. He says his plan was to retrieve the purse, then escort Angela inside the apartment and leave her there.

"But the purse wasn't there," I said. "Because I hadn't arrived yet."

"Right. Lee found the apartment unlocked and ransacked—"

"Courtesy of Pete Gutin," I added.

Monica said, "When Lee got back to the car, Angela was gone. She'd decided to take a swim as Suzie suggested. The drug reduced her motor skills so that she wasn't able to swim, and she wasn't thinking clearly enough to just float until someone arrived who could help her."

"That's terrible," I said. We were silent for a few moments.

Monica cleared her throat. "I heard the police picked up Pete at the Miami airport, by the way. He's on his way back here. Jenson says he'll be charged with robbery at the very least, and it doesn't look like he'll get to keep the money from his sale of the photos."

"So he's not going to spend his 'retirement' on a beach in the Caribbean?"

"Doesn't look like it."

Mitch leaned forward, tossing his crumpled napkin into the paper bag. "Since I came in late, I'm still a little confused on how the whole thing went down."

Monica and I glanced at each other. She waved a hand in my direction. "You were there at the beginning."

I took a deep breath. "Okay, let me see if I can get it all straight. Angela, Ruby, and Cara were at Club Fifty-two. Angela took the incriminating photos of Suzie, which Ruby knew about, but Cara didn't. Angela contacted two papar—ah—*press* people and offered to sell them the pictures. Monica and Pete. Angela and Ruby argued because Ruby wanted to sell them back to Suzie."

"Blackmail might be a better term," Ben said.

"True. Anyway, Ruby contacted Dwight, who set up a meeting with her. I'm not sure what happened on the balcony," I said, looking toward Monica.

"I interviewed Ruby today. Amazingly, now that Suzie and Nick and their entourage are in police custody, she's recovered her memory. She said once Dwight figured out she didn't have the photos on her—Angela had the only copy—he threatened her until she told him Angela had them. Then he pushed her over the balcony." Another cavalcade of fireworks lit up the sky overhead, and we were all silent for a second, watching it. I shivered, remembering how I'd seen her body fall.

Monica sighed and said, "At least she'll make a full recovery. Anyway, she shut up and stayed in the hospital, using her amnesia story to keep herself safe. My source informs me that Lee says Dwight called him and told him where to find Angela. Lee followed her as she left the store. He caught up with her on the sidewalk and tried to convince her to give him the photos, but he didn't have any money, and Angela walked away. He didn't want to come back empty-handed, so he managed to get her in the car and take her to the hotel."

"That's rather extreme," Mitch said.

Monica shrugged. "The relationships the personal assistants have with their 'stars' can be warped. The stars often treat their PAs like dirt and demand they be on call twenty-four hours a day. Many PAs don't really have a life outside of their work. They'll do anything for their star. It's a weird relationship. The PA usually knows the star better than anyone, yet they aren't a friend. They're an employee. It goes back to that king and court syndrome we talked about," Monica said to me.

"So you're saying that Lee would do anything for Suzie . . . even kidnapping and murder?" Mitch asked.

"Pretty much," Monica said. "Lee says Dwight asked Angela questions all night, but that she wouldn't tell him anything. She finally gave in and told them everything the next day—that Ellie had the photos in the purse. Dwight knew the power of having access to someone's digital identity and got her e-mail account information."

"I wonder why they didn't use the powder on Angela in the first place?" Ben speculated.

"They didn't have it until that morning. Sources told me that Suzie's dealer dropped by and left it with her then."

I frowned. "Why didn't they use it on Ben? I'm sure you weren't exactly cooperative."

"I let them *think* I was cooperative," Ben corrected,

"but I had my own agenda. When I saw the envelope, there wasn't much powder left. Maybe they were saving it in case I became less compliant."

"So once they figured out Ellie had the photos, she became their target," Mitch said.

I nodded. "Except Pete realized I had the photos and stole them from our hotel room. After I figured out that Chase and Cara didn't have the photos, I remembered the flower delivery, which led me to Monica."

"And the rest you know," Monica said.

"So her brother, Chase, wasn't involved?" Mitch asked.

"No. Except for sending the wrong purse. He had no idea about the photos. He was too wrapped up in the pill mill," Monica said.

"What will happen to him?" I asked.

"He's another deal maker. He's giving up his partner, the doctor, and his suppliers in exchange for several years in prison."

Ben said, "I'm still surprised that Angela only made one copy of the photos and then put it in the fake purse."

Monica shrugged as she said, "She must have thought it was a hiding place that no one would find and that it was safer than leaving the photos on her phone or computer."

"And the purse would be much harder for Ruby to get to than her phone," I added. "They had disagreed about what to do with the photos, and they were worth a lot of money."

"Oh! You'll be interested in this," Monica said, suddenly turning to dig through her bag. She extracted a sheaf of papers and handed them to me. "That's the listings from an online auction of all of Angela's designer clothes and bags. Her dad says the proceeds from the auction will go to set up a foundation to fight drug abuse."

Ben said, "I think she'd like that."

"I think so, too," I said. I made a mental note to get in touch with Angela's dad and tell him to keep the real Leah Marshall bag. Chase had said he'd get it to me, but I thought it should go in the auction.

Suddenly, there was a surge in the fireworks, which had been going on in the background as we talked. It was the finale and the sky filled with starbursts of red, white, and blue.

Nathan hopped up from the blanket where I think he'd been dozing, but he looked wide-awake now.

We packed up the blanket and gathered our trash, the kids still talking about the fireworks. Ben boosted Nathan up on his shoulders, and we joined the crowd moseying to the parking area.

Nathan looked down at me. "When do we have to go home, Mom?"

"Not for another three days."

"Good," he said with a nod. "This has been the best vacation ever. I don't want to go home."

Mitch wrapped his arm around my shoulders, and I slipped my hand around his waist as I said, "I wouldn't quite agree with Nathan."

"No, but the next few days have a lot of potential."

"That they do," I said, and Mitch gave my shoulders a squeeze.

"No more intrigue. Just sun, sand, and the water," I said. "And a few more of those deep-fried Oreos," I added.

"And milkshakes," Nathan said.

"No more excitement," Mitch agreed.

"Right," I said. "We'll have a really boring, uninteresting time for the next three days."

"Dull, even," Mitch said.

"Sounds good to me."

Author's Note

The first smidgen of the idea for this book came to me when I visited the Florida Gulf Coast with my family. Sandy Beach is loosely based on the city of Destin. I took liberties with the typography of the city, but I didn't change a thing about the beaches. They really are so beautiful it's almost hard to believe they are real: astoundingly clear water and pure white sand. We were stunned to have our very own "shark encounter" on our first day at the beach. It was one of those "I have to put this in a book someday" moments.

Sadly, the pill mill aspect of the story is based on real events. I first read about pill mills in the *Tampa Bay Times,* which described how Florida's crackdown on the illegal drugs had caused pill mills to use alternate "waiting rooms" in an effort to hide their activities from the police.

For information on the tabloid aspect of the story, these books were invaluable: *Tabloid Valley: Supermarket News and American Culture* by Paula E. Morton; *The Untold Story: My Twenty Years Running the National Enquirer* by Iain Calder; *Tabloid Love: Looking for Mr. Right in all the Wrong Places* by Bridget Harrison; and *Fame Junkies: The Hidden Truths Behind America's Favorite Addiction* by Jake Halpern.

To see photos of Florida's beaches, some articles I used for research, and other miscellaneous inspiration, look for the *Milkshakes, Mermaids, and Murder* board at Pinterest. You'll find me under "SRosett." Hope to connect with you on Pinterest, Facebook, Goodreads, or Twitter!

Acknowledgments

I'm amazed that this is the eighth Ellie book. Thanks to Michaela, my wonderful editor, for her continued support for the series. The team at Kensington is terrific, and I'm so fortunate to work with such wonderful people. Thanks to Faith. I so appreciate your positive outlook and your encouragement. A huge thank you to the reviewers, librarians, and readers who have spread the word about this series. I appreciate every mention, review, like, and tweet! Thanks to my writing buddies and online friends, the Deadly Divas and the Girlfriends Book Club. And, as always, the biggest thank you goes to my family: Glenn, Lauren, and Jonathan. I truly couldn't have done it without you.

In case you missed the last delightful
Ellie Avery mystery . . .

Keep reading to enjoy an excerpt from
Mistletoe, Merriment, and Murder
Available from Kensington

Chapter One

Wednesday

"**L**ook at me, Mom," squeaked a voice beside me. I glanced up from the green frosting I was slathering on a Christmas tree–shaped sugar cookie and saw my five-year-old son, Nathan, wearing the pale blue bed sheet that I'd made into a shepherd costume for the annual children's Christmas pageant. I had accomplished this sewing feat despite the fact that I'm not exactly handy with a needle and thread. Until a few weeks ago, fabric glue had been my go-to option when it came to creating Halloween costumes, but the pageant with its numerous rehearsals coupled with Nathan's rather energetic nature called for something sturdier. I was still stunned that it had worked. I'd actually made sleeves. I was grateful that zippers would have been anachronistic.

With the loose folds that draped around his neck and the strand of rope that Mitch had found in the garage for a belt, Nathan had looked authentically pastoral.

Now, though, Nathan had the neckline hitched up over his head into a tight-fitting hood that dropped almost below his eyes. He held his shepherd crook—a converted broomstick—horizontally in a fierce two-handed grip. "Luke, come over to the dark side," he said in a breathy whisper and swished his "light saber" back and forth.

I closed my eyes for a moment, half frustrated and half entertained. "Honey, I don't have time to play Star Wars right now." We'd had a marathon viewing session of the original *Star Wars* trilogy after Thanksgiving dinner this year and the movies had made a huge impression on Nathan. "Remember, I've got company coming. Daddy's taking you and Livvy to get a pizza, so you need to go change."

He whipped the hood off his head and his dark brown eyes, so much like Mitch's, sparkled. "Really?"

"Yep. And, no, you can't take your shepherd's crook with you," I called out after his retreating back.

With a quick glance at the clock, I went back to frosting cookies, slapping the icing on as fast as I could. I had two hours before the squadron spouse club descended on our house and I still had to make the cider, move chairs, start some music, light candles, check the bathroom for toothpaste blobs in the sink, and wrap my present.

Livvy strode into the kitchen, her ponytail bouncing. At least she wasn't in her angel costume. She had a book in the crook of her arm, her butterfly-shaped purse slung over her shoulder, and a coat of clear lip gloss on her rosebud mouth. "I don't see why I can't stay here," she said as she plunked down on a bar stool. She'd had a growth spurt during the summer and I still couldn't believe how tall my eight-year-old was. She

tugged at the cuffs of her sweatshirt, which was sprin-
kled with sparkly snowflakes. "I mean, I understand
why Nathan and Dad have to go—they're boys, but I'm
a girl. I should get to stay, too, right?"

"Well, honey, it's all grown-ups. Truthfully, I think
you'd be bored. We're just going to eat and talk."

"And open presents," she said accusingly.

"Another reason you can't stay," I said gently. "You
don't have a present for the gift exchange and everyone
has to have one for the game to work."

"But they're just white elephant gifts," she said
quickly. "You said the rule was they had to be worth
nothing and as horrible as possible."

Of course she was quoting me exactly. Our kids had
excellent recall for statements Mitch and I had made—
certain special selections only, usually having to do
with promises of ice cream and other special treats.
Christmas was just weeks away and Livvy and Nathan
were in agony. It seemed each day another package arrived in the mail for the kids from our far-flung extended families. It wasn't easy for them to watch the
presents pile up and know it would be weeks before
they could open anything. "I could find something in
my room to give away," she said in a wheedling tone.

"I'm sure you could, but you're not staying tonight.
You're going with Dad," I said in a firmer voice. The
lure of opening a present—even a white elephant
gift—was a heavy draw for her, but since no other kids
had been invited, I didn't think it was right to let Livvy
stay.

"But, Mom—" The garage door rumbled up. Rex,
our rottweiler—who might look intimidating, but had a
sweet temperament and would slobber all over anyone
who'd let him—shot through the kitchen, scrambling

across the tile, then the wood floor, legs flailing. He met Mitch at the door with his typical enthusiasm, wiggling and whining a greeting. Livvy hopped off her bar stool and gripped Mitch's waist to hug him and Nathan flew into the kitchen shouting, "Dad's home! Dad's home! We're going to get a pizza!"

Mitch hugged the kids, scratched Rex's ears, and gave me a kiss, all while setting down his lunch box and leather jacket. He told the kids to get their coats on while he changed out of his flight suit. A few minutes later, he was back in the kitchen in a rugby shirt and jeans, reaching over my shoulder for a carrot stick. "Looks good in here," he said.

I was shaking red sprinkles over the cookies before the frosting set, but I paused and glanced into the living room and the dining room. Sweeps of evergreen garland dotted with tiny white Christmas lights, red bows, and creamy white magnolias decorated the mantel of our gas fireplace. The Christmas tree stood in the corner of the dining room by the window with an assortment of gleaming ornaments interspersed with the homemade ornaments that the kids had made at school. Fat vanilla and cranberry candles in islands of evergreen were scattered over the tables and a potpourri of tiny pine cones, holly, and evergreen scented the air. "It does look good," I said, half surprised. "I've been so focused on checking off each item from my to-do list that I haven't stepped back and taken in the whole picture."

"Imagine that. You, focused on a to-do list," Mitch said, and I swatted his arm with the dish towel.

He dodged the flick of the towel as I said, "It looks great *because* I focused on that list." Mitch had some . . . issues with my list-making habits. He preferred the looser, more relaxed approaches to life. I liked to know exactly where I was going and what I had to do to get there.

He held up his hands in mock surrender. "Right. You're right. Without the list, we'd be lost."

"That's right," I said, smiling because I knew he was humoring me.

He grinned back and let the subject drop. We'd been married long enough that we both knew that neither of us was going to change our outlook on life. Agree to disagree, that was our motto—at least it was our motto where to-do lists were concerned.

He bit into a cookie, then asked, "Tell me again why you're hosting this thing? I thought you'd sworn off squadron parties after my promotion party."

I cringed. "Don't remind me," I said grimly. That promotion party was a squadron legend. "I said I'd host this party in a moment of weakness. Amy was supposed to do it, but her mom went into the hospital." I squared my shoulders. "This party is going to be different from the promotion party—nice and normal. Dull, even. Just good food, conversation, and presents."

"No flaming turkey fryer?" Mitch asked with a straight face. I rolled the dish towel again and he moved out of my range.

"No," I said as I went back to arranging the cookies on a platter. I transferred the platter to the dining-room table. Mitch followed me and began massaging my shoulders.

"I'm sure it will work out fine," he said, all teasing gone from his tone.

"Thanks." I felt my shoulders relaxing under his fingers. I wasn't a natural hostess. I worried too much and spun myself into knots. His arms closed around me. It felt so good to lean into his sturdiness. Five more weeks, I thought, then immediately banished the thought. Mitch's turn for a deployment was coming up in January and I was doing my best to avoid thinking about him leaving—I hated when he had to leave for months on end—but the deployment was always there in the back of my mind.

I heard the kids coming down the hall and twisted around for a quick kiss. "Y'all better hit the road. The spouses will get here soon and I still have to change," I said, lifting my shoulder to indicate my flour-spattered sweatshirt and worn jeans.

"I could help you with that," Mitch said with a wicked gleam in his eye.

Out of the corner of my eye, I could see Livvy standing in the kitchen, attempting to juggle her mittens. Nathan was running in circles around Rex, who was patiently watching him despite having his stubby tail stepped on.

"I don't think so," I said. With a significant glance at the kids, I lowered my voice. "I doubt that would speed things up."

"That's the whole idea. Speed is overrated," Mitch whispered before he glanced up at the sprigs of mistletoe I'd hung from the chandelier with red ribbon, then gave me a lingering kiss.

"I see your point," I said. "We'll have to finish this . . . discussion . . . later."

"Yes we will," Mitch said before herding the kids out the door to the car.

I hurried off to change into my favorite deep green sweater with the oversized turtleneck collar and a pair of tailored pants. I managed to get through the rest of my to-do list before my best friend, Abby, arrived.

"Don't panic," she announced, opening the front door. "I'm early. Here." She handed me two poinsettia plants. "I have more in the car." She spun around, her dark, curly hair flying over the fuzzy edging of the hood on her coat.

She'd brought ten plants, which we spaced around the house for the final touch of festiveness. Once those were in place, she made a final trip to her car and returned with a present and a peppermint cheesecake. "I'm so looking forward to this," she said, stripping off her coat and gloves. With her generous smile and curvy figure, she looked spectacular in a white sweater, black pencil skirt, and high-heeled boots.

I deposited her gift under the tree along with my hastily wrapped present and asked, "The third-graders are getting to you?" Abby taught at the nearby elementary.

She rolled her eyes to the ceiling and managed to look both worn-out and guilty at the same time. "They're so sweet, but eight hours of knock-knock jokes? And then when I get home, all Charlie wants to talk about is how much better front-loaders are than dump trucks."

"Is Jeff out of touch again?" I asked. Abby's husband, a pilot like Mitch, was currently on a deployment to an unnamed location in the Middle East. Communication between the deployed location and spouses at home was generally pretty good. There were morale calls, which were usually filled with static and an annoying time delay that made conversation challenging, but it was always good to hear that familiar voice on the phone. And now online video made staying close so much easier, but there were often stretches of time when the guys couldn't communicate for days, maybe weeks, at a time, depending on what they were doing.

"Yeah. I haven't talked to him for four days. There's nothing going on—no bad news, so I know he's just on a mission."

I nodded. You became quite good at reading between the lines of newscasts when you were a military spouse. "Tonight should be a good break for you. I promise there won't be one knock-knock joke. Come on, you can stir the cider and talk about anything you want while I light the candles," I said, leading the way to the kitchen.

"Enough about me, for now. This smells divine." Abby leaned over the simmering saucepan. "What's going on with you?"

I picked up the candle lighter from the counter and flicked it on. "I didn't get the organizing job for the schools." I'd heard through Abby that the North Dawkins school district was looking for an independent contractor to create and implement paper saving strategies throughout the district to help them cut costs.

"Why not?" Abby asked. "You're the best organizer in North Dawkins. How could they *not* hire you?"

I focused on the small explosion of flame around the wick of one of the candles as it lit. "No, up until a few months ago, I was the *only* organizer in North Dawkins. That doesn't mean I was the best."

Abby gave the cider a vigorous stir that sent it sloshing around the pan. "You're the best. I know how hard you work. And you're good. Don't get down on yourself. They probably had to delay the decision, or they lost the funding for it in the budget cuts—that happens all the time."

Another wick flared. "Gabrielle Matheson got the job."

Abby sucked in a breath. "No! How do you know? She didn't call to gloat, did she?"

I moved to the candles in the living room. "No, I don't think even she would be that tacky."

"I wouldn't put it past her," Abby murmured.

Freshly divorced and with two kids in college, Gabrielle had supposedly moved from Atlanta to North Dawkins for a fresh start. I knew her sister, Jean Williams, through the squadron spouse club. Jean's husband had retired from the air force, but Jean still attended some spouse club events—"the fun ones, anyway," was how she put it with a smile. Gabrielle had told everyone that she'd moved to North Dawkins so she could be near her sister, but I knew there was another reason. Atlanta was thick with organizers, but there was only one professional organizer between Macon and Valdosta—me. Or, there had been only one until Gabrielle arrived.

Gabrielle had called to introduce herself. Networking, she'd said. Her southern accent had oozed through the phone line, "Us professional organizers have to stick together."

I'd jumped at the idea, thinking it would be great to have someone in town to knock around ideas with. I'd even pitched my latest service to her, consulting with new organizers and helping them set up their businesses. I'd hoped this new venture would take off and I could eventually transition to full-time consulting so that when our next move came, I wouldn't have to start over from scratch again with zero clients. So far, I had two "newbie" organizers in two different states that I was working with long distance, via e-mail and social networking.

"Oh, honey," Gabrielle had said with a throaty laugh. "I don't need your help. I'm an old hand at organizing." She'd immediately switched to a new topic. "I think we should start a local chapter here," she had said, referring to the national association of organizers that we both belonged to. "Since you're so busy with your established clients—and I know you have little kids, too—I'd be happy to be president. Don't worry, you don't have to do anything. I'll take care of everything."

She'd signed off quickly and I'd been left with my mouth open and a dial tone buzzing in my ear. In the two months since she'd moved to North Dawkins, Gabrielle had managed to vacuum up quite a few of my new client leads and she'd also poached one of my most affluent regular clients, Stephanie, who, at one time, had my number on her speed dial. Two weeks after Gabrielle moved to town, Stephanie had called to let me know she wouldn't need me anymore.

"That's three jobs now where she's beat me out," I said, exasperated, as I returned to the kitchen and pulled mugs out of the cabinet for the cider.

"Here. Let me do that. You don't want to chip anything," Abby said. "How did you find out you didn't get the school district job?"

"Candy called me." I'd met Candy when I created storage solutions for a nonprofit group where she worked. She was in her forties, wore huge hoop earrings that always matched her clothes, chomped on gum nonstop, and had a bossy, tough-love kind of personality. She'd left the nonprofit and was now working in the school district office as an administrative assistant. "All she could say was that the director didn't pick my proposal. She asked me to call her back tonight, but I don't think I'll have time." I glanced at my watch. It was almost six.

"Oh, go. Call her. I'll get the door if anyone comes while you're on the phone," Abby said.

Candy answered on the first ring. She sounded slightly out of breath. "Just walked in the door from work. Now, you didn't hear this from me, and I can't say much, but I thought you should know what's going on. You're a good sort, the kind to get run over in a thing like this, so . . . officially, Gabrielle got the job because she has more hours available to work each week. Theoretically, she can get it done faster and she had a reference from a school in Peachtree City, which never returned my calls, so I couldn't verify she'd worked for them. She supposedly ran an organizing seminar for the teachers and revamped the school's workroom, which counted as more suitable experience than the organizing you've done for individuals."

"But even if I don't have experience organizing for a school—"

"I know, honey, I know. I've seen you work. You would have known exactly what to do. Anyway, that's all neither here nor there. What really made the difference was as soon as Gabrielle came in the office she schmoozed old Rodrick. That first morning, she just happened to have brought an extra latte, vanilla and skim milk, no less."

Rodrick Olsen was the superintendent. Candy's voice took on a gushy tone. "And wasn't that the biggest coincidence in the world? That she'd brought Rodrick's favorite? And didn't Rodrick look sharp in his pinstripe?" Her voice lost its sickeningly sweet exaggerated southern drawl. She was spot-on in her imitation. Back in her normal, rather gruff voice, Candy said, "Gawd, it was sickening. And he ate it up, let me tell you. She suggested lunch at The Grille, so she could completely understand all *his needs*." There was a clanking, which I assumed was Candy's big hoop earring clattering against the phone in her agitation. "So there you are. Just wanted you to know what you're up against—flirty schmoozing."

My heart sank. "I can't do flirty schmoozing. And I don't want to have to do that to get jobs."

"Don't worry, honey, she's the type of woman that men fall all over themselves for, but women will see right through her, just like I did. What goes around, comes around. Just be aware of what you're up against when you're both competing for the same job and the person making the decision is a male."

The doorbell chimed. "I've got to go. Thanks, Candy."

"Sure thing," Candy said. "You be sweet now."

Despite the plunge in my self-confidence, I had to grin at Candy's signature southern good-bye. "Bye, Candy."

Petite, pixielike Nadia, with her short, brown hair and elfin face, followed Abby into the kitchen. Nadia was one of the most intensely perky people I knew, which I figured was an asset for a first-grade teacher. She and Abby taught at the same school. Nadia was carrying a glass pan of fudge and had her camera bag slung over her shoulder. She was the official squadron photographer, but her photographs went way beyond the amateur level. She'd recently sold some of her photos of the local pumpkin patch to a regional magazine. She wore a cranberry-colored boiled wool jacket with black piping over a snowy white shell and black skirt.

Personally, I thought she took coordination of her clothing a little too far—she and her two daughters always matched, down to the hefty bows that she placed in their hair. I was sure that if the girls had been with her tonight, they would have been in some sort of burgundy taffeta party dresses complete with matching bows.

"There's been another one, did you hear?" Nadia asked as she handed the fudge to Abby and carefully set her camera bag on the counter.

"Another what?" I asked.

"Break-in," she said, clearly delighted to have the scoop on us. I didn't know how she did it, but Nadia always had the latest news on . . . well, just about everything. I thought she probably would have made an excellent investigative reporter, if she hadn't liked teaching so much.

"Another spouse?" Abby said. "Who was it this time?"

Nadia's expression turned somber. "Amy. They got in while she was at the hospital with her mom."

Tips for a Sane and Happy Holiday Season

A niche industry has grown up around holiday organization. There are endless plastic boxes and bins designed specifically to hold holiday decorations. The only downside to these organizing aids is the expense involved. Sometimes it seems you can spend just as much on storing your holiday decorations as on the decorations themselves. Here are some cheap and easy storage solutions that won't break your budget:

- Use Styrofoam egg cartons to store small, delicate ornaments.
- Look for plastic cord wrappers in the hardware section of your local superstore, which will usually be cheaper than the cord wrappers in the holiday section. Use these cord wrappers to wind lights, tinsel, and garland. Or, make your own cord wrappers out of sturdy pieces of rectangular-shaped cardboard.
- Save original ornament packaging and reuse at the end of the season.
- Wrap wreaths in plastic trash bags to prevent them from getting dusty, then hang in your storage area.

Chapter Two

"**H**ow terrible," I said.

"That's low," Abby said, emphatically. "Can you imagine targeting someone whose mother is in the hospital? Who would do that?"

Nadia and I exchanged a look. "It has to be someone in the squadron, doesn't it?" I said, voicing what we were thinking.

"It could all be a coincidence," Nadia said, doubt edging her voice.

"You guys worry too much," Abby said. "Before this, there have only been two break-ins on base and one in North Dawkins. That's not a pattern. That's coincidence."

"Still, I don't like it. Robberies don't happen on base very often. And, how likely is it that each one of those break-ins was at a house where the husband was deployed?" Nadia asked with a frown.

"Not every break-in," Abby countered. "Amy's husband isn't deployed."

"But she and Cody were away in Atlanta, with her mom, at the hospital. That means someone knew her house would be more vulnerable, like the others."

"It is strange," I said. "When did it happen?"

"At night, like the others," Nadia said, raising her eyebrows. "They drove to Atlanta in the evening. Amy came back the next morning to pick up a few things and found the back door open."

Abby rolled her eyes. "Isn't that when robberies usually happen—in the dead of night?"

I ignored her. "Do you know what was taken?"

"I heard a laptop computer, MP3 players, and some cash," Nadia said.

"It does sound like the others," I said. The other robberies had all taken place during the night and small but valuable electronics and money were taken.

The doorbell rang and I hurried off to answer it. I swung the door wide and said, "Hi, Marie."

Her head was nowhere near the door frame, but she ducked a little anyway as she stepped inside. I guess being six-foot-two probably made you overly cautious about door frames. Marie said hello softly and stopped short in the entryway, like she wasn't sure what to do. She pushed a swath of her long orangy-red bangs out of her eyes and looked around the house. Her slightly protruding eyes seemed to widen even more. "Your house is lovely . . . so pretty . . . so clean. I don't know if I want you coming to my house tomorrow, after all," she said with a nervous laugh.

Despite being in her late twenties, Marie had the gangly arms and legs of a teen, which didn't really go with her more stocky midsection. It was horrible, but every time I saw her I was reminded of the Sesame Street character, Big Bird. It had to be a combination of her height, her soft-spoken manner, and the mismatch of her stringy arms and legs combined with her thicker core. I quickly tried to banish that association from my mind. You know you've been watching too much children's television when it starts to influence how you see people.

"Oh, don't worry. This is definitely not the normal state of our house. There are usually toys and books everywhere." I had an organizing consultation scheduled for tomorrow with Marie and I was afraid that with her timid and hesitant manner, she might cancel. "Come have some food and let me take your gift and coat."

After a slight hesitation, she reluctantly released the red package. I wondered if she was thinking about leaving, claiming some forgotten appointment or errand, but then she smiled nervously and handed me her coat. I sent her into the kitchen and made a mental note to check on her later to make sure she was having a good time.

Everyone seemed to arrive at once and soon the sound of conversation and laughter began to drown out Mannheim Steamroller's "Deck the Halls." I was in the kitchen chatting laboriously with Marie—yes, she and her husband had been assigned to the squadron almost a year ago; yes, they liked it here; no, she didn't like it that he was deployed; yes, she was looking for a job—when I heard Abby call my name, I excused myself, glad for the interruption.

I hurried through the crowded room to her. "What's wrong?" I asked.

Abby was frowning. "I wanted to warn you. Gabrielle is here."

"What? Why would she be here?"

"Jean brought her," Abby said. My eyebrows shot up and Abby hurriedly said, "What could I do? They came in with a big group. I couldn't let Jean in and turn her sister away, could I?"

"No, but I wish you had." I knew I was being unreasonable, but I couldn't help it. "Abby, that woman is sabotaging my business. I haven't even told you what Candy said about her."

"Oh, Ellie, sugar," a syrupy voice, dripping with long southern vowels, sounded behind me, "Your house is—um—charming. So cute and domestic. It must be just perfect for your little family. It's so nice of you to host this party at the last minute, even though it's quite a squeeze in here. And I love all this neutral paint. It must make decorating a breeze."

Wow—had she just said my house was too small and that it was bland? I gritted my teeth, determined to be nice. I would take the high road.

Jean was standing slightly behind Gabrielle and I thought I was seeing double for a moment. I hadn't realized how strong a resemblance there was between the sisters. I'd met Gabrielle at a chamber of commerce meeting, so I knew what she looked like and I'd had plenty of interactions with Jean through the squadron, but I hadn't seen them together. Side by side, they looked not just like sisters, but more like twins. There were differences in their style of dress and—more prominently—in their attitudes, but they were both the same height and had black hair, green eyes, and heart-shaped faces with high Slavic cheekbones.

Jean stepped around Gabrielle and handed me a

plate of brownies iced in swirls of chocolate frosting. "Hi, Ellie. I invited Gabrielle along tonight so she can meet more people." Jean's dark hair, which was threaded through with strands of gray, was pulled back into a low ponytail held in place by a rubber band. Under her quilted down coat and wool scarf of neutral brown tones, she wore jeans and a green sweatshirt embroidered with elves.

In contrast to Jean's unfussy clothes and faint makeup, Gabrielle looked incredibly stylish, if a little overblown, in a Christmas ribbon–red wrap dress with a plunging neckline and black heels. Her makeup was thorough and flawless, her dark hair—no glint of gray anywhere—floated about her face in luxurious waves, and the scent of lilies drifted around her.

"Um, yes, I know. Here, let me put those gifts under the tree. Help yourself to some food," I said as I escaped. Really, how could I have thought they were alike? Now that I looked at them, I kept seeing differences—Jean had plain, short-trimmed fingernails. Gabrielle's long, acrylic nails were polished a glossy red. After introducing Gabrielle to everyone, Jean filled a plate with food and plunked down on the couch beside Nadia. Gabrielle avoided the food, except for a few carrot sticks. There was also a sensual air about Gabrielle that was completely absent from Jean. The plunging neckline of the dress, the flowery scent, and the way she held herself—one hand on her thrust-out hip—looked almost as if she were expecting a photographer to pop out and snap her picture.

Impatient with myself, I shook my head. *Stop being catty*, I told myself, and went to get more napkins. I couldn't help but notice that Gabrielle was the center of attention wherever she was. She drew people to her.

There was a sort of energy and sparkle about her. No wonder Rodrick had been captivated by her.

Everyone had arrived and the party was in full swing. I cruised through the house, chatting and making sure everyone had food. Abby was slowly herding everyone into the living room so the gift exchange could begin. I filled a plate for myself and hurried into the kitchen to get a mug of cider. The kitchen was empty except for Gabrielle and Marie, who were on the far side by the breakfast table. Gabrielle, who had her back toward me, pressed a business card into Marie's hand. "You should give me a call." Gabrielle spoke quietly, but I could still hear her. "My hours are much more flexible than Ellie's and I'll give you a twenty percent discount on whatever she quotes you."

Marie shot a guilty glance at me, then said, "That's okay—I've already got an appointment, with Ellie, I mean. I'll just keep that." Marie shifted around the back of the table and quickly escaped into the living room.

Furious, I slapped my plate and mug down on the counter and marched over to Gabrielle. "I can't believe you did that." I was so angry my hands were shaking and there was a tremble in my voice.

Gabrielle glanced languidly over her shoulder at me, then turned to face me with a little sigh. "Ellie, sugar," she said in a long-suffering voice, "don't be upset. It's just business. A little friendly competition."

Words burbled up inside me, but when I'm upset, I get tongue-tied and all I could do was sputter, "Friendly? That's not friendly!"

"There are plenty of clients to go around for both of us," she said in that infuriatingly calm tone.

"Then why are you poaching mine? You're intentionally going after them, I know it!"

"I can't help it if they're not satisfied with your services, now can I?"

The muscles in my core tensed and I felt my face flush. "What you're doing is wrong. You and I both know that." I stepped toward her. "I'm a nice person, but I will *not* let you do this to me."

Gabrielle's gaze shifted from my face to the living room. Our house had an open floor plan and I suddenly realized everyone in the living room could see us arguing. The only sound in the room was the faint strains of "Silent Night" playing in the background. *Great.* I briefly closed my eyes. Everyone had probably overheard us, too.

"Don't worry, y'all," Gabrielle called, addressing the room. I opened my eyes to see that she'd swept by me, picked up my mug of cider, and was strutting into the living room. "Just a professional disagreement— Ellie and I could go on all day debating decluttering strategies."

Every head swung back toward me and I managed to force a smile to my lips. "I think it's time to start the gift exchange."

Abby jumped up. "Right! Okay, here's the rules. Everyone draws a number . . ."

I tuned Abby out and busied myself cleaning up the kitchen. By the time I came back inside from emptying the trash, I felt calmer, and embarrassed, too. I couldn't believe I'd let Gabrielle get me so riled. From now on, I would avoid her.

I slipped into the living room and watched the gift exchange until it was my turn to open a present. The game was complicated and involved options for swapping gifts and strategies to hang on to the gifts you wanted. I kept losing the gift I opened, a stationery set embossed with prints of holly and mistletoe. Most of the envelopes were missing, which was why it was a white elephant gift.

There were only a few presents left when Gabrielle opened a package that contained a flat box made of rough wood with a long opening a few inches wide near the bottom. "What is it?" she asked. "A birdhouse?"

"Sort of," a spouse new to the squadron, Cecilia, replied. She was four months pregnant and worked out each day with the neighborhood stroller brigade, which despite having the name "Stroller Brigade," was a neighborhood workout open to anyone who wanted to join. The stroller was optional and it was such a good cardio workout with a mix of lunges, squats, and push-ups for toning that I still joined them when I could. I had to hand it to Cecilia. There were some days when the power-walking workout left me exhausted. If I had tried to do that workout while I was pregnant, someone would have probably had to wheel me home in one of the strollers. But Cecilia always powered through the workout. She adjusted the portable—and broken— sewing machine that was on her lap. It was the gift she'd "won." She pushed her glasses up her beaky nose and said, "It's a bat house."

I laughed out loud, along with everyone else, over the strange present.

"What?" Cecilia said. "Bats eat mosquitoes—they're really good to have around." An outdoor girl who'd grown up on a farm, she was still upset that she couldn't ride a horse while she was pregnant.

By the time the dust had settled and the game was over, I'd lost the stationery set for good and was the owner of a three-inch-high Lucite paperweight. It was shaped like the classic round-cut diamond with a flat top and faceted sides that narrowed to a sharp point at the bottom. I recognized it. It had been a giveaway from a local insurance agent. His firm, Jim Excel Insurance Associates, was etched onto the top of the "diamond" along with a phone number. We'd had one a few years ago and, after taking it away from Livvy and Nathan several times because the point was so sharp it could cause major bodily injury, I'd tossed it in a box of charity donations. Now I had a new one.

"Oh, but that means I'm left with the bat house," Gabrielle wailed with a pout when she realized she couldn't swap with anyone else.

I thought the bat house was *so* deliciously appropriate for her. Every witch needs a few bats, right?

Nadia shook her head over the white elephant gift she'd won, a jigsaw puzzle of intricately detailed butterflies, which were repeated over and over again to make the puzzle even more difficult. There was a helpful note jotted on the box that stated several pieces were missing. "This one is way too hard for the girls—four hundred pieces—and it's missing pieces. Imagine how frustrating that would be, to get to the end and not have all the pieces after all that work."

Abby held up her prize, a wooden duck decoy, and said, "Well, at least I can decorate with this." Trust Abby to come up with the white elephant gift that could legitimately be turned into home decor. She had great instincts when it came to arranging furniture and accents. I was sure she'd find a place for the duck on her mantel or on a bookshelf and it would look spectacular and no one would ever guess it had been a white elephant gift.

I turned to Marie, who'd won a figurine of an elf with a chipped nose. The hat was held on with a piece of tape. "Guess you can't decorate with that."

I expected her to laugh and agree with me, but she said earnestly, "I'll find a place for it. I'm sure I can use it."

I wasn't quite sure what to say to that. How could you use an elf figurine? And a broken one, at that? Unless she planned on turning it into one of those funky found-art pieces that recycled trash into sculptures, I couldn't think of anything.

Hannah, the low-key squadron commander's wife, won a small painting with flaking paint and an elaborate frame. Unlike the last squadron commander's wife, who'd become a close friend of mine, Hannah was so self-effacing and quiet that it was easy to overlook her, so I was almost surprised when she called for everyone's attention at the end of the party. "Don't forget the squadron Christmas party is coming up. It'll be at the Peach Blossom Inn and we're having a gift basket auction to raise money for a terrific local charity, Helping Hands."

People began to drift back to the kitchen to grab another quick bite of food or refresh their drinks, but the party was waning. It wouldn't be long before I was distributing coats and waving everyone off. I breathed an internal sigh of relief, a reaction to getting through the party with no major mishaps, except for the spat with Gabrielle, but that was nothing compared to the flaming disaster of our last party.

I relaxed into a newly vacated seat next to Jean and asked how her husband liked retirement. Simon's last assignment had been at the squadron and he'd had a big retirement party during the summer.

"Loves it. He absolutely loves it." She leaned toward me, confidingly. "I was so worried that he would go stir crazy with all that time on his hands, but he got involved with Helping Hands and between that and golf—he's always busy."

"What is he doing for Helping Hands?" I asked. I knew the local charity, located behind our church, had an annual food drive and ran a food bank all year long. They also built homes for low-income families. It was nothing like the scale of Habitat for Humanity, but I thought building even one or two houses a year was quite an accomplishment.

"He started out helping in the food pantry three days a week. It was like pulling teeth to get him to go with me the first time, but once he got involved, he loved it. He's on the board as the financial manager now and does just about everything. And," she leaned in a little closer, "Helping Hands just got a significant donation." She raised her eyebrows for impact. "Significant. It's really going to help. This year has been rough for so many people with the economy tanking the way it has. Donations have been down all year, but now it looks like we'll be able to break ground on two new houses. Simon will probably have less free time than when he was on active duty."

"That's wonderful about the donation," I said. "And you're still doing your online resale business?" Jean combed through garage sales and other online auctions for items she could resell through her own online storefront.

"Yes." Jean held up the white elephant gift I'd brought,

a beat-up set of Hot Wheels toy cars, and said, "These will probably go fast."

"You're kidding."

"No. I'll put up a couple of nice photographs and price them right. They'll probably be gone in a few hours. In fact, a lot of this stuff that people think is trash could sell," she said.

Hannah held up the painting. "Even this?"

"Maybe," Jean said. She didn't sound so sure. "I could give it a try. Want me to list it?"

"Sure."

Nadia and Cecilia handed off their gifts to Jean and I added the paperweight to the collection. An hour later, I was practically shoving Abby out the door. "I should stay and help you clean up," she said.

"You already did. All I have left to do is start the dishwasher. Now, go on, you've got a babysitter to pay. And don't forget to lock the house up tonight!"

I couldn't hear her reply, but it sounded a bit like, "Yada, yada, yada."

By the time Mitch came home and we got the kids in bed, then did the final post-party sweep of the house and talked a bit about our days, it was nearly one in the morning. I'd just relaxed into my pillow when the phone rang.

Abby's voice had a tremor in it as she said, "Sorry to call so late. Don't panic. Everything's okay, well, except that I've been robbed."